No Animals We Could Name
Stories

TED SANDERS

Graywolf Press

This publication is made possible in part by a grant provided by the Minnesota State Arts Board, through an appropriation by the Minnesota State Legislature from its general fund and the Minnesota arts and cultural heritage fund with money from the vote of the people of Minnesota on November 4, 2008, and a grant from the Wells Fargo Foundation Minnesota. Significant support has also been provided by the National Endowment for the Arts; Target; the McKnight Foundation; and other generous contributions from foundations, corporations, and individuals. To these organizations and individuals we offer our heartfelt thanks.

Published by Graywolf Press
250 Third Avenue North, Suite 600
Minneapolis, Minnesota 55401

www.graywolfpress.org

Published in the United States of America

ISBN 978-1-55597-616-3

2 4 6 8 9 7 5 3 1
First Graywolf Printing, 2012

Library of Congress Control Number: 2012936217

Cover design: Kapo Ng @ A-Men Project

For my mother,
who would have been happiest of all.

Contents

Introduction

This is the music I have been waiting for, which is to say: the music made by the intersection of the visual, the sonic, the emotional, the tactile, the dramatic, and the gonzo. Ted Sanders is a fearless, wild, tremendously sensitive writer, who seems to write not only about the three dimensions of the world we live in, but also about the fourth, the fifth, and the sixth. How else can one account for this sentence, concerning the ontological condition of a halibut: "He swims on his side, affecting flatness." Or this, of a ghost hovering over her sleeping former husband: "Here in the night about this bed, you find yourself thickening down out of dark, gathering in his thoughts, shaped by his insistence." Or this, of a magazine resting in a woman's lap: "It arched over her thighs like a bird drawn by a child." Sanders tunes into all the stations at once, constructing a sound like no other, finding the spark of life in everything we can see, and can't. It doesn't seem like an accident that there are a lot of animals here: bears, fish, deer, lizards, lions, horses, octopi. Reading these stories is like looking into the eyes of an animal, finding there both recognition and unbridled otherness, a gaze returned to you that both is and isn't from a reality you already know and that may be ringed with fur, or legs. Even the machine in "Assembly" has its own odd life, its own agency, its own powers of invention.

This is the music of now. We see life everywhere—in our computers, in our phones, and as animals disappear we feel again the fresh, hard, erotic force of what we're about to lose. We can't quite return their backward glance. Our computers, closed, emit that pulse of light in a heartbeat rhythm, safe in dreamland. Sanders isn't writing about any of this per se, he is writing about men and women and children and animals, about beauty and loss. But he has hit upon a poetics of what it feels like to be alive right now, that blur of life that seems to be in everything, all the time, distributed in unpredictable, distressing, and deeply pleasurable ways simultaneously. The ghost, after having made a kind of spooky midnight love to her living husband, departs: "You curdle dearly from his skin."

This is the music of joy. Not easy joy, not necessarily permanent joy, not the joy you might expect. It is the joy in what is. The halibut, writes Sanders, "watches the light in his own eyes." Can anyone read that and not feel both thrilled and yearning, does anyone not want to watch the light in his or her own eyes? In story after story, Sanders reminds us that the light is there. The rest is up to us.

—Stacey D'Erasmo

No Animals We Could Name

Obit

The boy who falls asleep to the story of the bear will grow old and wordlessly die. In the end, he will die across his pancakes, coughing up blood in a restaurant in a distant town, blood freckling the arms and throat of his latest wife, the table, the dark stone floor where bright ice and dark water from his spilled glass will also fall. All of these events will occur, and more. But the boy who will become this man is still young. He still lives in the yellow house where he was conceived. He was conceived as the sun shone over spruce trees into the front bedroom, onto the face that would become his mother's, not far from the hall where the dog slept then, dreaming beneath the soft sounds falling through the open darkwood door.

The woman who lay in the buttress of sun slanted against the front window of the yellow house will explicitly recall her memories of that experience, that day. She will continue to believe in these recollections steadfastly, long after the man who lay with her then has died. She will continue to believe in them even though, as she knows, there were a number of instances in the yellow house over the surrounding days that could, practically speaking, have been the act that led to conception.

The step that will never be fixed—the middle step on the short stairs of the front porch—will upend beneath the foot of the man as he comes to the yellow house on another sunny day, not so far off. He will by then have nearly forgotten what it is like to consider this house his own. The boy—who from his bedroom window at the front of the house will have watched his father come up the walk, through the shadow of the spruce tree—will hear the snap of bone. Neither man will ever forget this sound.

The dog that will die unseen in winter—far from home, where the gate will have blown open in the snow—will be named after the dog that slept in the hall in the yellow house. The boy, grown into a man, will have named this new dog. He will remember the old dog, the one who lay in the hall and dreamt of berries and beasts, the sound of his owner's voice. This dog, the first, dies beneath the kitchen table, his feet stirring, as the bear's story is being told.

The woman who will die in a hospital bed late into the night—senseless and mute on morphine, breathing slow and

The man who will wake in the night to the implausible pain of his own stopped heart will remember—as he is folding to shallow while her family, around her in and out of the room, waits for her to die— once lay in another bed wishboned around the man, watching a basket-colored sun make urchin shapes through the spruce tree in the front yard. The man, moving above her, over her—with rigid arms and fisted shoulders, feeling the cool intermittent press of her breasts against his ribs— looked into the mottled sheet of sun that lay across the woman's face and the rumpled bed. He considered the wide hazel irises of the woman's eyes, eyes drawn to the window, out into the sky over the front yard. The man believed at that moment that he would remember this sight of her: the sun across her skin, falling between her just-open lips, where a fine mindless shape was curling, her skin lit and blooming, her carved arms raised around her head like a harp's arms, as if the delicate gesture unfolding through

his knees in the dark—standing outside the room of the boy, listening to the still-young woman he once married sing to the boy a song a bear might sing. In the shadowed hall, he imagines the glint of peppermint. And the woman—the woman who will die in a dim hospital room, the mother of the boy who will die in a restaurant, the wife of this man who will die beside a bed in which a different woman will lie—this woman sings the bear's song to the boy, to the visiting man in the dark hall, to herself.

This man, who will later break his leg on the front step, will eventually marry a woman who is unable to conceive. To the boy, the new woman smells like the earth around trees, or honey and medicine, or wellwater. She will come to love the boy, will love the man he will become, will love the boy's child in turn. Years later, after the death of the father, them were being sung word-lessly into sight in her face. The woman will survive this understanding.

The bear who lives in the woods licks peppermints from the palm of the old woman. From the steps of her porch each morning, the old woman feeds the peppermints to the bear—one after another after another—in order to keep him tame. The bear has no home that the old woman knows of. When the old woman walks to the white stream above the lake, the bear walks with her, and there as the old woman sits and watches, the bear slaps fish onto the bank. The bear eats his fill, and the old woman returns home, taking one fish or two with her, bent like silver moons inside her basket—all she can carry. She cooks the fish over a fire, gives silent thanks to the bear. Late each night, at bedtime, the bear returns. He sits at the

this new woman will listen as the boy's mother recounts the moment the boy was conceived. The woman who smells like wellwater will hear the sight of sun's spread across dusty glass, the spread of warmth up the insides of raised arms, the rumble of low sounds made by the husband, the sight of the sun itself—and she will know from her own memory the tree through which the sun shone, the window through which the sun must have fallen, though in her mind the room has always belonged to the boy. She will imagine, correctly or incorrectly, the sounds made by the man on that day.

The treehouse that will never be built will be described many times. A hackberry tree stands in the yard where the man lives alone, where he will later pretend to introduce his son to the woman who smells like wellwater, though in fact they have already met. The bottom of the porch steps and sings to the old woman as she falls asleep. The bear sings deep and strong, a song of thankfulness and want. This is how the story ends.

The boy who will retell the story of the bear learns it from his mother. She tells him the story at night in his bed beside the window, and she describes the whiteness of the peppermints, the gleam of the fish taken from the stream, and she sings the bear's wordless song to the boy, letting the bear's song press the boy to sleep—the boy who as a man will die in front of strangers, coughing blood onto his food. The boy dreams of the bear's song, fertile, low, and wide; he will dream of the song as a man. He will tell this story to his own child, will mistake it for remedy, will elect to fail to sing the song he knows.

leaves of the hackberry tree are perennially pocked with galls, and just over the man's head, high above the boy's, the tree's fingers open into a gesture of grasping, and the man imagines out loud to the boy the treehouse he believes he could build for them there. The boy tells his mother. The man will mention it to his new wife. The man and the boy discuss the treehouse at bedtimes, with ambitious talk of trapdoors, rope ladders, spyholes. The man, eventually, will be survived by the possibilities of the treehouse; the boy will describe it, much later, to the young woman he believes he does not love.

The song that will be sung instead to the boy's child is sad and sweet. The boy knows this song too, but the young woman who will

The young woman who will sing to the boy's child will never know that the boy himself dislikes the extra verse. But this woman will sing just the same as she is sung to. Her grandfather sings her this song, and she will sing it to his child will sing an extra, unfamiliar verse, one the boy would never have otherwise heard—not a verse so much as a small chorus, more eager than the rest of the gentle song, a song that is not a lullaby, nor even the bear's song, but that has a lullaby's earnest swoon, and the extra verse will feel to the boy, for years, like being startled from half-sleep. He will come to believe that he no longer loves the woman who sings this song.

sing it to the boy and his child in the car, on the way to the hospital, the day before the boy's mother will die. She will sing it to the mother herself, deep in the last full night. Long afterward, elsewhere, this woman will die in a different car. She will be survived by a different man to whom she will also have sung this song.

Hesitantly, suspiciously, the man who fathered the boy will ask the woman he once married about the circumstances surrounding the conception of their son. He will, by then, have forgotten things the woman will continue to remember.

The tree under which a stranger's daughter will later play—kneeling into the bed of brown needles, pressing a hashwork of white and red grooves into her skin, peeling bulbs of sap from the bark and murmuring to herself—is the same tree that stands aside the front walk, limbs nodded deep over the half-wanted patio furniture tilting loose legged and flaking in the shade. It is the same tree through which the sun for years has fallen on its way to the front window of the yellow house, the house the man has already left behind.

The boy's child will never know the yellow house. He will never firmly believe in his memories of the woman who once sang there. He will know different houses, different songs. He will know different mothers. He will

The bear in the story told to the boy does not enjoy the taste of peppermint. He licks the old woman's palms, slaps fish to the shore for her, but while he is drawn to the whiteness of the peppermints, the bear imagines himself wounded by their bite. This truth reveals itself near the story's end, know the bear's story, but not his song. Nonetheless he will die in sadness, far from the girl he will never learn not to love. but the mother will never reveal it to her son, his father, the dog in the hall. She will have no cause to reveal it because the story, in the mother's telling, fails to end. Instead, it is survived by this tune, by the sad braided rumble of the bear's voice.

Neither the man nor the boy nor any of the women loved by them each will ever notice that the bear's story, as told by the boy's mother, does not return from song. They will fail to suspect the things that will befall the bear, the old woman. Nonetheless they, and others they love in turn, will sing songs to themselves that resemble the bear's song. They will encounter and remember days full of voice. Celebrants and mourners will weep, throats torn open by the pull of this singing; lovers will share breath, possessed by moments of unassailable faith; children will croon inaudibly over busy new hands; dogs will dream and mutter, safe in warm houses, paws trembling; bones will mend; trees will seek sun. In time these things will grow and turn bare. And after all there will be survivors.

Flounder

HERE IS THE HALIBUT: HE LIVES ON THE SEAFLOOR, A GREAT swimming slab, shimmying into the bottom's silt. He swims on his side, affecting flatness. He is meant to work this way. His top side, as he swims, is in truth merely his right side, where both of his close-set eyes now bulge. This top side—his right side, all that he can see of himself—is dark and mottled and always up, and on his bonewhite left side, always down, nothing remains of his face but the delicate swell of half of his jaw. Whatever sense of symmetry the halibut has, or of elevation, or orientation, he has had to learn it for himself because he has known a different body; he is born upright. When he is the size of a hand he undergoes the measured shift of certain bones, certain surface features. In particular, his left eye migrates to his right side. This movement becomes a slow pain that he will always feel, a pull of displacement, a creeping injury. With it comes a realization that resembles pain, but which dwindles with time into discomfort: the discovery that from each eye he can see the other. And though at times he briefly forgets this ability, this condition, in much the same way that a man may disregard the constant sight of his own nose, nonetheless the halibut finds it difficult to become blind to himself, and his considerations are not those a man might have; the nose, after all, does not look back. And sometimes when the halibut lies nearly buried beneath the silt and only his eyes and gills are exposed, he thinks to himself that it is often difficult not to stare, that up is an abstraction, that everything that cripples could be considered a wound. And because he does not know the quality of his left side, he chooses to believe it is a scar.

HERE IS THE MAN, FISHING FROM A BOAT FULL OF OTHER MEN, using a long strong pole that fits into a metal holster against the rail. The line is long and strong, ends in wire. The man has paid to be on the boat, to use the pole. Men in thick tan coveralls with hoods help him, help the other men who have also paid. The men in coveralls are busy and bearded, appropriately dressed, and the man with the pole watches them, does what they tell him. He nods a lot, says okay. He is very cold. The man enjoys learning things, knows many, many things already, like the shape of Nevada or that planes fly because their moving wings are sucked upward or that the moon tugs the sea from side to side. He knows that one cubic meter of water—scarcely enough water to drown in—weighs twenty-two hundred pounds, a metric ton. This particular thing, he does not believe.

IN AN INCIDENT TO COME, LATER IN THE DAY, THE HALIBUT will swallow a drifting piece of squid that is wrapped around a small thick treble hook, and this man will be at the other end of the line, far, far away in the light. The pole will already be bent beneath the weight of all the water passing along the line, the line arcing through the water between the man and the fish, between the boat and the seafloor—far more line than the distance alone implies because the press of the moving water will have given the line a magnificent, vertebral curve. Neither the man nor the fish will know just how far the line arcs outward from a plumb line straight up and down. Perhaps the men in coveralls know it, have worked through the math, but they will be unable to envision the fact of it. There will be no place from which the entirety of that line can be seen—looping out into the dark and cold, like the tense wooden curve of a slender bow, splendid and tight and thrumming as the water slices itself around it.

When the halibut takes the line, the man will not set the hook. He will not even attempt to set the hook; the men in coveralls have told him it is pointless to try. They have described to him, as best they can, the generous hyperbola of the line beneath the water. One will remind him: *Too much play.* The man will think of translational distances. And when the halibut first takes the line, the man will not know for certain what has happened—will certainly not know, for example, the things the halibut will know—but he will nonetheless feel through his hands and through the pole a sonorous weight on the line. He will come to believe in an implied movement there, like the sea's motion made concise, pulling on his palms, his forearms, his biceps, his feet planted on the deck, his thighs near his knees. He will feel this in some of the same ways that the halibut, moments before, will have first felt the terrible weight of this alien pull—again, not quite a pain, but a pressure, a vital gravity—anchored in the deep narrow pocket of his mouth, at the top of his throat pulling, a frightening and essential tug, stretching out from him and away, up toward the light. The silt the fish has lain in will become a cloud—will briefly blind him, far from the sight of the man.

BEFORE ANY OF THESE THINGS COME TO PASS, AN OCTOPUS drifts beneath the boat. The octopus is not a fish. The octopus is one answer to the riddle *What creature has legs but cannot stand?* Another answer is a kangaroo in space. The man on the boat knows both these answers. He learned the first from a restaurant placemat; his son has since invented the second. Of course, among the many items the man does not recall, despite all he knows, is the fact that the octopus does not have legs, but arms. And even if the man did remember this, he might dismiss it as a matter of semantics. As for the octopus, the man does not imagine that it troubles itself with semantics, or that it even, strictly speaking, invents names for its parts, or that it fancies itself an element of riddles. Nevertheless, in certain circles, the octopus is considered an intelligent creature. Some humans, in fact, wrestling with their own limitations of understanding, of communication, of empathy, make it their business to study just how intelligent the octopus may be. Octopuses have been taught, in the company of humans, to recognize symbols, to open jelly jars under water, to solve simple problems of cause and effect, such as blue equals pain. In one aquarium, an octopus has taught herself to climb out of her tank, to make her way across the floor to a neighboring tank of crustaceans, to drag herself up the side of that tank and in to where the lobsters cower. She takes a lobster tightly in her arms and returns back to her own tank. There she eats the lobster, hides the empty carapace under rocks. She does this by night, finishing before the aquarium workers—who are human—return each morning to find another lobster mysteriously absent. For a while, some of these humans will suspect others of themselves in the disappearance of the lobsters, but this is not the octopus's fault.

BENEATH THE BOAT WHERE THE MAN WHO KNOWS THE AN-swers to the riddle regards his borrowed rod—where the men in coveralls help men underdressed for the cold pull in massively flat, white-bellied fish—an octopus tangles itself in the taut curve of the man's line. The line is meant to be invisible, the color of water, and when the octopus strikes that strange, dimensionless blade, it is cut, and its arms flick, like a hand closing. It is caught then. The physics of its entanglement have to do with its bonelessness, something the man will scarcely be able to imagine. But as the octopus struggles, the man above comes to understand that a weight is on the line, and another man—in coveralls—encourages him to pull her up. By *her,* he means more than just the line. And so the man turns the big reel. He turns for minutes. The line feeds onto the spool and so must be shortening, but it seems only to tremble, not emerge, where it runs up into the air from the water's surface. This uniformity of a man-made length will mystify the halibut, has beleaguered the octopus, numbs the man.

As the man works the rod and the reel—his arm tiring, his back grimacing collaboratively—he feels ever more sure that there may be

a heavy dead weight on the line. He braces himself for a disappointment, either strange or mundane—as though he could in actuality have
snagged a boot, a tire, a rubbery clump of seaweed, or a body or a part
of one. And when the thing truly on the line comes up from the water
below, the man is stunned, thinks for a moment he has done something wrong or that something wrong has been done to him, because
a writhing blurb of seething orange has a hold of the line, an object
of a scandalous color, an organic orange like that of certain flowers,
or a certain rustic-seeming breed of scented candle, wrapped in strips of
raffia, or certain suns. It bobs there, bright and rich, the size of laundry,
half-immersed in its reflection in the uncolored water. Threads of white
roil within the orange. Two men in coveralls reach out, chattering and
laughing, and one palms the line, hauls the orange mass up and aboard.
The other holds a baseball bat. And when the churning bulk they've
pulled from the water slaps, wet and heavy, to the deck, its arms unfurl
and furl, and a round tubule on the side of its head opens and closes,
and the man still holding the rod sees a shimmering copper eye, a black
oblong pupil. It reminds him strongly of a goat's eye. The line is so
tangled in the octopus that to the man it seems to run through the octopus, imperceptible except where it draws deep crevices in the octopus's
skin, cutting bloodless through its flesh, as though the line could go on
quietly and invisibly injuring the octopus forever.

The man with the baseball bat begins to beat the octopus. He uses
the bat. He uses a great deal of his strength. The octopus squirms complexly, multifoliate. Its colors change, change moving over it in discrete
waves as it dulls sullenly into brown, brightens into embarrassment.
The man who has caught the octopus watches. He marvels. He considers the size of cells. He thinks how the sound of the bat against
the octopus is like a sound he believes he could have imagined, but he
understands he has never heard this sound. Later, he will consider trying to describe the sound to his wife, and he will think of pillows hit
by tennis rackets, but they would have to be wet pillows, or better: an
apple the size of a chair being struck with an ax. Or maybe a massive

slab of wet meat, pounded with a broad hammer—although this last act strongly resembles, in practice, the deed he merely wishes to approximate; furthermore, the thought will only make him recall his mother, and cube steak. In the end, he will not tell his wife about the octopus.

On the boat, the man watches as the octopus—whose flushed arms are writhing over the deck, clinging in places, fixing themselves briefly to the bait box, to the housing of the cabin—seizes randomly on the bat with two arms. They constrict and wrench the bat cleanly from the grasp of the man in coveralls. For a few woozy moments full of laughing and raised voices, an instant where the men standing around lean away, the octopus brandishes the bat over its head. The bat swings in a loopy, threatening circle. It strikes the window of the cabin and bounces away. It strikes the octopus. The man in coveralls reaches in and pulls the bat free, still laughing, cursing. He bends and goes back to work. He grunts now. Later, the men will take a long time untangling the body of the octopus from the line. They will cut the line at last. They will slide the octopus wetly, heavily, into a white box along the rail. The man who has paid for this experience will think, as he watches, that the octopus looks like organs, or a placenta. He will wonder what it is about water that could allow such a thing to be present in the world.

THEY GET THE MAN ANOTHER ROD AND REEL. ON THIS ONE, the line is red and again ends in wire. Some of the other men discuss the octopus. The men in coveralls act as though the incident was not much out of the ordinary. They describe the flavor of octopus, or rather they do not, because they make the *tastes like chicken* joke. The man dislikes this joke, but he laughs at it; they all do. The man tries to conjure the taste of chicken into his mouth, but cannot.

Later, as the man cranks at the reel with his already tired arm, pulling up the halibut that has swallowed the treble hook that bounced over the silt on the seafloor, he knows he has not caught another octopus. This weight is heavier by far—feels more cumbersome and momentous, feels full of one type of inertia or the other, feels inexplicably like hauling up a great, sturdy doormat. A man in coveralls leans over and hefts the rod in his layered palm. *That'll be your halibut,* he says. He tells the man that it won't fight much on the way up but that it'll be a long job bringing him in. The man turns the reel. Elements of his arm—biceps, triceps—already drown in their own spent energy. The back of his right hand hurts, begins to feel slightly dismantled, subject to rearrangement. He watches it. *Three hundred feet here,* the man in coveralls says, and asks if he's feeling it, laying his thick hand on the moving arc of flesh between the man's shoulder and neck. The man nods and leans into the line that feeds onto the turning spool. He settles up against a rhythm he believes he is only just learning: letting the length of the rod drop as he cranks at the reel, and then pulling the rod back upright with both hands, hauling up the line and the fish at the other end, putting—as men say—his body into it. His spine is a magnificent thing. The flat muscles in the small of his back begin to ache, becoming solid. He does not know the names of these muscles, where they begin or end.

It does not occur to the man to wonder how he knows to draw the fish nearer this way—reeling in line as the pole falls, then pausing to lift the pole again with the strength in his back, the tight slicing line thrumming splendidly down the pole's length and off its nodding tip. The men in coveralls have not described this technique to him. He does not have a memory of being taught how to do this particular thing. Nevertheless, his body understands it. His muscles and joints—tiring, swelling—organize themselves unknowingly, carving the motion from the man's purpose. And because the man does not think to question how he has come to understand this movement—even now as his body folds and unfolds over the line, as he watches the water take its space around the boat, as he listens to the wet line being drawn through the mechanisms of the pole and the reel, as he briefly straightens the fingers of his right hand and imagines the tangible rewards of his work—even now he does not contemplate the difference between understanding and discovery, discovery and invention, invention and belief. He will have the opportunity to consider many of these things on other occasions.

The wire emerges from the wrinkled water. A white shape moves alongside the boat, and the man stops reeling. The shape looks the size of a bed. It goes slim and disappears. Two men in coveralls lean over the rail on either side. *Big one,* says the man on the right. He holds a large silver hook in his hand, the size of a child's arm. The man on the left does not have a net. He has a fat silver revolver instead. *He'll fight now,* this man says. A third man stands behind him, leaning on the baseball bat—not the man who killed the octopus. The white shape reappears in the water, a pointed sliver growing patiently wide like an opening eye.

THE HALIBUT SPINS SLOWLY WITHIN THE WATER, TOP OVER bottom, listening to the pull in his mouth. So much light, and the water so loose. He watches the light in his own eyes. He lets himself drift right side up, right side down. He watches himself look back through the water below. He does not see the seafloor. He does not know how to see the seafloor. But as he drifts, the determined pressure in his mouth returns, and he is pulled partway out of the warm, wrapping water into some new and terrible element, and he feels, for the first time, a sensation something like what the man who knows the answers to the riddle calls cold. And then a sharp crisp sound comes, impossibly near, loud but thin, and with it another tug of pressure, and real pain. The fish turns, sinks back into water, swims. He swims down.

The men lean over the rail. The boat displaces many tons of water, many cubic meters. Below them, in the water, there is a thin slanted column of powder and warmth, cavitation, where the bullet has passed. And that bullet: how far would it go as a torpedo before it became a stone, a stone in the shape of a crumpled finger? The fish's own blood threads the water, and a clouded trail of its own mess, blood and feces, brooding in a thick plume back up to the bright burning surface, where the boat is a dark, steady footprint in a disintegrating cloud, and in that cloud long shapes bend and flicker, gesture into the water. The fish goes down, down; his body is a muscle. He sews through the water, side to side or up and down, weaving back into a deeper dark until he senses the bottom just below, feels and then begins to see the clouds of silt drifting from the seafloor. The mystery of the weight in his mouth doesn't end.

The man who knows the answers to the riddle does not know that the halibut, like the octopus, can change colors. This is merely one of the things the halibut and the octopus have in common. The man also does not know, but would perhaps have been able to guess, that the halibut changes his color in order to match the shade of the seafloor where he hides. The man knows the word for this: *camouflage*. The man knows how to spell the word. And the halibut is so good at camouflage that he can imitate the patterns of textured rock, or of striped silt rippled by currents, or of a checkerboard. The feat is a willful act that involves the eyes, an understanding of one's surroundings, and the learned discovery of the chemical endeavors of the skin—though of course the halibut does not know these things about himself. It does not occur to the fish to wonder how he knows to alter himself this way, even now on the seafloor, far below the man, as he begins to make himself go dark against the dusky silt. He attempts to hide from the pain in his ribs, the pressure in his mouth; this is what he knows. He makes himself go dark in a growing circle that emanates from the burning spot of hurt in his side, where he can see that he is torn, where he can see blood and bright bits of himself rising into the water. He watches them rise, watches his body begin to turn the deepest shade he can conjure. And perhaps because the halibut does not question this ability, he is able to believe, as he colors himself, that only his upper half—his right half—becomes dark. He believes that his left half—pressed against the bottom now—glows bone white and sickly. He does not stop to consider that he cannot know this for certain about himself; he will not consider it even when he is drawn again into the open cold above, exposed and upended and made heavy beyond reason, pulled by a clutch of new pains; he will not be able to imagine, even then, the ways in which he will be seen.

The clean spade of the boat's bottom drifts high above him, away at the surface, the place he has been and will be. The motes of silt, the dark particles in the water—they are illuminated scarcely by the faint light filtering from above. Some of these bits begin to settle across the halibut's side. If he had been given a different understanding or had been taught certain things—if he had been the man—he might at that moment have considered how, at that moment, he looked like a cold bed of burnt coals, only recently disturbed, beneath a furling cloud of ashes that had only recently begun to resettle. But for now, all he may see for certain of himself is his own reciprocal stare and those tiny, blown-loose pieces of his flesh. He may breathe. He cannot know that the hook has worked its way into his gills and will not come free. He may open and close his mouth around the red line, but the length of the red line arcs from him and away, through the debris about his body, disappearing out into light, or darkness, far from here—up and out into a density he also does not understand.

HERE IS THE MAN ARRIVING HOME. HE DOES NOT HAVE THE fish. He has instead—on a dark plastic strip rolled in a small metal canister—the undeveloped potential for a picture, in which the fish hangs dead from a peeling metal bar next to three other fish, all big but none as big as the man's fish, all with their smooth, bonewhite bellies bared. A square of paper with a number on it has been stuck to every fish, giving the weight of each. The squares of paper have been stuck to the fish with thumbtacks. The paper on the fish the man has caught says *112*, which is a big number; it has already made him think of orders of magnitude. The man is in the picture too, and he will later discover that he looks handsome in it. But he cannot see this picture yet, and when he comes home, having flown from the sea, having showered more than once, he does not have the fish. He tells his wife and son about the fish, about certain events that transpired on the boat, but he does not have the fish. He shows them what he has instead: a receipt, a carbon in triplicate, documenting an account he now has at a fish bank. He has deposited his fish there. He can now withdraw fish, though the fish bank is far away. And different kinds of fish are like the currencies of different countries, and so for the massive flatfish he has caught and given, he can procure so many pounds of smoked salmon—but not one hundred twelve—or a number of swordfish steaks, or shark, or fillets of steelhead trout, or rockfish, or mahimahi, which is the pastoral name for the dolphin fish, a name no one can stomach. He even believes shellfish might be available to him, though of course they are not technically fish. And he tells his wife all of this, that all of these things could be shipped to them, overnight, and what is not sent fresh could be sent canned or frozen. She, listening, is amazed and happy. The son grins proudly. Together they begin to invent plans with what they have coming to them, and the man begins to believe the things they say. But when at last the man sees the picture, he will look at the fish, its scales, and he will wonder where the bullet hole is. He will wonder if the paper that says *112* covers it, or if it could be found on the dark side of the fish, or if it is merely unseen. He will imagine that the skin of such a creature can be parted after all, and smoothed again by hand, like feathers or vegetation, or water, undisturbed.

Airbag

One

THOUGH SHE DOESN'T OWE ME ANY, DORLENE PUSHES AN
apology my way every few miles. I'm the one that should be sorry, letting the conversation hang like I have, like it's a hand I won't take. I
can't yet manage to do any different. At the farm, when I step out of the
car into the late September cool and open her door—because it seems
like the thing to do—I turn away. To be honest, I only pretend not to
watch, craning like I'm peering up toward the farmhouse. And even
though seeing the house again does have me jangling, Dorlene is a hell
of a distraction. A couple of what must be Tom's art-and-design kids
slouch across the lawn, headed down past the garage, but those kids
can't really compare. Maybe not even Triti herself. What I'm saying
is: though I've got my head turned toward the house, I'm pouring a
highway of thought into my peripheral vision over at Dorlene. To see
how she manages. I figure she'll clamber out, ass first, feet dangling, but
instead she scoots herself to the edge of the backseat, face forward—a
tiny, unbelievable thing—and she pops right out, stiff. She's airborne
for a blink, sticks the landing, her arms and legs apart at just the same
mute angles, like a paper-chain person. She looks dispensed. And then
she's limber again, throwing the door shut with both hands and all her
weight. Her head doesn't even come as high as the door handles, not

much higher than the tires, really. She could maybe stand upright inside the wheel well. Maybe. I can still hardly gather up the idea of her.

"Your door's open," she says in that voice, and she steps up and slams that one shut too, one little foot lifting. She cocks her head at me. I go ahead and look down at her outright then, because you can't go on not looking. I'm cool about it, I think.

"I do apologize again for that awkward car ride," she says. "I hope you understand. Those fucking airbags, I'm serious to god."

"It's okay."

"No, it's a complication. And it's out of kilter already." She moves her hand between her chest and mine, like she's singing. She had to sit in the backseat because she's so small, an airbag could kill her—just the concussion of the thing. According to her. Back at the bus station, she checked my dashboard and excused herself to the backseat, and that's how we drove. Hence all the apologies. Back at the station, she said, "They inflate by controlled explosion, did you know that? Like rocket exhaust." She kind of half jumped at me and threw her little stick arms out, and went "FOOMP!" which with that painful squirt of a voice—an unbelievable voice, really—sounded like an animal noise of alarm. A little dog, or a monkey. I don't know if she noticed my flinch.

Now Dorlene smooths her tiny dress, a rust and brown plaid thing with pleats. A little kid's dress, probably. Her sandals are the size of butter dishes, and inside them her naked feet look long-toed, almost like hands. And her hands? I don't look at any of her for long.

I'm caught up in Tom's idea of a joke, I know that much. Picking Dorlene up at the station, driving her out here to Tom's farm for the party, him not warning me and all. At the time he said he just needed someone who'd have room for her in the car. A joke all right, but at the time I took it differently. What with Lisa and all, I mean. And Triti. Plenty of room in the car these days. So I said I'd pick this friend up, this former student, really, this Dorlene, despite my nerves about driving out to the farm with a stranger, a woman. All that bedeviled conversation. When I asked him what she looked like, he gave me this: "You'll know her when you see her." And when I wanted to know what the hell that meant, he just laid me one of those closed-lip grins of his, his eyes fairly fucking twinkling. "You'll know her when you see her," he said again, all sphinxy.

I nodded at him like I got it. I figured it'd come to me. People give you that line, and then the thing—the thing you're supposed to know when you see it—starts to take on the color of a surprise. Something you'd appreciate, or hate. And you start to wonder what kinds of things *those* are. So at the station, as I was waiting for Dorlene beside the bark-filled flower beds by the ticket window, I was mostly on the lookout for somebody spectacular—attractive, I mean—or maybe somebody hugely fat. Maybe both. If I'm honest, by the time the bus showed up, a half hour late, I could've drawn a picture of the woman I was waiting for, like Lisa, only taller, and fiercer, a tank of a girl with long dark hair, or red, a real killer.

So I didn't even notice Dorlene. I mean, I saw her get off the bus, but like anyone would I dismissed her as a kid—a very together kid. She had a miniature suitcase, with the trombone-slide handle and the wheels. She made a beeline for me, but I was looking past her for the thing I'd know when I saw it, until she got close and I saw she was holding up—figure this—a greeting sign like you see in airports in the movies, white and rectangular. Big black letters read: DAVID BRESLIN. But I was so invested in the bodies still trickling from the bus that for a second I didn't recognize my own name. Or I recognized it, but I think I thought it belonged to somebody else in this particular case; I laid my eyes on her, and the sign too, and went right back to the bus—just for a second, but still: I feel a little stupid about it.

Dorlene tittered about my confusion all the way out here to the farm—her in the backseat on account of the airbag, her little suitcase in the front seat on account of all the stuff still in the trunk, all that miscellaneous crap I claimed from the house last time, I don't even know what all anymore. I drove—humming past nearly done fields of corn and soy, passing every little while through gritty brown blooms thrown up by combines—and Dorlene chattered, apologizing for the seating arrangement, teasing me, talking about herself. The fact she's willing to joke about it shows you she's not shy. She tells me all kinds of things, like how the reason she looks the way she does is because her particular kind of dwarfism—this is her word, *dwarfism,* like it's a religious movement or a philosophy—just makes her all around tiny. She looks like an actual miniature person, so small she might be a toy. Or like something you haven't ever seen before. Her body's not stocky. She's well proportioned, willowy, even. Her hair is brown and straight and ordinary. Mostly it's her nose that's off—long, and built along the same plane as her forehead, giving her face a rodenty slant, but not in an unpleasant way. Her eyes are extremely dark. Plus she's got that voice, high and nasal, almost like her voice can't make it through her mouth and so instead resonates out from somewhere behind that nose. Sometimes I can hardly make out what's she's saying. And it doesn't help that her voice is smudgy around the edges, like a deaf person's voice. I figure it's her throat: maybe her vocal cords don't come together, or apart—whichever would make her voice so high and displaced. I've seen pictures of vocal cords before, but I've only got a dim idea how they work. They're extremely vaginal looking, if you want to know the truth, but that's a whole other thing.

And now that we're finally here, Dorlene is still apologizing with that voice. She props her hands backward on her hips and sticks her chest out, says she's sorry again about the backseat.

"It's okay," I say.

"Well, it doesn't seem okay. I mean, you seem pissed. You've seemed pissed this whole time, David, I'm serious to god."

"No, no, I'm not pissed. Why would I be pissed?"

"Well, you don't talk much."

"I'm not much for small talk." That's what I say.

Dorlene doesn't bat an eye. She peers down at herself and pokes her belly with a tiny finger. "Christ, I'm hungry," she keens. She looks back up at me. "That's all right, then. I make you uncomfortable."

"Not really." Up at the house, Tom goes by carrying a white plastic bottle. I start to wave, but he's far off and not looking our way. No sign of Triti anywhere, not really. I decide I will say something like the truth. "Or, okay, I guess. Unsettled, maybe."

"Unsettled." The word leaks out of her like a squirt of air from a balloon. And here's what I mean about her voice: *unsettled,* when she says it, only has two syllables. "Okay, that's good."

"Is it?"

"So ask me something."

"Ask you something."

"About me. People tend to be curious about me. It's a curious thing. You're not curious?" She says: *cyuh-yuss.*

And here's the thing: I am curious. I'm pretty fucking deep in already, if you want to know the truth. I'd really like to ask her something like: So is it that your vocal cords never split, or that they never met? Or maybe is that a doll's dress, or why are your toes so long, or can you swim, or where do you keep your crackers, but I don't want to ask a question that could be taken the wrong way. I'm beginning to doubt that Dorlene is the easy-to-offend type, but you just never know.

"I guess I wouldn't know what to ask you," I tell her.

"Ask me how old I am. No one ever asks me that until later." She gazes up at me, cocking her little head again.

"That's because it's not polite." I haven't even thought to wonder about her age—not because I'm polite, but because she's outside the yardstick. My best guess figures her for about twenty-eight, but honestly I wouldn't be shocked to hear it swing ten years in either direction. Thirty-eight would put her in my range, and I guess that'd be a comfort.

"Polite," she says, and laughs, pressing both her hands across her belly: *oh-oh-oh-oh-oh.* She rocks back on her heels. "That's quite funny of you, David."

I don't know what's funny, but she seems to mean it. "Well," I say. "I guess we should go on up."

"Cigarette first," Dorlene says. She wiggles her fingers at me.

"What?"

"Cigarette. You smoke, don't you?" She grabs at the air between us. I haven't lit up this whole time, not even when I was alone on the way down to the bus station, on account of who I might be picking up. It comes to me slow now, looking at her little grasping hand, that I shouldn't have bothered. Dorlene wants to smoke.

I fish the rumpled pack out of my jacket, swimming in the very idea. I pass her down a cigarette. It's huge in her hand, as big around as her fingers and half again as long. It's ridiculous, of course, completely absurd. She snaps the filter off and then she starts to twist the paper, pinching as she goes, squeezing tobacco out the ends. Both her hands bend into tiny teacups. Tobacco sprinkles down around her feet. Some sticks to her palms. She's a real pro at it, you can see that right off. In no time she's got it twisted down to the thickness of a juice straw. She holds it up to me. "It's better when I can roll my own, but this'll do in a pinch."

"I guess it will," I say, and I hear a little squeaky shine in my voice.

"Now, will you light me, please? We'll smoke, and then we'll go up."

I've no doubt that's what we'll do. I light us both up, and we smoke here in the little splintered herd of cars piled in the crook of the L-shaped drive. Dorlene smokes her tiny cigarette like she won't get another. She even does a Frenchie now and again, smooth as a cat. I wonder— because of the cars all around us—if I appear to be alone.

"I'm thirty-two, by the way," she says abruptly.

I nod like I don't care. "That's older than I would have guessed."

"My, you *are* polite."

Lord Jim starts barking, far off. His usual big, deep, warning barks. He's somewhere past the outbuildings, deeper in the southwest corner, at the unmown end of the property. I can't spot him, but I get a little chill. Down around my legs, Dorlene listens too. She has her nose up in the air, like she's scenting. She looks mousier than ever. Or something more sleek and keen than a mouse—something more in the middle of the food chain. And I can't believe that I haven't thought of the dog yet at all, all the way here. That I've neglected to imagine the spectacle coming down the pipeline, I mean.

"You know about the dog?" I ask Dorlene.

Dorlene drops her nose and starts to crack her knuckles, prissing her cigarette way out at the tips of two bent fingers. Underneath the far-off pound of Jim's barks and the swells of talk from the house, her fingerjoints pop and click—tiny little sounds just her size, like beans being snapped. "I've seen pictures." She looks toward the barking, but she's surrounded by these cars she can't begin to see over. She doesn't sound worried, exactly, but there's trouble in her voice. Lord Jim goes on hammering the air. "What's it? Lord Byron?"

"Jim. Lord Jim."

She arches her eyebrows. "Well, that's not even real."

"He's something," I say, but I don't even know what I mean. He lopes into view just then, way off in the lowlight along the cropline—a huge and bobbing white square. He disappears into the high, faded corn.

"I do like dogs." She puts her emphasis on the word *like*.

"I do too."

"I never thought Mr. Shamblin would get another dog after Willa died."

Mr. Shamblin, she says. Willa. I don't know much about Dorlene, just some of Tom's wet-eyed ambiguities about this repeat girl in the Seattle summer program, his favorite student. I don't know how much she knows. She still has her head tipped aside, listening, though the barking's stopped. Her neck is long and sweetly bent, her slight shoulders round with muscle in the ordinary places, and beneath her collar, across her chest, the fabric of her dress snugs across the swell of breasts. I hit my cigarette and cross my eyes down at the glow. I wonder if she knows how Willa went deaf and blind at the end, how that good dog became a doddering, snuffling husk. "I wouldn't say Jim really is Tom's dog. He came with the farm. He's more Triti's than anyone's. She's crazy about that dog."

"Triti. She's the caretaker?"

I start to laugh at that one—partly because Dorlene's soft *r* when she says Triti's name makes it come out *Tweedy*. But also, that there would even be a caretaker. That Triti would ever be called something like that. And it seems like Dorlene ought to know better, but maybe not. It's not even clear why Tom took the farm in the first place. It was the kind of place he and Helen might've wanted for themselves, but Helen had been dead five years when Tom closed on the farm. He makes noises about the day he'll move out permanent. Instead he comes out only for emergencies, or for mundane pleasantries like mowing. Or for the rare party like this one, when he invites the students and the faculty and a few outsiders like me. The rest of the time, it's mostly just Triti. Triti and the animals. I shake my head. "Triti? No. She just, I guess, wanted to live out here, and Tom let her stay for cheap. I mean, she does take care of the place, but it's not a job or anything. Someday she'll get tired of not giving up on it, and she'll go someplace else. Or Tom will finally realize he's never giving up the house in town, and he'll sell the farm. Either way, Triti will leave. I don't know what she'll do then. She would hate to leave the dog, at least." I suck on my cigarette. I feel like I've said too much, or said the wrong thing. Plus listening to myself talk, I'm not sure *caretaker* is the wrong word for what Triti is out here after all, these days. Her and her steely presence, her patience, her sobriety.

"Why did Triti want to move out here?" Dorlene asks me.

I shrug. "It's away."

"I heard you had a thing."

I don't let her see my surprise. "We did, yeah," I tell her, and hope that'll do. A broad bubble of shouts and laughter arches onto us from over past the garage west of the house. Peopleshapes amble back and forth. I half expect to see Triti go ironing by up there just then, but the sun's got everybody backlit. I don't feel much like heading up yet, and I guess Dorlene doesn't either, because we just stand there a while longer, letting the cigarettes go slow.

We finish about the same time. I try to pace the last finger of mine to hers, kind of eyeing it, but I get this feeling like she's doing the same to me, and maybe that's what made them last so long. This hits me somehow, levels us a bit, I'm not sure why. We go up to the house. I make my steps small. No one's out back except a few of the grads. We both get looks, me by association, but whereas I ignore them, Dorlene actually nods and tosses out hellos. We walk on by the kitchen, where slabs of massed talk flicker out an open window. Past the house, on the west side of the lawn, where a big tree went down in the spring, Tom and a bunch more students encircle a big pile of brush: Tom's promised bonfire. Ernest stands in the front leg of the driveway alone, watching them. The kids are his too, of course, but they avoid him as devoutly as they flock to Tom. Tom plays the piper down below, his voice rolling up the lawn, round and slow and smiling. The fallen tree's mostly sliced up now, but a patch of trampled, unmown grass makes a chalk outline for where the carcass has been. All the dead twiggy stuff has been dragged out into the short grass, and that's what they're trying to light. A stack of burnable logs sits off to the side. Several of the biggest slices of trunk have been rolled out for seats.

In the drive, Ernest's got a rolled-up newspaper in one hand like a baton. He beats it against his thigh now and again. The sight of him is a little jarring—we used to be neighbors, after all. Friends, in a way. But he's the only person I see that I know besides Tom, so I start over toward him. I don't know what the hell to do about Dorlene—I don't know if she knows anybody either. But she stays close, like we're together or something.

When we get up to Ernest, he says, without looking over, "They're using lighter fluid." I get the impression he knows he's talking to me, but I don't know what I did to announce myself.

I nod. "Lighter fluid, huh?"

"They went through a whole bottle already. And on to a second," he says, real flat.

"Oh my," squeaks Dorlene, and when Ernest hears that, he does look over. He bends at the waist with his arms still crossed.

"You're Dorlene," he says in that same tone of voice.

"I am."

"I heard about you."

She doesn't even look over at him. "Did they really use a whole bottle?"

"I'm Ernest Baines," Ernest says, like using both names will mean something to her. But Dorlene just walks off toward the brushpile, her ankles disappearing into the grass. We watch her go.

"Holy god," Ernest says when she's out of earshot.

"I drove her here. She was in my car."

"Did she have a carseat?" Ernest says. I don't tell him about the airbag thing—about how she's so small it could kill her—even though I'd like to tell someone.

Tom spots Dorlene. He spreads his arms out wide as he walks up to her, but they don't hug. It's quite a sight, him towering over her, like a circus bear. Until now it's been Dorlene who looks not really real, or real in a different way—synthesized, maybe. But now it's Tom who seems make-believe. Kind of an absurd hulk of a thing, a monster. Next to him, Dorlene looks practically like a perfection.

"Holy lord," Ernest says.

Dorlene starts wagging her finger at Tom. You can tell she'd have it in his face if she could. She points at the brushpile, the bottle of lighter fluid in his hand, scolding. But Tom just laughs and shrugs, shakes his head. I can imagine his protest even from here.

Ernest turns and looks me up and down. He sighs. "So Dave, how are you?"

"Pretty good," I say. I add, "Hanging in there," and right off wish I hadn't.

"And how's Lisa?" Ernest slaps the newspaper against his knee— *whack, whack, whack.*

My head clouds over. They're still neighbors, and he's asking me. "She seems good."

"She's lost weight."

"Yes."

"A lot of weight."

"Thirty-five pounds," I tell him.

Ernest nods. "So, you're still talking, then. I see." How much Lisa and I talk these days is no business of his, so I don't say more. I've been out of the house for almost a year and have barely seen Ernest since. I'm realizing right now that he's not a friend, not so much. Proximity might've been all we had going for us back when we used to talk more, when we were neighbors still. But maybe proximity is all any relationship has going for it. I try to think of something to say, and then Ernest murmurs, "Look at that, look at that now." But all he means is just Dorlene down there, still talking to Tom. Meanwhile, the kids bomb the brushpile with lit matches.

I ask Ernest how Brenda is, trying to rile him. It's been years, and we didn't know her long—she moved out several months after we moved in—but we were friendly for a while, the four of us. Afterward she was always coming by to take or leave the kids, and out in the driveway you'd see her and Ernest sometimes, stilted and smoldering. We didn't keep in touch.

Ernest scoffs. "Yes, how is Brenda." He lifts his rolled-up paper like a sword. He goes into a fighting stance, and he starts on like he's fencing or something, stabbing and parrying out at nothing, the whole bit. His shoes scuffle across the driveway stones. "From what I hear?" he says, and then he kind of lunges and stabs down toward the ground, throwing his back hand up over his head like he's in Shakespeare or whatever. "Sluttish."

All at once there's a flash from below, and the thump of tearing air. A big fantail of fire, all orange and black, blooms from the brushpile. Me and Ernest both startle. Ernest jerks up erect and steps back beside me. Down below, Dorlene's been knocked off her feet, almost lost in the grass. Tom bends and scoops her up with one hand—under her belly, like he's scooping up a cat—and he trundles toward us with her under

his arm. I find I'm walking down to meet them but I don't know why. I
leave Ernest standing there.

"I am serious to fucking god, Mr. Shamblin." Dorlene is stiff as a
stick, her hip pressed against Tom's. Her dress hangs down between
her legs. "Put me the fuck down." Behind them, the flash of fire has
vanished to black and smoke. Nothing's caught. The kids chatter and
whoop.

Tom comes up grinning, hanging on to her. "You've met Dorlene."
He's wearing a long pink polo that's tucked I don't know how far down
into his pants. His pants always ride low, and with Dorlene on his hip,
they're sliding into a dangerous zone, but the polo stays tucked.

"David," Dorlene says to me. She's managed to cross her arms.
"David, please tell this man to put me down."

"What, you're friends or something now?" Tom rumbles. "A little
time in the car, and now this?" I don't know if he's talking to both of
us or just Dorlene. He hitches her up against his hip again, re-getting
his grip.

"Mr. Shamblin," says Dorlene. "David." She hooks her eyes on mine.

Ernest speaks, right behind me—practically in my ear, close enough
so I can feel his breath on my neck and smell the dim piss-taint of wine.
"Tom, Tom, Tom. This hardly becomes you."

What that even means, I'd like to know. But Tom laughs and sets
Dorlene down. She alights like a dandelion tuft, starts smoothing her
dress again. We all watch and then Tom turns to me. "Triti," he says.

For just a second I don't even recognize the word, and when I do I
blink and shake my head. "I haven't seen her. We just got here."

"I need to find her."

"I haven't seen her," I say again, shrugging, and fuck if my face
doesn't burn.

"Well." Tom turns and considers the brushpile. He drops a two-
handed wave of resignation toward the kids still there, then smiles
down to Dorlene. "You wanna see the house?"

We head up and in through the back porch, the four of us. The house smells like food and age and Triti. The adults have gathered in the warm kitchen: Martin and Clara, red-faced Bob Everitt, a handful of faculty I know by sight but not right off by name. Fat Susan—partly here on neighbor credentials, like me, but also because she's co-owner of a gallery in town—has the back seat at the table alone, her mitts around a wineglass as big as a melon. She waggles her fingers at me. Little kids yammer somewhere back deeper in the house, a sound that takes me stupidly by surprise. Triti is here too, standing with her back to the sink, facing us and holding wet hands in the air like she's prepping for surgery. Water piddles off her elbows. She's cut her hair a little shorter, and the inside curtain of it, hanging to her shoulders, has been dyed pink. I haven't even decided yet what I'll say to her. Looking at her now, standing here, I realize I've pretended I might say nothing.

Triti doesn't snag on Dorlene at all. Her eyes slide up over Dorlene and onto me, right behind. I mean, everyone looks first *at* and then *away from* Dorlene, but only Triti seems not to notice her. A small but detectable hit ripples around the rest of the room as people spot her. They fix their faces as far from surprise as they can, most of them mustering up something like a happy expectancy, some of them checking Tom, all of them careful not to stare. But nobody manages to keep their conversation up; only the kids' voices from the other room keep the moment from sinking all the way down to silence. It's awful, and I wonder if this is how it always is for poor Dorlene. But she just stands there right out in the middle, hands slid inside her pockets like paper in envelopes.

Tom waits another beat or two and then says, his voice all girled-up with glee, "Now that's how you silence the rabble." Everyone waits for him to go on, to flood the uncertain space that's bubbled up. He steps in behind Dorlene, his face thoughtful and impish, and I can see he's either working up his joke or already has it and is just weighing the delivery. At last, he dangles a hand low over Dorlene's head. He booms, "Everyone, this is Dorlene. I know she only comes up to here on most of you"—and he shifts and curls his hand so that he's making a vaguely lewd gesture of height just at the level of his own crotch—"but don't think that means she's going to do you any favors."

Grumbles and titters sprout up all around. Fat Susan lets out a loud puff of air—*whuh!* Bob Everitt squawks and Ernest chuckles low. Triti's eyes roll faintly and she shakes her head. Tom shrugs for everyone, turning and grinning. "What?" he says. "What?"

Dorlene raises her arms. She holds them up like some little prophet or something, and everybody quiets and looks at her—I sure do. Tom stops mugging and beams down at her. She lifts her voice, and it hums so high it sounds like a ringing that's just in my own ears. "That's good advice I hope you didn't need," she says. "But I *am* Dorlene."

And just like that she pretty much has the whole room. Laughter and friendly voices—relieved voices—rise. And I try to think if in my whole life I have ever said the words "I am David," or if I ever would, and I try to imagine what kind of thread of connection somebody would have to have with themselves to be able to say such a thing and to find that it's not just received but received *well*. And while I'm thinking this, I realize that someone in the room is clapping, and it hasn't seemed inappropriate, and for a split second I worry it might be me.

"She is Dorlene," I say to Ernest.

"Mm," he says.

Triti's eyes are on me. She still has her forearms up in the air, her hands like mittens. "Tom took all my towels," she says across to me, and her voice rattles me, but I'm distracted by the sight of Clara Pope shaking Dorlene's hand. It occurs to me that this is a thing I myself did not do. I'm not sure I regret it; Clara has bent herself into a captivating, awful shape, clearly unsure how to handle the mechanics of the act. She looks like she's just barely overriding the instinct—a maternal one, maybe—to squat down to Dorlene's level. The effort does regrettable things to her ass. I'm embarrassed for them both.

"Towels . . . gone," Triti says to me. She shakes her wet lifted hands. Triti's words come through to me like they're on a wire, through the chatter that's risen back up. She's tuning herself to my frequency, throwing a private conversation across a crowded room—a kind of invisibility, a concentration.

And I'm hearing her, I am, but the fact that I'm hearing her—that she would talk to me this way at all—makes me a little sick, drags me back across the months. I shrug at her and press a smile and shake my head. Triti bends and begins to wipe her hands and forearms on her jeans, leaving dark smudges across her thick thighs. She keeps her big black eyes on me the whole while, her face as blank as an animal's.

"Interesting," Ernest says beside me, but I pretend not to hear him. I let myself get drawn back into Dorlene making the rounds with Tom. Everyone watches, one way or another. The spectacular handshakes, the looks on everybody's face as they drink in Dorlene, the eager ginger way they bend to and touch her—it's all fantastic. Dorlene has a whole battery of greetings, all of them old-fashioned and flirtatious. She stands in front of poor giggling Bob Everitt, practically underneath his outrageous potbelly—a fucking alarming sight, I can tell you—and tells him: "I fancy you a troublemaker, Mr. Everitt. I hope you won't disappoint me." And somehow even with all her fairylike slurring, she still sounds prim and precise. Bob fans his fingers and flops his wrist and all but whinnies at her.

Ernest, watching, makes little noises of satisfaction now and then. After a while, Fat Susan hisses at us, trying to get our attention. She tips in toward us, her boobs blobbing over her hands, threatening to snap her wineglass off at the stem.

"*Pssst,*" she says again, giving us both the *p* and the *t* of it, baring her teeth. Ernest raises an eyebrow, and she pushes a slow slurring whisper at us: "*Who—is—that?*" She tugs a hand free and points down, again and again, like Dorlene was under the table or something.

Ernest mimics her, pointing down at the ground, raising his eyebrows even higher. Susan nods. Across the room, Tom is protesting innocence high over Dorlene's head. A couple of younger guys I don't know laugh, looking from him to her like autograph hounds. Tom says something about Dorlene's flat head. "So you can put a drink on it," he clarifies. Dorlene rocks on her heels.

Ernest holds his finger and thumb an inch apart for Fat Susan, indicating a tiny thing, a little bit. He makes his face a question.

"*Yes,*" Susan hisses, eyes darting. She mouths her question again, giving it no throat but lots of saliva, the words crackling so wetly you don't even need to read her lips: *Who—is—that?*

Ernest whispers crisply back at her. "That's Dorlene."

Across the room, a little snigger pops out of Triti. She's slipped into the laundry room doorway now, watching us, her hands folded into her armpits. Susan scrutinizes Ernest like he's a cobweb in a high corner.

"She's a student," I tell Susan. "Of Tom's. From the summer thing he does in Seattle."

Susan leans back and lays her hand flat on the table. "She looks so young." She slips back into a dead whisper on the word *young.*

I check out Dorlene again, how she has her hands locked behind her waist, how she's so pert and erect and attentive. "She's not, though. She's thirty-two."

Ernest looks over at me and makes a sound like a detective.

"That's still young," says Fat Susan.

"Dave likes them young."

"How does a person like that even manage on their own?" Susan asks, not seeming to hear him. I'm hardly sure I've heard him right myself. "Is she married?"

"Now *that* is the question, isn't it, Dave? Or maybe it isn't."

Triti's still watching, listening. Her jaw is like stone. I point to a used paper plate on the table in front of Susan. Something red has recently been devoured there, scraped down to its stain. "Where'd you get the food?"

Fat Susan raises her wine and drops her head, giving me a vampish gaze. She waves a balloon hand toward the dining room. "Oh, *honey*," she says.

I push off, leaving Ernest behind, and excuse my way through the kitchen. I don't watch Triti watch me go. But as I sidle past Tom and Dorlene, Dorlene—I swear—reaches out and briefly snags me, giving my pants a fleeting tweak, like I've caught on a bramble. I glance down, and she slims me the corner of a smile. I've no idea what kind of look I'm giving her in return, but blood rushes to my face. She opens her mouth and flashes her eyes, and she tells me, thinly but unmistakably: "Hungry." I nod before I know it. I sort of stumble past Bob and slide through the butler's pantry into the dining room.

I find myself almost alone. A couple of students—a guy and a girl—are making their way down Tom's long homemade table, which is just obliterated by food. Further on, the front parlor is full of kids—faculty offspring, loose and loud, flickering between the dark furniture. They've got some game going up on the TV screen. I try to let my head clear. I tell myself Ernest doesn't know as much as he thinks he does. I wait for him to come slinking out after me, snarking—or maybe Triti—but nobody does. I can still feel that faint tug on my pants, so foreign and low.

The couple at the table nod and smile at me. I nod and walk on by. I pass the open door to Triti's room without looking. I know anyway: her bed like a magazine, quilted and trim and square. I wander into the front parlor. Eight or nine kids, half of them rapt before the jangling TV, some clinging to controllers. Every few moments, the room reacts to something that happens on screen, the kids flinching and howling, but all I see are scrolling colors, flashes, shapes shrinking and growing. Tiny figures move. Someone must've brought these things here, hooked this stuff up to Triti's set. Beside me, a couple of the Gottlieb girls—I think—are sitting on a trunk.

"What is this game?" I ask.

I get a gangly, one-shouldered shrug in return. Neither of them takes her eyes from the TV. "I dunno." The TV whistles and bangs.

I go back to the dining room. I take a paper plate and step in behind the two grazers. The sight of all this food makes me struggle to imagine what kind of thing Dorlene might want to eat. Why she's hitting me up for it, I don't know, but I think it over hard. The spread out here is chaotic: Tupperwares, or whatever passes for that these days, and trays and bowls and plates with lids cast aside or foil pulled half off, almost everything inside tan or green. Bags of chips yawn from the back rows like artillery. The food itself is that pretentious mix of the refined and the intentionally lowbrow they always have at these school things: pita triangles and Jell-O salad and stuffed mushroom caps and macaroni salad and Brie, and some kind of little quiche thing maybe, and who knows how many hopeful homemade dips—I see three different guacamoles alone, and something that looks like salsa but isn't. There's a bowl full of curling red chips that I figure for sweet potato. Despite the extravagance, I don't find much I'd eat. Besides chips, there's not much store-bought stuff, stuff you can trust. Voices knife up briefly from the kitchen, sparring good-naturedly.

On Dorlene's behalf I reject the smaller-is-better approach right away; I figure it's probably stupid to imagine that most of the eating mechanics couldn't be overcome. I'd follow the lead of the two students, but they aren't so much taking food as they are browsing, pointing and murmuring knowingly to themselves. They nod at a round Corningware thing full of purple spheres, shining in a glaze. Abruptly the one beside me, a tall girl with a sultry swayback and a pooch that pops out from under a braless tank, turns and drapes a slack hand above another dish filled with a brown-and-yellow bubbly crud. It's been cut into already; the insides look thorny, wet, and coarse. "Try this," she says to me, her voice like a rumpled bed. "It's amazing."

"All right." I carve a two-bite spoonful onto my plate. I've got no plans to eat it. Experience has taught me that what other people want to eat most is whatever I don't—not that that's narrowing it down. But I tell myself this yellow stuff looks promising, not identifiable right off, sophisticated. The girl plucks simple grapes, green and red, from a bowl with her long fingers. I take another half spoon of the yellow stuff. "Did you make this?" I ask her.

"Oh no. I'm allergic. But T—— made it,"—and here she gives me a name, but it's a name I've never heard, something French or Danish or something, something like Terry but with an *n* in it, and she pronounces it I'm sure exactly right, and the sudden shift her mouth and tongue make startles me—"and so I know it's amazing." She halves a grape with her front teeth. "He's amazhing." She reaches out with her hand and actually lays three long fingers against the rim of my plate. She chews. She pats the edge of my plate, real soft, just barely, twice, holding the crown of the bitten grape between that same forefinger and thumb. "Enjoy," she says, and she drifts away from the table, taking the guy with her.

After they go, I consider dumping the yellow crud back into the dish, but I don't want to get caught. Instead I push it as far to the side of my plate as I can, making a gooey skidmark. I spy a plastic-wrapped plate of Triti's cookies that no one's busted into yet, and I slip a cookie out from under the wrap. I take a handful of Cheetos and a few of the red chips. I take a cluster of green grapes. I stand there and I eat the cookie and I stare into the yellow stuff, imagining the swayback girl in different stages of allergic disfigurement or death—nothing personal, just a thing she's got me wondering about—and after a minute she and her guy go prowling across the lawn outside, headed down toward the brushpile, her lifting grapes and taking them into her teeth. I steal another cookie.

I take some stuff I'm pretty sure is tabouli, and two of the round purple things, which are so slippery they're instantly problematic. I take some cheese squares, a few crackers, a wobbly blob of Jell-O salad that I fussily quarantine for its own sake. I get a clear plastic fork.

And now I've got my plate, loaded in a way I'd never load a plate for myself, and hell if I know what I ought to do next. I feel sort of stranded. From the kitchen, Tom's voice still booms, and I have trouble even beginning—mentally, I mean—to orchestrate the act of taking the plate on in to Dorlene.

I venture into the butler's pantry, up behind Bob Everitt. I lean into a shadow. I don't know if Dorlene's even thinking of the mission she's got me on. In the kitchen, Ernest is talking to a woman in a sagging tan. Tom stands at the laundry room doorway, and just over the hump of Bob's shoulder I see Dorlene beside him. I shift a little and then I freeze because there is Triti: she's kneeling in front of Dorlene. She's gotten right the fuck down to her knees, eye to eye, just like I suspected Clara Pope wanted to. I can't see Dorlene's face, or Tom's, but Triti's shines with pleasure as she chatters and nods, looking for all the world like some chirpy preschool rah-rah gushing to a toddler about her finger-paints or her teddy or whatever. She kneels like you would kneel for a dog. And as I watch she looks over at me, finds me. Her eyes are dark with glee, sharp and deep.

I turn and leave. I pass Triti's room again. I head out the front door and onto the open porch. The presence of the porch swing surprises me—I don't know why—but I go ahead and take a careful seat on the peeling slats. I eat a cracker and swing a little and look out over the lawn. Nobody's gotten the brushpile lit yet. The kids down there look to be lost between tries, an idle cluster talking and glancing stupidly around. Somebody upwind's got some weed going, somewhere out of sight. A round of Triti's laughter comes bulldogging out the kitchen windows, down the house, big sudden heartfelt *hunh-hunh-hunh*'s. Tom's voice rides it loud, unintelligible, undercut by a sharp trill from Dorlene. And then, fleeting but plain—bobbing momentarily to the surface of that sea of noise—I hear my name slip from Triti's lips: *Dave*.

And I suddenly just feel a thousand, feel spread thin and sick again, retrograde. I can't figure out how I ended up back here. Here on this swing, here at this house, here with Triti nearby at all. This is not what I wanted. And look—even though I maintain that everything that crumbled would have crumbled no matter what, still I can't help nosing at the rubble I'm crawling through now. I nose at it and I hate like hell the freedom of suspecting that different flavors of ruin might have been available to me. I doubt that Triti can say the same. The Cheetos on this sad plate I've put together look like sickly little neon turds, embarrassments. I pick one up and flick it out into the grass. I expect it will alight and glow there, but it disappears.

I swing. I eat the pineapple. I light a cigarette. I go ahead and toss more Cheetos into the lawn. Whatever they're talking about inside, I imagine Triti's got Dorlene fooled by now. And Tom's a lost cause, of course. Not that you can't trust Triti, but you do have to mind the gap between what she says and what she's thinking, because of her stranglehold on it all. She has magnificent control, I mean. Her telling me just now that her towels were gone, for instance: it's no surprise that her first words to me after five months weren't a greeting, any reminder of my absence. No, she squeezed those words out smooth for me, like pearls. And that is maybe her exact nature, now that I think of it— pearl-making. It comes to her like breathing. And I guess I don't know after all how you can trust a person like that in the long run. I'm going to say I can't—not in the long run, I don't think so. I doubt anyone will warn Dorlene.

The slippery stuff on my plate has been sliding around, slopping together; the Jell-O is compromised and mostly inedible. I pluck grapes from the mess of my plate, some of them frosted in the yellow stuff. They go into the lawn, too, one by one. They bounce and tumble in and out of the grass. I give myself points when one reaches the gravel drive that leads back to the road. I watch the sun drop toward the hill out west and I listen to the house leaking sounds, words I still can't quite make out.

Jane

HE KEEPS YOU. HERE IN THE NIGHT ABOUT THIS BED, YOU find yourself thickening down out of dark, gathering in his thoughts, shaped by his insistence. Ask him what you are. You resemble pain, a pressure rising, a scent, a sound his heart breeds in his ears, anything that thrives on attention. But it misses the mark to say you are in his thoughts. Better to say you are of them, or even better: that you are his belief in you. And as he lies beside his silent wife and burns you to life—teaching you your body, dictating the way he means your limberness to move—slowly you learn that possession is the sinew of ghosts.

You haven't walked in this place, this sleepy house of his. Because every ghost is restricted to its most vital paths, your territory here is no more than his devotion to you. And his devotion is a narrow, brimming well. You've touched nothing here, not really, not by your own hand. You haven't let slip a single sound, but that's to be expected: because he doesn't ask you to speak, you cannot. He doesn't wish to hear you utter certain things, wouldn't like to hear you suggest, for instance, that your claim to each other is the old one between men and women, a concession. This is a secret of sorts. He keeps it as killably small as he can.

A mirror rises from the dresser across the room. You are not in it. The mirror multiplies the dressertop clutter—a wooden box, two tilting picture frames, the squat jar full of hair clips and bands, jewelry mounded in a shallow basket, this coffin-shaped bottle of perfume. The mirror casts back a swatch of the dark room, too—the window above the bed, curtains closed across the night; the green bedside clock, its numbers turned to hieroglyphs and lies; laundry accruing amorously in the corner. And of course the bed itself beneath you in the dark, that draped country. On one side of the bed, a thick sweep of fair hair curls. But nowhere do you see yourself, not you—you don't believe so. At most, perhaps a swell in the shadows describes you, or there: a deviation in the square of the room. You can't be sure; every conviction is his. He teaches you instead that what you cannot discern, you must allow him to believe. See how you learn.

HE DEMANDS THAT YOU BE BEAUTIFUL; HOW COULD YOU deny him? As if this flesh, now, could be disowned. Swelling upon him here in the dark, over the clouds of his breath settling across his shoulders, you are entirely composed of the paints that comprise him. He colors you, believing he does you a disservice. He thinks of your face like riverstone, like fine wind-shaped sand, and your eyes full of color, hazels and coppers and others too, as varied as the shapes of shadows in a rockfall. He fathoms the structure of your nose, a delicacy, ended in a fleshy tip that talking draws down and releases, like a rabbit's, but he is mindful of how if you are to talk to him, he must watch your mouth because your lips—you mouth it: *my lips.* You tear them apart cleanly where you open for him, like water itself around flesh, and he will agonize to watch them linger, to know that he will never discern the tiny noise they make at parting. Your hair is a rainbow-black snake. It is a curtain or an exquisite spill. It is ink somehow spun into thread, into rope, into a limb, all these things—tonight or another, another. *God the hair on you,* he might say, and he doesn't say now but thinks how you might pull yours around between your breasts, how it might lie there, an enviable pet, and how you might stroke it, knowing you are seen, the inside of one wrist grazing your nipple through your shirt. He imagines your legs, trailing behind you, sloping into the floor, knit like a mermaid's. Where your thighs thicken, your skin recedes dark up under your hems. Or you have no hems, no anything, only bare skin up and up, sculpted soft around a curving god's eye of shadow, deep in your naked lap. From your hips, your curling torso rises—a long smooth segment of an undescribed coil. You drape your weight onto one sapling arm, your naked fingers thin and kicking slowly across the carpet, your elbow overstraightened into a tender, bent-back swell. Your other arm reaches up, reaches out, reaches maybe for your cigarette, for hairs fallen into your face, for a gesture in the making, for this. You shift beneath the liquid of your shirt, liquid yourself. Or of course you are shirtless, radiant, waxing dusky in the places where a woman should, down your face and your front—these, and these, and these, and here. You spill heat like breath onto the carpet between your thighs.

The folded sheets sag between the quiet wife and him. This has been your way, yours and his—you occupying him so soundly that you consume this landscape. Outside you in this room, so many dearly foreign things abound: cold sluicing down from the window, the clock's clean slanted green, the expansive sounds of a furnace, the texture of a wall, a door's tilt and shadow, a wife's breath and pliability. But you come between him and all of it, all of this, becoming as he admits you—a lens, or a shape-stealing shadow, or a trapped slab of air between panes of glass.

You listen first to his breathing. Or if you do not listen, exactly, you espouse its rhythm. Perhaps you are unable to listen, just as you have been unable to speak. He fixes you here with these rules, rules he makes but doesn't know. For instance: you have mass, but may exert no force; you are hot, but fail to rise; you are meant to be filled, but cannot truly surround. The only physical law you obey is his gravity, and the only freedom he grants you is the attitude of your compliance. And so as he lies beside his wife and thinks of you, you do this, you do: you willfully abide becoming full.

You understand him. It is easy. You are answers to everything. You must be. You become the limit of his fascination, a towering and rapacious thing. And you might imagine that you make yourself canyon walls closing where rapids rise, that you are rich flora arching over a sodden path, that you thicken like the surface of a wound, that above all you insist he go only where you allow it. Imagine you could accomplish such a feat. You can. You are weak and strong because of your faith that things are just so: that you are the turn of the knife that carves you.

All of this is given. All of this is given. And of course it cannot be forgotten that you are an accumulation of moving parts. You know what this means to him, to you. He has collected his thoughts of you, compelled by all the possibilities of blood pooling, and you unlimber gladly into them. You do this because he obliges you. For example: you may stand crooked over a bed, your dark hair tumbling down around your lit face, all your sullen, waiting parts exposed. Your back gleams, a story pouring through the shapes of shine your skin makes. And him, he may draw you against him, asking you to be brazen and trembling, mutable and firm. This you can do. You are the sight of you, the touch of you, your scent and sound and will—or in a given instant: the mettle of your body's rootbone, taken in the heavy hooks of his fingers. See how you learn. He forgets everything he knows about restraint, surrenders to you your voice, and certainly now you could confess to him: *I cripple you*, you do, and this is what binds you, this old deed—these slow drooping strings of salt and blood and marrow.

AND AFTER, MUCH AS HE HAS BEFORE, HE LIES JUST SO—JUST so he lies. You curdle dearly from his skin. Now you truly are smell and sights, warmth, the thick sweet air of a sequestered room; he breathes you slow but slight. You have already begun to dissipate, had always been meant to begin, pushed apart by a coldness, or by little more than some named heat's absence—and what is your name? As for him, his need dwindles, all his insistence sagging now, not now. You begin to rise from the bed, going surely to rags, thinning into threads, into dusted beams of cobwebs. Beneath you, the clock burns. The curtains hang. The mirror yawns. The wife there breathes and breathes.

There is no name for the jagged thoughts that tumble into the space you leave; as you now exist—sad to say—you are not precisely an element of such imaginings. But first and last you pretend—as you drift and fade into some dark corner made for you, or for which you are unmade—you pretend you know how in the night as you unspool, this wife watches her husband where he lies feigning, lies hoarding indifference, his hands casket-crossed on his chest. You wonder what has been traded for this. You see and suspect, despite all your blindnesses, the way her eyes shine in silence like bones in the dark.

Putting the Lizard to Sleep

I WAS A DAY TOO LATE PICKING UP THE LIZARD; HE WAS ONLY
dead, but I was late anyway. I set a tiny bell tinkling as I came in the
door on the third day, and I loitered stupidly beneath it as it rang down
around me and away.

A broad woman in a broader navy suit had commandeered the counter, talking to the vet girl from the other day. The woman nodded and
leveled heavy hums at the girl, who stood there starched into her white
top—thick, farmy arms and a thick, farmy neck. I tried to recall her
name—something fluid with *g*'s and *v*'s. Like Guinevere, but not that.
Neither of the women looked up for my bell. The broad lady leaned
against the high counter, an anchor-rope arm curled across a cat carrier.
I watched her bend over it, heard her pour a few sweet sounds into it.
She wasn't giving any of that to the vet girl. I listened to them talk. They
said *hairballs* and *medication* and *intestinal,* and a lot of other words
that went down at the end. Mostly they said *hairballs.*

I fingered through a rack of the clinic's business cards on a stand by
the door. I tried to look purposeful. Eight different compartments for
the cards, but only two different names among them. Dr. Kipp wasn't
one of them. I let myself get suspicious. I looked through them all.

"I can help you here, sir. Can I help you?"

I jerked around, knocking over a column of cards like dominoes. Another girl sat behind the high counter. She stretched herself to see me,

craning her neck, tendons carved out of her skin there—it seemed like it would have been easier for her to stand. She smiled at me. She wore glittered eyeshadow.

"I didn't know you were there," I said, fumbling to right the business cards. I made a bad job of it. I went to the counter, slipping between the wall and the lady with the cat. The lady glared and didn't move down, but she corralled her cat carrier in a little closer to herself. Her cuff buttons scuttled across it.

I looked back at the girl and shrugged. She blinked.

"Can I help you?" she chirped.

"Yeah. Yeah, I'm John. Collins?"

"Like the drink," she exclaimed, straightening in her seat and sparkling her eyes.

"What?"

"Like the drink. You know. You must get that all the time." She covered her teeth with her lips. She became mannequin serene—like she could move only while talking. She sat frozen. I didn't know what to say. Finally I told her this was the first time. I said, "Actually."

"It wouldn't be the first if you were hanging around with my crowd." Then, wagging a finger at me: "We must be hanging around with different crowds."

"Yeah, maybe."

"Can I help you?" she said again. Fresh as the first time.

"I'm here for Rafael." I spelled out the name for her. She clicked at the computer. The other vet girl told the broad lady that she'd be right back with her medicine. The lady nodded imperiously, said she'd be waiting. I flattened against the wall as she veered away from the counter; she walked through the space I'd been occupying. I watched her vet girl head down the hall—Genevieve?

"Lhasa apso?" said mine.

"What?"

"Rafael Lhasa apso?"

"No. Rafael lizard." She clicked once. Again. I felt a little weird. I wondered what Rafael the Lhasa apso had been in for. Worms, maybe. "Oh, okay," she murmured after a minute, her voice suddenly funereal. She pushed herself away from the counter on her wheel-footed stool, still looking at the screen, her wrists perched on her wristpad and her red nails straining up off the keys, hands like scared spiders.

"So did you want to pick up his remains today, then?"

That's what she said: *remains.* I came at the word a little slowly, in that oblique way you do for a word you weren't expecting—a way that can make you realize a thing you hadn't before. Remains, right—that's what stays, the mess you leave. What a bold little novelty it was to try to imagine Rafael torn from his shape that way. I wondered what Evan would think, whether he would understand. I plucked at my pants and said please.

The girl got up, squeezing me a sympathetic, lipless smile, and came out from behind the counter, saying, "It won't take a minute." She was hugely, startlingly pregnant. She swayed down the hall the way the other girl had gone, through the last blank door a long ways back. I caught a glimpse of a garish, laminated poster beyond, a swirling and colored cross section of innards.

I took a seat across from the woman with the cat. The woman's jacket was bunched up behind her neck, rising above her hairline, making her look hung up by something, rigged. She'd taken the carrier out from beneath the towel and was hunched over it again, sticking a carrot through the wire.

"It's a rabbit," I said, watching. She looked up at me.

"He is a rabbit," she said.

"I thought it was a cat."

"I'm allergic to cats."

"Oh. What's his name?"

"Thumper," she said, turning back to the cage.

"If I'd heard that, I guess I would've known. Thumper. That's got to be, like, the Rover of rabbitdom. Spot, Boots, Whiskers, all that." She looked back at me again. I gave her a long pause and she made me think through it all. I shrugged and said, "Mittens."

"My daughter named him. She's five." She said it like a killing stroke.

"My son is five. He named our lizard."

"What's your lizard's name?" She was sitting all the way upright now, intent on burying me in her attention, holding the carrot like an ice cream cone. I glanced at the rabbit, brown and impossibly sleek, eyes almost closed and his nose wriggling, ears pressed like sleeves to his flanks. He had the dullest expression on his face. A bright-red towel with blue and baby blue butterflies on it lined the floor of the cage. It should have been green. I frowned at the rabbit. I wondered how long rabbits live, if you let them.

THE LIZARD COULD'VE LIVED FOR TWENTY YEARS, I FOUND out too late. Twenty years if you let him—longer than a child. Twenty years is a large chunk of life, a sizable fraction of a life. A fraction with a name. If you imagine twenty years forward in a life—or backward maybe, for that matter—you come to a barely believable place, and watching the lizard with Evan I found that I couldn't picture him at either end. The lizard, I mean: Rafael. He stared back at us, sometimes with two eyes, more often with one. He was a hunter too, but far down the food chain. Far enough to have the telltale wide-set eyes of prey.

Rafael lived in Evan's room. He stayed there even from Friday to Tuesday when Evan was gone to his mother's house, and Sara and I kept the door open so he wouldn't be alone. He had his own cage, of course, but we liked to see him standing tamely at the glass, the thrum of his throat his only motion, and we would go in to speak sweetly to him and be seen by him—though I often felt myself invisible, standing there, the way the curve of the earth is invisible to a man. I made my comforts small. Fingertips seemed to impress Rafael, but smiles were wasted on him.

He was a good lizard. We all liked him. We took him out a lot because he was the kind of lizard you could do that to. We'd asked for
that kind. He sat in our hands, not much longer than any of our palms,
scenting the air or our skins with his tongue. His toes felt like pencil
points, or like blunted pushpins when he climbed your arm. It more
than tickled. It felt like it hurt. The cats stalked about nearby, furious.
They bristled and quivered insanely whenever we brought him out.

"I think we should name him Smiley," Evan said, bent over the lizard
in his hand. "Because he's smiling."

I looked at Sara. She blinked at me. She shook her head.

"I don't know, buddy," I said. "I'm not sure that's his name. He's
sort of dashing. He should have a dashing sort of name."

"What's dashing?"

"Like the Three Musketeers. Like Robin Hood."

"What's a dashing name?"

"Like D'Artagnan. Like Tristan."

"Rafael," Sara said.

"Or Galahad. Galahad is a very dashing name."

"Yes, it is," Sara said.

"What's the one Sabby said?" His name for Sara.

"Which one? Ask her."

Sara raised her eyebrows. "Rafael?"

"Rafael," said Evan slowly, picking up the lizard by his hips and
turning him.

"Be careful," I said. "Not by the tail."

"I know."

The lizard was the kind whose tail would fall off in an emergency—
a lizard emergency. It was supposed to grow back, but from what I could
tell, they didn't ever grow back right; our lizard book had pictures. I
read that chapter several times, in the bathroom even. A lost tail might
grow back in the shape of a bulbous knob, or a stubby spear, or often
in the shape of a head—a lizard's head. The worst ones were cloven and
lopsided, like soft lobster claws.

"Be careful, Daddy," Evan always said to me, sharing my fear. "Be careful of Rafael's tail."

Rafael ate crickets alive, a troubling trait. He was a good lizard anyway. Not including the crickets, he only ever bit someone twice, and both times that was Evan's mother. She invited herself in a lot when she came for Evan on Friday afternoons. Also she wanted Rafael to like her—craving, I imagine, the casual prestige of being the lizard's favorite. Sara said it was her way of pissing in our house. After the second time Rafael bit her, she breezily theorized that he must not like the smell of her lotion.

"Maybe he does," Sara said. "Maybe it smells like crickets."

"I never thought of that," Evan's mother said, looking at Evan. "Who knows what lizards smell?"

"Let me smell," said Evan, and she did, but if he learned anything from it he kept it to himself. I couldn't have told him any more; her scent, when I got close enough to detect it, seemed like nothing I knew.

In time, I came to hate crickets. I hadn't before. Since they had to be eaten alive, we always had crickets at home—livestock for our pet. I tended them like they were chickens—useless chickens. The crickets had their own cage, with their own food and water, and a sparse but functional toilet-paper-tube decor. I replenished their population every week with a bag from the pet shop. I hated them; they stank. They smelled much worse than Rafael ever did, and their behavior was more questionable. I suspected that they ate one another, at times, though I couldn't be sure. Also, they weren't supposed to chirp, but every once in a while we'd get one that did—completely maddening.

After the first few weeks, we began to keep the crickets outside. Evan—who at times seemed as interested in the crickets' miniature ecosystem as he was in Rafael's—made a place for them, in the pot with the rose of Sharon tree. The tree wasn't doing much, didn't have much of a future. It had been withering under the eaves for over a year, waiting for Sara to plant it in the yard. She watered it occasionally—or I assumed she did—but it hadn't bloomed over the summer, and by then the dirt around the base of the tree had become a little round pasture of brittle leaves. We kept the cricket cage in the pot, in a little hollow Evan shoveled out by hand there. Evan fed fallen leaves through the slots in the lid of the cricket cage. Or at least I think he did.

From there, seven crickets a week went to Rafael. I admit I relished their fate. I tricked them by giving them a special kind of food that fattened them up for Rafael. The woodcutter's dumber children, Sara called them, trying to disapprove. But she, like us, enjoyed the spectacle of their demise. Rafael's feeding times were more comical than graphic, full of a mute and alien violence. He struck at the crickets one by one, lunging like a clumsy snake and taking them whole into his mouth. The act itself was eminently fast and bloodless, so pristine that it made me frown to think of the gory fuss raised by beasts like tigers, or wolves. Mammals in general. Nothing savage or even self-aware came into Rafael's face while he murdered his meals.

And the crickets were always white when they went in, white as popcorn, because I had to dust them with a powder beforehand; Rafael got his calcium that way. I took the crickets from beneath the rose of Sharon tree and dumped several of them into a plastic canister full of the white powder. I shook them up until they were completely covered in the stuff, like chicken breasts in a bag of bread crumbs. Everyone said it was important. For proper maintenance of your lizard's health.

"Don't forget to dust them," said Evan, who knew all about it. When I put the cricket cage back beneath the rose of Sharon tree, he rebuilt the drifts of leaves around its edges.

"I won't," I said, and I didn't. I didn't mind. I figured the experience was a trauma to them. I shook them maybe more than I needed to.

And so when the crickets went in they were white like mice, beacons against the dark-red sand in Rafael's cage. I wondered if they knew how they looked. Evan and I watched them scurry, Rafael towering among them.

"They look like ghosts," Evan said.

"Yeah. They do."

"Are they dead?"

"What do you mean?"

"Are they dead, after you put the dust on them?"

I smiled and took a breath, rolling the thought around like a taste. What a thing to say, to imagine. I got a sudden revelatory sense of everything he must not understand—a huge and reeling space. I let out a little laugh. "No, man, they're alive. They're just white."

"Oh." Evan turned back to the cage, his chin on his fingerbacks. I watched him watch the crickets scramble, captivated by his solemn face, suspicious that it stirred from within. Like a sequestered pond disturbed by trickles from an encroaching underground stream.

Within months, Rafael did lose his tail—just as we'd feared. One afternoon just after Evan's mother had come and taken him away, I found Rafael, his tail half-gone where a clean new wound shone: an open circle of raw, pink flesh. I felt sick, violated, confused. I thought immediately of the pictures in the lizard book, about the worst of the replacement tails I'd seen. Plus the meat he was showing, the actual inside of himself—I couldn't stand it. I called Sara at work, but she was already gone, so I paced around and waited for her. I walked in and out of Evan's room and thought about calling him at his mother's house. But I had never called him before, not him specifically; I didn't want the first time to be for this. I paced and waited. Whenever I came across the cats, I reminded them they were bastards. Just in case. More than once I looked in Rafael's cage for the missing length of tail, but I couldn't find it.

When Sara came home she took it better than I did, at first. I believe she may have had more confidence in the process, like it was a magic trick. But then she discovered that Rafael seemed to be partially paralyzed—below the waist, as it were. She took him from the cage, and when he walked up the throat of her forearm his whole back half simply dragged behind, his rear legs trailing limply. And his tail, of course, with its huge and unapologetic wound. Sara cooed at him sadly. She looked from him to me and back again.

That evening we took Rafael to Dr. Kipp, who we did not know. We called our usual vet, and they referred us to this other place that had more experience with lizards and the like. Also, they had emergency hours. Dr. Kipp met us at the door—he was short and dark, very erect. He unnerved me. He took us in back, where he examined Rafael and then conferred with us solemnly, tapping a forefinger against his black caterpillar mustache between sentences. He called Rafael *the young man*. He told us that Rafael might simply be suffering from an injury that was pinching a nerve in his spine, causing a temporary paralysis. Dr. Kipp spoke in a way that suggested this was common, though he didn't specifically say so. The therapy for such injuries, he explained, involved steroids and warm baths. Also digital manipulation. Sara and I looked at each other.

"Massage," Dr. Kipp said, his hands in his pockets.

"We know," Sara said.

I cleared my throat. "We were wondering how something like this could happen. The tail."

Dr. Kipp shrugged. "This is the design of the lizard. It is meant to occur."

"Yes, no—I know. But I mean, what kind of thing could cause it? How could it have happened?"

"You do not know how it happened."

"No."

Dr. Kipp shrugged. "It could have been any number of things. If the young man's tail became trapped somehow."

"Trapped."

"Under a rock, in the lid of the cage." Between Dr. Kipp and us, on the huge stainless examination table, Rafael bobbed his head and licked his eyes. He looked tiny in the big black shoebox we'd brought him in. Ordinarily such a box wouldn't have held him, but now he sat motionless, propped up on his front legs while his back half slumped. He looked like a seal. Sara stared at him, chewing her nails, pressing one hand into her mouth with the other.

"I frankly don't see how," I said.

Dr. Kipp sighed. "Sometimes even the smallest provocation can cause the autotomic response." Our lizard book had said pretty much the same thing, almost verbatim, but I resented him using the word like that, a word we weren't likely to know. I did know it, of course, because of the lizard book. I'd even unearthed the etymology: *autotomy,* like *lobotomy,* where the *-tomy* part means "a removal or a cutting, an excision." The *auto-* part means "self." This is what lizards do, when threatened. Dr. Kipp leaned over the table and peered at Rafael. "And so we may be experiencing some minor swelling in an unfortunate location. This is common. But here: if the young man was truly trapped—if he struggled about during the incident, or had been subjected to violent movement—permanent damage may have been done to his spinal cord. In this instance, he would have to be euthanized. I'm sorry." He said all this leaning over the shoebox, examining Rafael, like he was talking to him and not us. Dr. Kipp tapped his mustache.

Sara pulled her hand from her mouth. "He wouldn't survive like this? I mean, just live?"

I found myself nodding. "People are paralyzed."

Dr. Kipp sighed again and straightened. "Has there been defecation since the incident?"

We looked at each other. "I have no idea," I said. Sara shrugged and shook her head, her fingers back in her mouth.

"He is likely unable. We will wait and see, will we? It's difficult to say without knowing how the injury was managed."

Sara said, "We have a child in the house."

Dr. Kipp raised his eyebrows. "A small child?"

"He's five. Rafael's his pet."

He nodded and shrugged again. "Boys," he said. Sara bent and began to murmur into the shoebox.

Dr. Kipp gave us five days. He sent us home with a plastic syringe and a tiny supply of steroids. Sara took care of all of it. She squeezed Rafael's delicate jaw open—the way you do with any animal, only on a tiny, fragile scale—and squirted the medicine down his throat. Every night, she ran a tiny bath for Rafael in the bathroom sink, a puddle of warm water just about chest deep. Chest deep on a lizard. Each evening she fussed over the water's temperature. She palmed water across Rafael's back. She tiptoed her fingertips up and down the length of his spine, talking quietly to him. She knelt on the floor, the counter edge pressed into her armpits. She squeezed the gruesome stub of his tail. "He likes it," she said to me as I watched. "It helps him." And he did seem to like it. His eyes went to slits, and he lifted his chin. "Look at him," Sara said, letting water drop onto his head from her fingers. "Little baby," she said. "Poor young man." The cats, shut in the bedroom across the hall, mewed and pawed at the door.

By Monday, Rafael still wasn't better. Sara gave him two baths that day. After dinner, I leaned in the doorway as Sara hummed in the bathroom, splashing softly in the sinkwater, humming to Rafael. Evan would be back the next day. I hadn't called him, hadn't told him or his mother anything about Rafael, about what had happened; I'm not sure why. Rafael wasn't getting better. He hadn't crapped. We couldn't tell if he'd eaten or not. The crickets' whiteness faded with time, and after a few days they became hard to find.

I said to Sara, "Tomorrow's the fifth day."

"Fourth day," Sara said, not even looking up. "You're always doing that."

I counted in my head, mouthing the days, discovered she was right. I left the room, closing the door behind me. I released the cats. They smoked around my ankles and slid into the living room, heads hunkered stealthily down.

On Tuesday, on the drive from his mother's house, I told Evan about Rafael, about him getting hurt—that he was going to die. I assumed he knew nothing about it. In the growing dark in the car, I told him about the accident—about the autotomy, although I didn't use that word. I told him about the paralysis, Dr. Kipp, Sara's baths. After hearing it all, Evan didn't ask me how it happened. The accident, I mean.

Once we got home, Evan and I sat on his bed, across the room from

Rafael's cage, across from Sara sitting on the floor, curled over her knees. We'd taken Rafael reverently from the cage so Evan could see, then returned him.

"Maybe he will poop tonight," Evan said.

"I don't think so, buddy. I don't think he can do anything back there."

"Maybe he'll get better when we put him to sleep."

"No, buddy, he's going to die. We're going to help him die."

"Euthanasia." The word I'd put there crawled out of his mouth.

"That's right."

"And what's euthanasia?" Sara said. Like it was a quiz.

"Um, it's when he's going to die, and we help it."

Sara laughed to herself and began to blink fast through something—some kept thought. I didn't know what it could be, but then I think she said, kind of soft up into the air: "That's any damn thing."

I said to Evan, "We make it more peaceful."

"More peaceful."

"Yes."

"I hope he will be better then."

I stared into the cage. A couple of crickets, at least, still haunted the place, but I couldn't see them. Rafael himself was out of sight as well. We still hadn't found the rest of his tail.

"What are you thinking?" I asked Evan, not looking at him.

"Nothing."

"I was thinking I wish we knew how he got hurt." I looked at Sara while I said it. She had her eyes on Evan.

"Well," Evan said, and he paused. "Well," he said, "I was thinking, I do think he will be better." He swung his hanging heels against the side of his bed—*thudud, thudud.*

"You never know," Sara said to me.

Hours after bedtime, in bed ourselves at last, Sara asked me if we couldn't keep Evan home from school the next day, so that he could be there at the vet when the euthanasia took place. I thought about it, about the act—I imagined a syringe bigger than Rafael himself, his skin wrinkling beneath it, his soundless thrash.

"I don't know that I want him to see that," I said.

"Why not? Shouldn't he? I think he should."

"Picture it," I said.

"I have."

I sighed and rolled into her, pressed my forehead against her cool shoulder.

"Believe me, I have," she said.

I said, "He should go to school."

We took Rafael in the next day, Wednesday. I took Evan to school first. In the morning, saying good-bye for the last time, Evan said to Rafael, "See you later," and Sara told him to say *See you on the flip side.* On the way to school in the car, Evan asked me what *flip* was, and I had no idea what to say at all, not at all.

"That's different for different people," I told him at last. When I got back home, Sara had Rafael in the bathroom one last time. I couldn't say what for.

As it turned out, it wouldn't have mattered if we'd taken Evan with us to the vet that day; not one of us witnessed the act. With a lizard, you can't be there when it happens. They don't let you stay, and here's why: the moment itself can't be guaranteed. Apparently, lizard vital signs are so hard to detect, even on a normal day, that you can't be sure if the lizard is alive or dead. The vet injects the drugs, and then you have to wait—twenty-four hours—to be sure they've taken effect. Dr. Kipp had neglected to tell us this. The girl at the counter, the girl with the thick, farmy arms, explained it to us stoically. We asked her her name, like it would help.

"How do you know if they haven't?" Sara said to the girl, thick and impassive. She and the girl each had a hand on the shoebox between them, Rafael inside. "How do you know if the drugs haven't taken effect? If he starts to move, is that how? That's how you know—he moves?"

"Essentially, yes," said the girl. "The animal begins to shows signs of regaining consciousness. It happens very infrequently."

"But how do you know twenty-four hours is even long enough?"

"Twenty-four hours is many times longer than long enough. Twenty-four hours is a precaution."

"How could you know?" Sara turned to me. "How could they know that, babe?"

"This is what they do," I said.

"What would happen if he doesn't die?" Sara said to the girl. "If he's still alive, what do you do?"

"Then we administer the drugs again. It happens *very* infrequently."

"You have seen it happen," I said.

"It has happened."

"Oh my god," said Sara.

The girl looked at Sara, back at me. "We could contact you, if you like, but people generally prefer not to know."

"I would want to know," Sara said to the girl. And then, to me: "I want to know, baby."

I said, "I don't think that's anything we need to know. And it won't happen anyway."

"Extremely unlikely," said the girl.

We left him there then. We said good-bye to him first; Sara cried. At school that day, Evan made abstract art out of paper-towel tubes and orange pipe cleaners the size of batons. No one from the vet ever contacted us.

AND SO ON SATURDAY, A DAY TOO LATE AS IT TURNED OUT, I found myself back at the vet, waiting for the pregnant girl. I stared at the rabbit lady. She gazed back at me, unperturbed. She had let her hand with the carrot fall back at the wrist. Thumper sniffed at his door.

"My son's lizard," I told the lady, clarifying. "His name was Smiley."

She raised her eyebrows, smiling with the middle of her mouth and frowning with the ends. "Five-year-olds," she said. She turned back to Thumper.

"Yeah," I said. I got up. I walked around the vet's waiting room, a strangely big space, full of imitation plants and a busy, barnish smell. Down the middle of the room ran a long row of wooden shelves, filled with bags and cans of cat and dog food, special-diet stuff for chronically ill animals. I thought about what Thumper the rabbit might think of the smell in here, but Thumper was probably all about carrots right now. What could carrots smell like to rabbits? Maybe like steak, or like chocolate cake, or maybe like carrots, only fantastic. I wondered what was keeping the pregnant girl.

Toward the back of the room I found a small display case of glass and mirrors. On the shiny shelves within, skulls had been laid out in rows. Animal skulls, all kinds, many shapes and sizes, the smallest scarcely as big as a fingertip. They'd been mounted on sloping glass slabs. In front of each stood a trim little placard, giving the names in Latin and English. I squatted and took my glasses off, lifted a hand to shade the glass. I squinted.

Glaucomys sabrinus, flying squirrel. A smaller one was *Mus musculus*, mouse. Another one, swollen and round, was *Agapornis roseicollis*, lovebird. *Holodactylus africanus*, African clawed gecko. *Rattus rattus*, black rat. *Sylvilagus audubonii*, rabbit.

The farmy vet girl returned. The girl who'd taken Rafael. Her name came to me suddenly: Geneva. I could hear her behind me, but only the reflection of her uniform hovered in the glass, white and doubled. She and the rabbit lady murmured. I eavesdropped on the instructions for medicating Thumper as I looked back through the rough reflections at the skulls. I ran my eyes over the tiny cranium of *Sylvilagus audubonii*. The skull looked so small and so terminally savage, robbed of its adornments—full of secret planes and holes that scarcely admitted the substance, the relevance, of vital structures like ears. I tapped on the glass. I pictured Thumper gagging on a stubby plastic syringe. I thought about Evan, what he would make of these, and I wondered when it is, exactly, that a human skull begins to shed its softness.

"Mr. Collins?" The pregnant girl stood beside me, fiddling awkwardly with her bulging shirt at the navel. I guessed she would ordinarily be a handwringer.

"Where's Rafael?"

"Mr. Collins?"

I stood up, turning. A smell came off the girl in a cloud, the essence of some synthetic Victorian flower; it mixed with the bite of the disinfectant in the air all around, pulling my thoughts into vapor. My vision swelled.

"Oh man," I said, fading back a step.

The girl advanced. "Mr. Collins?"

"Stood up too fast." I smiled and fended her off. "Where's Rafael?"

Her eyes dipped into the rounds of her cheeks. Her mouth curdled, gathering words. A sudden horrible thought came to me, watching her. A wondrous thought. I thought of Evan and felt a little tremor beneath all my skin as it shrank.

"He's not *alive*, is he?"

"No, no," she said. "No. No. He was euthanized. It went fine. It was very peaceful. But I'm afraid, when you didn't come, yesterday, we did accidentally cremate him. We did cremate his remains. I'm so sorry." All this in a rush. Like she was relieved I'd suspected so much.

"I called," I said.

"You did?"

"Yesterday." My voice drifted. I watched over her shoulder as the rabbit lady left without glancing back in my direction. I found myself wishing that her apparent failure to do so was in fact an exertion.

"Who did you talk to?" the pregnant girl asked.

"What? I don't know. A girl. You?"

"I wasn't here yesterday." She looked back at the desk. Looking for Geneva, I guessed, but I couldn't see her.

"No, not her," I said. "She told me her name. I don't remember it."

"I can find out."

"No, no. It doesn't matter." I rubbed my eyes, took another queasy step back. "About the girl."

"I'm so sorry. I really am."

"We were going to bury him. My kid is five. We made a stake with his name on it."

"Oh," she said, putting her hands across her mouth. "I'm so sorry, Mr. Collins."

"It's not your fault. I don't know." I eyed her slowly, wondering if she was part-time. Back at the front desk, Geneva had rematerialized. She had an ear cocked our way, pretending to look down at a clipboard. I stood there trying to think what to do, or how to do it, and as I did, a strange slack feeling watered from my chest down my arms—relief, I realized after a bit, a shameful little strain of it. Plans I'd only queasily committed to seemed pointless now. I pursed my lips. "He was a good lizard," I said at last.

"I'm sure he was. I'm real sorry."

"What about ashes? Do you have ashes?" She grimaced. "You don't have ashes? What do you have?"

"They only fire the incinerator one night a week, and unless we have an animal where the owner wants the ashes, we do, you know, a group . . . thing. All the euths at once, I mean."

"So you wouldn't have Rafael the dead lizard ashes—you've got, like . . . petshop holocaust ashes."

She frowned. "We do a group burn unless there's a request. A special request."

"Could be a little corn snake mixed in there, then, or some Lhasa apsos. Emu, maybe."

The girl scratched at her forehead with a big crimson nail. She was losing some of her interest in being stricken—because of the emu, maybe. "I'm sorry, I don't know what to say," she said. She put her shoulders up by her ears. Her breasts rolled into each other atop her belly. "There's no charge for the cremation. I mean, of course there wouldn't be."

"Yeah, well, right. Okay. Thanks. Look, here's the problem." I cleared my throat, and it shuddered. I wondered what the stuff was that they gave to Thumper. "My son," I said. "My son, he felt pretty sure I'd come in here today and Rafael would turn out to be alive, you know? Because of the waiting-to-see thing. He's five, he doesn't really get it. I guess I wanted to have . . ." I paused and looked up at her. She had her head cocked like a bird's. She reminded me of the kind of owl that has one ear permanently higher than the other on its head, to help pinpoint the tiny sounds of prey. Eyes the size of grapefruits, relatively speaking. Owl grapefruits. I glanced back at the skull case, the girl. She tried to smile at me, but her teeth had gone shy. "I wanted evidence, you know? *The* evidence. I wanted him to see what dead is. We want him to understand that Rafael isn't going to be around anymore, anywhere, at all. Ever. He has to get that."

"Yes," said the girl.

"Look, if I come home without the lizard he's gonna say maybe he's still alive and I'll say no, they burned his body, and he'll say yeah but maybe he's really a fire lizard and he flew out the chimney or, Christ, I don't know. He's a kid. It's all cartoons." I wiggled my fingers through the air.

"Okay, hold please?" The girl turned and hustled away, leaving me standing there. She wobbled around the corner, disappearing down the hallway. Geneva went after her, leaving me alone. I didn't know what to do. Maybe I'd caused difficulties; maybe, even, I'd gotten the girl into trouble somehow, and I felt a little bad about that.

I went over to the hallway. I listened for voices coming through the door at the end, but all I thought I heard was something crying, some animal—a puppy, maybe. Beside the hallway entrance, a huge sagging bulletin board announced the PET OF THE MONTH; yellow schoolhouse letters had been pinned to the board in an arc. The pet of the month was named JEZEBEL. An overexposed picture of a fat gray cat wearing a prairie bonnet hung below. Someone held her, belly up; fat human thumbs had her by the armpits. Beneath the picture a hand-printed list hung:

JEZEBEL LOVES
warm laps
dress-up
Charlie Chan
sunshine
lunchtime, dinnertime, breakfasttime, anytime!

JEZEBEL HATES
getting wet
the neighbor cat
Venetion blinds
birds on the loose (squirrels too!)
industry

"Industry," I said. In Jezebel's picture, a crescent of her tongue stuck out from between her teeth. Her eyes looked wild, one rolling slightly off center to the left. I lifted my glasses and looked closer, as close as I could get. In the background of the picture, a bowl of colored candies sat out on a coffee table, and a green afghan spilled over the arm of a couch.

I heard the door at the end of the hallway open, footsteps on the floor. Voices murmured low. Both of the vet girls rounded the corner, and the pregnant one stopped and looked around, not seeing me. Geneva headed back behind the counter.

"Here," I said.

The girl jumped and grabbed her belly. "Oh my," she said.

"I'm sorry."

"Oh goodness," she said.

"Charlie Chan, what's that about?" I said.

"What?"

I pointed at Jezebel's list. "Charlie Chan."

Geneva spoke up, from way back behind the counter. A computer screen lit her face. "The dog. It's their dog."

"The dog," I said, and looked back at Jezebel.

"Mr. Collins?" said the pregnant girl.

"I'm sorry."

"It's okay. I'm sorry too." She said this earnestly, almost enthusiastically, like we'd just discovered we hailed from the same hometown.

"You *are* sorry," I said.

"I am. But we talked about it, and . . . okay." She set her shoulders and dropped her chin, rolling her eyes up at me gravely. "We do have disposable carriers. I could give you one."

"Wait, what?" I said. "You what?"

"A box, if you want one. A disposable. Doctor puts the small animals in a Ziploc bag, and then we pack the bag in a disposable carrier. A cardboard box. To take home, right? It's got our name on it. It's what you would have had, to take home to your boy." She took a step back and made a game-show gesture, turning and opening both hands brightly toward the reception desk, as though offering me something I'd earned.

"Whose idea was this?"

She dropped her arms. "Doctor's. And—oh!—also he said not to charge you for anything. I mean, we'll take care of the euthanasia. Because of the oversight."

"Dr. Kipp."

"Yes."

"You would do that?" I said.

"I'm sorry?"

"You think I should take a box. An empty box."

"I'm sure, Mr. Collins, that it's not my place to say." She clasped her hands together beneath her belly and gave a tiny bow. She was very pretty. I thought of sailors trapped in the stomachs of broken ships. I looked at Jezebel's picture again, her fat-handed owner and the M&Ms, Charlie Chan somewhere out of sight back there.

"I could do that," I said to the girl. I followed her to the desk and waited while she slid a folded-flat box from a shelf and popped it into shape—a white box far bigger than Rafael would have needed, but the smallest they seemed to have. It was about the size of Evan's head. The girl took it to a table against the back wall. Geneva stopped what she was doing and leaned back alertly in her chair, looking on.

"Your name's Geneva, right?" I said to her.

She glanced at me. "It is."

"I remembered that."

"People tend to."

"I didn't, almost," I said.

"I was there with your lizard," she said. "It was painless."

We watched as the pregnant girl packed the box full of loose paper towels, plain white ones as blank and purposeful as her face while she worked. She laid a dozen or more single sheets into the box, one at a time. She closed the top of the box, where it came together into a handled peak, held shut with cardboard tabs that she thumbed into place. It looked like a little house. The girl put a white sticker on the front of the box and brought it to me, smiling. Geneva had turned back to her computer.

"There you go, Mr. Collins." As though it were all right. I spun it around to look at the sticker she'd attached. It said LOT#1367-GL. She'd put it on crooked.

I shook the box. The girl flinched. I couldn't get the paper towels to make any noise, but I thought I might be able to discern one, sometime, in a quieter place, and wondered what it would be like. The box did have the name of the place on it, like she'd said. A logo stretched around two sides, and I recognized it as a bigger version of what was on their business cards: an ascendant parade of silhouette creatures treading a thick line the same shade of blue as themselves. Some little rodent led the way, followed by a chinchilla, a cat, a dog, and a woman with a bird on her shoulder. The cat straddled the corner, longer than it should have been. The bird brought up the rear, holding its wings aloft and looking as though it meant to make off with the woman. The rest of the animals seemed unaware of the danger. I held the box at arm's length.

"The chinchilla looks funny," I told the girl.

She looked at the box in my hands.

"That's a turtle," said Geneva, and when I looked at the box again, I wondered what I'd been thinking. I tried to recall if I knew whether chinchillas were rodents or not, and then for a second I couldn't remember if turtles were reptiles or amphibians. I started to rotate the box in my hands, putting the procession into motion. I went at turtle speed.

"*Raaaaah,*" I breathed when the bird came around the second time.

"Mr. Collins?"

"No, I was just—the bird. Birds on the loose." The girl frowned, gave her shirt a pluck. "I will take this," I told her. I went on holding the box out between us. "Thank you. We'll see."

"I'm sorry about our mix-up," she said. "I'm sorry about the loss of your pet." And because I'd never heard anyone say that before, I thought—for a second—that she meant that Rafael had lost something.

"No, he didn't," I started to say. I fumbled stupidly through some words. I said thank you again and started to leave. The girl seemed to be waiting for it; she waved as I backed out the door. Geneva frowned from her chair, gazing vaguely off to the side.

I carried the box to the car, cradled in my arms. I couldn't bring myself to use the handle; I don't know why. I settled the box in the passenger seat. I started the car but didn't go anywhere. Instead I sat looking at the box. I sat there doing that for a while, and then I reached over and upended the box. I drove all the way home like that.

"OH GOD," SARA SAID, MAKING A TENT WITH HER HANDS and covering her eyes. "Is that him?"

"Not really, no," I said.

"What do you mean?"

I'd carried the box in by the handle, and now I bent and set it on the table. I stepped back and pulled my arms from my coatsleeves, trying to think if I should have said yes, or something else. Sara asked me again where the lizard was. She watched me from the couch, all frozen and waiting. Suddenly she wilted, reaching for the box and pulling away, confusion running through her face.

"Oh my god. Is he alive?"

I stopped and considered her, surprised. My head felt like a bird's. I tried to imagine her thinking such a thing. "That's what *I* said." I touched my chest.

"Oh my god."

"No, he's not alive. He's not alive anymore. He died like they said. They put him to sleep. It went fine."

She nodded, chin working. "So where is he?"

"There was a mix-up. I couldn't get him."

"What do you mean? Did they just throw him away?"

"Ah. They . . . burned him."

"They *burned* him?"

"Well, it's one of the options—for that. The wrong one, but he was definitely dead. I mean, technically they cremated him. That's what I should have said."

"They cremated him."

"Yeah, if you don't want the remains, then they can cremate them. I told you that."

"Oh god," Sara said, nearly crooning, touching her lips. "He's *remains*."

"I think it was bad timing. Last night was incinerator night."

"But you called," she said through fingers. "I thought you said you called."

"I did."

"Did you tell them that?"

"Yes, but, you know, they couldn't . . . you know. What would they do?"

"Did you get your money back?"

"They didn't charge us. For any of it."

"Well, yeah."

"They didn't charge us for the shot, even. The stuff, you know."

"Oh, baby," she said, real sad. She leaned down the length of the couch and tore herself a handful of tissues, one at a time. They fled into her hand like tiny blue ghosts. She piled them on her stomach and pressed one to the corners of her eyes, her nose. "Oh shit," she said. "Fucking little lizard." I stayed standing. She had all the couch anyhow.

"But anyway," I said. "I got the box."

"The box." She pointed. "This box."

"It's the box they would give you. Normally. To bring him home in."

"It's empty?"

"Yeah. Well—actually, it's full of paper towels."

"Why?" she said. She sniffed. "Why is it full of paper towels?"

I opened my mouth. Air came in. I thought about the vet girl, the glitter in her eyeshadow.

Sara didn't wait for me. "They said, 'Sorry, we incinerated your dead lizard, but take this nice box full of paper towels anyway,'" she said.

"I asked for the box."

"Why."

"Because of Evan." I looked at the back of my hand. Sara's tissue went still.

"You're going to bury an empty box," she said at length.

"Yes."

"You're not going to tell him."

"That's my thinking."

She gazed at me. She shrugged and dropped the ragged tissue on the floor. "Well," she said, "here, then." I hesitated, then leaned forward and grasped the box with both hands, tossing it to her. She hefted it, shook it beside her ear. "Feels empty. Sounds empty."

"Does it? It's not."

"It feels pretty empty. It's big."

"Yeah." I watched her turn the box over in her hands. She didn't say anything about the sticker. "I guess we'd better buy a shovel."

"I guess you better, babe." She eased the box down onto the table. I squinted at her and she blurred a little.

"Okay," I said, and just as I was saying it the box gave off a sudden soft *whick,* and a flit of movement. I jumped, and Sara did too, but it was only the tabs on the box top popping free. The box cracked open. Sara spread her thumb and forefinger along the line of her collarbone.

"Oh shit," she said, breathing, and we watched the mouth of the box yawn slowly open, the raw ends of cardboard scraping and stuttering apart. Eventually Sara sat forward and closed the flaps, fingering and pinching the tabs quickly back into place. Like she had done it before.

"Thank you," I said.

"What a thing to say." She poked the box. "Evan will know there isn't anything in there."

"No, he won't."

"You can tell when you touch it." She poked at it some more, scooting it.

I shrugged. "So he won't touch it."

"He'll want to. He will anyway. He might."

"So what am I supposed to do?"

"Maybe you should put something in there."

"What, like an effigy?"

"It doesn't have to *look* like a lizard, but for god's sake it should at least *feel* like there might be a lizard in there." She sat back and plucked another tissue off herself. I looked around the room.

Sara pointed to a heavy retractable pen on the table. "Here. A pen."

"Not heavy enough. Too clackety, too."

She shrugged, worked the tissue into her nose. I wandered around, looking over our busy shelves and opening our few cluttered living room drawers, surprised by all our stuff, and by how little was like a lizard.

"How about a candle?" I peered into the candle drawer. "Part of one."

"Maybe."

I broke off a lizard's worth of cranberry candle, pulling it free from the wick like a shrimp from its vein and feeling the weight of it in my hand. It smelled like Christmas. I brought it to the table, rocking it back and forth in the cradled cup of my palm. Back and forth. I was pretty sure it was wrong, a machined thing. I tipped the box over onto its side and laid the candle down atop it. The candle began to slowly roll, picking up momentum. It rolled off the box and dropped into a magazine, open on the table. It lay there.

"We need something else," I said.

"Something meaty seeming."

"Yes."

"Lizard sized."

"Yes, the weight of him."

"Sausage link," said Sarah. She blew her nose, dropped the tissue on the floor.

"Sausage link," I said. Right off, I knew it was the right thing. A picture of one popped into my head, one with little lizard legs, scurrying— steam coming off it. Then I tried not to picture it, which was much harder. "Do we have sausage links?"

"We have had them," Sara said. She picked up the pen from the table and started writing something on the palm of her left hand.

"What are you writing?"

"I'm not," she said. "I'm drawing."

I went into the kitchen. I went to the refrigerator. I opened the freezer and dug around in the cold, under the pizzas and behind the ice cubes. Most of the stuff in there was old and foreign—a box of pink Popsicles, a bag of peas with onions, a tiny Tupperware with a brown and orange chunkiness inside. And way in the back I found a box of sausage links, frozen in place by a blurb of furry ice. Some of the skin of the box stayed behind as I tore it free. Inside, only a few sausage links remained, glommed together like a little stack of logs. I broke one loose and dropped the rest in the garbage. The box, too. I ran my thumb across the sausage link, smoothing the icy ridges where I'd broken it away from the others. The feel of the thing relieved me somehow—its cold stoniness, its pasty and impotent complexion. I wrapped my hand around it and gave it a squeeze.

"Do we have any Ziploc bags?" I called to Sara.

Her voice came back. "We're out."

"How about Baggies?"

"We don't use Baggies anymore. We use Ziplocs."

I went to the drawer where we keep that kind of stuff, but all that was in there was a loose roll of wax paper and a bunch of those little cake-decorating tips.

From the other room, Sara said, "I'm only going along with this because I think he did it."

I tore off a ragged rectangle of the wax paper. It looked like Vermont, or New Hampshire. "Will tape stick to wax paper, do you think?"

"Do you hear me, John?" She called me John.

"I hear you."

"I think he did it."

"I hear you saying that."

"You know what I mean."

"Yes, Sara, I know what you mean." I examined the wax paper, trying to determine if one side was different from the other. The box didn't specify.

"This is the worst thing I've ever done," Sara said. She emphasized *I've*. Or I thought she did, just slightly, and right then I thought I might tell her about how I'd gone through the garbage a day or two after Rafael got hurt—how I stood on the front step, angling the big black kitchen bag into the yellow porch light, pawing through all the

kitchen refuse, removing and inspecting the little white trash bags from
the other rooms, the bedrooms, one by one. I unwadded balls of tissue, paper towels, toilet paper. I didn't even know what I was looking
for—or, rather, I knew precisely what I was looking for but did not
know for certain what it would look like. I looked through everything;
I found nothing like what I thought I might.

Sara got up from the couch. I imagined I could hear the tissues from
her belly falling to the floor. I put the wax paper and the sausage link on
the counter and started to roll it up.

"So it's wax paper," Sara said from the doorway.

"That's all there was."

"Here, then." She set the box from the vet down in front of me. "And
here." She held up her left hand. A piece of transparent tape drooped
from the tip of her middle finger. I reached to pull it loose, and as I did I
saw a dark patch on the skin of her palm—a fat stripe of ink. Also what
looked like a mustache, or giant lips, straddling the stripe. But then the
shape crumpled as Sara bent all the rest of her fingers into a fist, leaving
just the finger with the tape pointing at me.

"It's double-stick," Sara said.

"I see that."

"That's what there was."

"So it's double-stick." I took the tape and wrapped it around the
wax-paper tube, sticking it to itself. I opened the box and parted the
sea of paper towels. I felt a little confusion there; the paper towels
weren't blank after all. They had herb plants printed on them, stenciled in green. Their names in blue, someone's handwriting, I'll never
know whose. I saw basil twice. I pressed the wrapped link against
the bottom of the box, thinking it might stick because of the tape. I
covered it again and closed up the box. It was easy, overall. I hefted
the box gently, testing it, but I already knew. I started to say it was
kind of creepy and then didn't. It was, though. I handed it to Sara and
she must've felt the same, because she grimaced as she shifted it; she
gave it right back to me. She wiped her hands on her pant legs. I went

back to the refrigerator and opened the door, looking for a place to make room.

"I don't want that in the refrigerator," Sara said.

"Oh, right." I opened the freezer.

"No," Sara said. "I don't think I want that."

I looked down at the box. "What are you talking about? It's sausage. It was in there already."

"No, I don't think it belongs there."

"Why not?"

She grimaced again and made a fluttery gesture with her fingertips and thumbs, like she'd been into something. "Just . . . no."

"Well, what the hell am I supposed to do with it? I can't just leave it on the counter."

"I don't want it on the counter anyway. Put it outside."

"Evan won't be here again until Tuesday," I said. "That's like four days."

"Three. Three days." She held up her hand and mouthed silently, *Sunday, Monday, Tuesday,* making three imaginary dots in the air as she went. She didn't count today.

I looked out through the sliding doors over the patio. I stepped up to them and put my hand against the glass, gauging October's cool out there.

"How cold is it in a refrigerator?" I said, squinting.

"I don't know. Fifty degrees."

"That seems high."

"Thirty degrees."

"Well, that's not right."

"I don't know why you're asking, then. It doesn't matter."

I took the box outside, closing the screen door behind me. I set the box down on the concrete under the eaves, beside the patio wall. Sara watched me through the screen. She looked gray. She chewed her nails. She had her head tilted and she bobbed it slowly, almost in a circle; I couldn't tell if she was nodding her head or shaking it.

"What if something gets into it?" I said.

Sara took her hand out of her mouth. "I was thinking that."

"It's food, I mean."

"Oh my god." Sara turned and faded back into the house. I cast around for something to put on top of the box but found nothing that wouldn't crush it.

"Sara?" I called, and almost immediately she resolidified at the door. She opened the screen and handed me one of the red plastic milk crates from Evan's room.

I took it from her. "What was in this?"

"What wasn't?" She slid the screen door closed again. I caught another glimpse of the dark drawing on her palm.

I put the milk crate upside down over the top of the vet box. I pushed it with my toe, and it skittered across the concrete.

"Put a rock on it," Sara said, but there were no rocks. I saw only one heavy thing, the rose of Sharon tree. The leaves, already feeble, and yellow now, had begun falling in earnest for winter.

I went over to the tree. I imagined I could still detect the stale-rotten smell of the crickets, rising from the dirt where we'd kept them. They'd been gone for days, though; after dropping Rafael off with Dr. Kipp I'd come home and taken the cricket cage to the dumpster, letting everything inside tumble rudely around as I walked—leaves and twigs and toilet paper tubes, the two cutoff bottoms of Dixie cups, dead crickets and live ones, tiny cricket turds like thistle seeds. I pitched the entire thing. The whole container, everything in it. I cracked the lid open first, just a little bit, I'm not sure how much.

"John?" Sara said through the screen.

"Yes, okay." I stooped and began to drag the rose of Sharon tree across the patio, the heavy stone pot scraping. Leaves shaken loose began to fall, palmfuls of them. I dragged the tree right across in front of the doorway where Sara stood. She *tsk*ed at me twice as I went by—twice—but she didn't say anything. I hefted the tree up onto the crate. I used my legs. The plastic lattice sagged beneath the weight, but it held.

"Might as well be good for something, right?" I said. When I looked up, Sara was gone. One of the cats ghosted by, further back in the house; I couldn't tell which one.

TUESDAY NIGHT, I WAITED FOR EVAN IN HIS MOTHER'S DRIVE-way. I hoped to avoid talking to her. The week before—the day we'd taken Rafael to the vet for the last time, the day Geneva had taken him stolidly from us—Evan's mother called us, long after bedtime. Sara and I were forked on the couch, reading.

"Evan said Rafael was sick or something? Or dead—I'm so sorry, is that true?" Her voice made the phone hum.

"When did he say that?"

"Today at school."

"Why were you at school?"

"The Harvest Party, John. The party? I took cupcakes."

"Oh." I hadn't heard of the Harvest Party. I felt pretty sure I hadn't.

"You should go to something sometime. It's fun, the kids are fun."

"I can never keep track. I don't get the schedules." I took a pen and wrote *E—harvest party?* in the margin of the article I was reading. I held it up to Sara.

"Just ask for one. Or ask me," Evan's mother was saying.

"Yeah, I'm bad at that," I said. Sara shrugged at me and shook her head. She waved dismissively at the magazine, her brow furrowing. She mouthed something at me. I squinted to see—it looked like *Fuck that.*

"So what happened to Rafael?"

"Right, Rafael," I said.

"Did he die?"

"Well," I said, and I laughed. Sara frowned at me. "Maybe." I laughed some more.

"What does that mean?"

I explained the whole situation to her, badly. I began at the end, for some reason, and only seemed to recall for myself—as I spoke—how things had begun. "He lost his tail, I guess is how it happened. It started because he lost his tail."

"How did he lose his tail?"

"I don't know." Sara watched me talk. She'd put her open magazine in her lap. It arched over her thighs like a bird drawn by a child.

"Did Evan have something to do with it?"

I took a breath. "I don't know that."

"Hmm. So Rafael is at the vet now?"

"Yes."

"And you'll find out tomorrow."

"Yes. Or the next day, I'm not sure."

"Did Evan go with you? When you took Rafael in?"

"What? No. He was in school. This was this morning."

"Why didn't you take him?"

"Why would I?"

"So he could be there, so he could know what was happening," she said, and over her Sara was saying to me, "She wanted you to take Evan? Tell her there was nothing to see."

"There was nothing to see," I said into the phone. "There wasn't even a doctor. It was . . . it would have just been a different place to end things."

"But still, some context would have been demonstrative. I don't want him to think Rafael just went out the front door and isn't coming back. That's basically what's going on, right?"

I rolled my eyes at Sara. "Demonstrative? Of what?" Sara stuck out her arm and began to snap at me, wiggling her fingers at the pen in my hand. I gave it to her and she bent into her magazine, scratching.

"Of the process, John. Of what's really happening."

"There was nothing even to see there. Just a waiting room."

"That's better than nothing."

"What do you want him to think is going on? You want him to blame the veterinarian? Or the girl that works there? That would've been more like it, the way it happened."

"Not blame—associate. With an understanding."

"You know, it's not like I didn't explain all this to him."

"Well, that's good. I'm sure you did, and I do think that's good. I talked to him, too." Sara raised her magazine into the air at me, holding it high in both hands. I dropped my glasses back down onto my nose. In the sky of a big blue travel advertisement—over an open sea—she'd written: *NOT HER BUSINESS,* in thick, gone-over letters.

"What, at school?" I said into the phone.

"Yes."

"You talked about death at school today. At the Harvest Party," I said. Sara dropped her magazine back into her lap.

"Yeah, we went for a little walk. We went out to the playground for a little bit." I tried to picture them, ambling together out the side door of the first-grade wing, kicking through the forbidden buckeyes near the parking lot, their heads bent. Some dear and kept conversation under the yellow leaves there, just the two of them.

"What did he say?"

"He said he was sad."

"He did?"

"Yes, and we talked about how some things get sick and die, and how that's just a part of nature. And also that just because someone gets sick, it doesn't mean they're going to die."

"Rafael is going to die, Beth." I looked at the clock over Sara's head. She had her eyes laid on me like a cat's. "I mean, he is probably dead now."

"Well, I get that. But maybe I should've known about it so I could answer Evan better when he asks about it. You know what I mean?"

"Yeah, well. I know what you mean," I said.

Sara got up. She took her magazine and slid into the hall. Light unfolded briefly from the bathroom, winked out again. Evan's mother and I went on talking. We got around to the distribution of long pants and short pants between our two houses, thick jackets and thin. We talked about lunches, hot and cold. We made arrangements.

And now, a week later, with the box from the veterinarian waiting on the patio at home, I felt relief when Evan came out of his mother's house alone. In the house, TV shadows rose and fell behind the curtain along the driveway where I idled. Evan tottered down the steps, his backpack as big as his torso. He'd been bundled beyond reason, so I took his coat off before he got in. We left, and drove halfway home in nearly complete silence. I watched him through the rearview mirror, where he sat in his red turtleneck, huge in his fat blue car seat—an absurdity. He looked out the window. He didn't mention Rafael, not for miles.

"So, Rafael?" I said at last.

"Yeah, Daddy?" He rolled his head to look at me in the mirror, his plump lips—his mother's—pink with cold. His eyes as much like hers as mine. I had no good sense of how much of my face the mirror allowed him.

"I went and got him," I said.

"Oh," said Evan. Not a disinterested *oh,* I knew. Sometimes, when you're five, you don't know how to answer. An *oh* is like a lob.

"I got his body, I mean. The doctor said it went well. The euthanasia? He died very peacefully. It didn't hurt him at all."

"Oh."

"That's good, don't you think?"

"Yeah."

"It's sad, though."

"Except now we can get a new lizard."

"Well," I said. I tried to think what to say. For a minute I had no idea what a person would say.

Evan said, "Maybe they have another Rafael at a different store."

"Oh buddy, I don't know. I don't think we're really ready to get a new lizard right now. We're pretty sad, Sabby and I are pretty sad. About Rafael. I don't think we want a new lizard right now."

"Well, sometimes when pets die, it's nice to get a new one. To not be sad." He shrugged his mother's shrug. He looked out the window again and I did too, for a moment.

Then I said, "Yeah, but sometimes it's nice to just be sad for a while." I watched Evan watch the trees go by on the roadside, smoky brands in front of the setting sun. "I think maybe we should just be sad for a while," I said to the mirror. "He was a good lizard."

Evan didn't answer. Shadows ran in and out of his face. A few minutes later he said, "Look, Daddy. The trees are attacking the sun."

We went home with dinner, burgers in paper and a fish sandwich for Sara, which she finished before I even sat down for myself. Afterward, the three of us went outside and we stood on the patio around the box, Evan and Sara and I. I removed the rose of Sharon tree and set the milk crate aside. It had gotten colder, much colder, and dark outside. The orange porchlight had burned out months before, had become ancient with spiders and bugs.

"Tomorrow we'll bury him. You and I," I said.

"He is in the box," Evan said. His breath plumed.

"Yes, he is. His body is."

We looked at the box, with its blue animal parade. All of them hunted, hunting, I saw now. Even the little rodent, whose hapless imagined prey stalked around the corner from where I stood. I didn't move to see.

"Why is he in a box?"

"Well, he's dead. He's there because he's dead."

"Did they put him in the box?"

"Yes."

"For you to take him in?"

"Yes."

Evan said, "Did you see him?"

I hesitated, just for a second. "No, I didn't."

I turned to Sara and she was right there, tearing at her mouth's corner with her teeth. She was staring at my forehead, and I tried to think if I knew what kind of thing that meant, or if it meant anything at all.

And then as I stood there, with Evan between us, beneath me, suddenly I was losing my sense of years passing, of having passed, and I was falling back with my memories swept in the curved stretch of my arms, and I thought about the things you learn about the people you choose to know, and the sad fading mystery of how you let those things come loose from the people, from the reasons you love them, from the reasons you don't.

Evan rolled his head back on its hinges and looked up at me. "Can I see?"

Before I could even take in a breath, Sara said, "Sure you can."

I looked up at the sky. High over us, spilt-flour clouds, lit from the ground, slid by past the branches of new winter trees. Leaves rattled low in the yard. I felt my heart rising in my chest, Evan's eyes on me from below.

"Sara . . . ," I said into the air.

"I'm sorry," she said immediately, even as my voice still fell.

"Can I, Daddy?" Evan asked.

"No, buddy," said Sara. "I'm sorry, it's not such a good idea."

"I'd rather we didn't," I said.

"Why?"

"It's better not to see some things."

"Then why did Sabby say I can?"

"Why are you asking me that? She's standing right here."

Sara exhaled and, I think, slid a tiny halfstep away from me—or maybe she just shifted her weight that way.

Evan rolled his head back in her direction. "Sabby why did you say I can?" All in a breath.

"Evan, honey, I don't know. I just wasn't thinking. But listen to your dad."

"Can I, Daddy?"

"No, Evan, no."

"Would it be scary?" he said, although by the way he said it I could tell it hadn't really occurred to him that it might be. And as I tried to gauge the issue for him, for a minute I forgot that Rafael wasn't in the box at all, and I had no sense myself how scary the contents might—in reality—be or seem. Or which would have been scarier by now, after four days outside: the real or the not.

And then Sara said, "You might think it was scary if you saw, buddy, but it isn't really. It's just body. The only thing that's scary is that Rafael won't be around anymore. He won't be our pet anymore, our friend. That's scary and sad, but it'll be okay."

"That's right," I said, though I had no idea, that moment, whether it was or not.

Evan dropped out from beneath my touch. He went to his knees and elbows in front of the box. He put his chin into his hands.

"It's just body," he said.

We watched him, and then Sara spoke again. "Evan, do you know how Rafael got hurt?"

"Well," Evan said, and the top half of his head levered like a puppet's as he spoke. "Well, I think nature did it, is what I think."

Sara turned to me. Her face had become brittle, her upper lip curling. She shook her head. "Oh, it's nature all right," she said.

Evan rocked forward, pushing his nose inches from the box. His toes tapped against the concrete. "Rafael, Rafael," he whispered.

IN THE NIGHT, THAT NIGHT, I WOKE UP BEWILDERED. IN A backward avalanche of panic. Slaps at my neck, my chest, a small voice calling in soft alarm. *Daddy? Daddy? Daddy, Daddy.* I sat up quick into cold, piling my breath in the back of my head. Evan bent into me over the edge of the bed, heat unfurling off him, his white undershirt glowing and swinging in the dark.

"Evan? Buddy, what is it? What's wrong?" I scoured him up and down with my foggy eyes. I slapped at the bedside table for my glasses, but they were never there. Evan's face looked dusky and swollen, and I put my hands unthinking on his cheeks. His skin felt so hot and so torn

from its usual shape that I tried to smooth it with my thumbs, to see if
it had broken.

"What is it, Evan? What's wrong? What's wrong?" I slid my hands
down Evan's arms to his palms, turning them up and tilting them toward me. Blood pounding in my ears put my voice under water.

"Rafael, Rafael," Evan cried, twisting his hands in my grasp and
taking me by the wrists. The pull of it took me to my feet. He led me out
of the room. I left Sara there where she still slept.

The patio door stood open, the blinds pulled back. A faint pre-
morning blush fell through and lit pink angled shapes across the kitchen
tile. Cold crept along the floor and around my feet. "Outside, Daddy."
Evan went to the first panel of the patio door and pressed his palms and
forehead against the glass, looking out and down. He had no pants on,
I saw now, no underwear even. I came up beside him to the open door.

"Evan, were you out here?"

"Well, I was," he said, looking up at me. "But Rafael."

I sagged. "Evan, did you try to see Rafael?"

"Yes, but they ate him." His voice rose as he spoke. He put both fists
into his crotch, bending into them and lifting one foot after the other.

"Okay," I said. "Okay, let me see."

I stepped out, my bare feet crumpling up onto their sides to get away
from the freezing concrete. Bird voices unfolded tersely from the air
around me, flickering into strings of ornaments. The sun hadn't come
up yet. In the corner of the patio, the orange crate had been turned upright, empty. Further out, the box from the vet lay on its side, its flaps
gaping like the mouth of a tiny whale. A cluster of paper towels nearby
made a ragged, small-headed ghost—dropped there and given acciden-
tal shape, I could just see, by the clutch of a tiny fist. I went around the
far side of the box, noticing as I did that the rose of Sharon tree still
stood against the patio wall. I'd left it there, and an animal had gotten
into the milkcrate, into the box. A raccoon, probably, or a possum. So
stupid of me, to forget the tree. Evan watched me from inside, his dim

shape swaying, his forehead and hands going suddenly white where he pressed himself flat against the glass. The little tip of his penis.

"Was there an animal?" I called to him.

He spoke into the door, muffling himself, steaming a circle onto the glass—*Yes?*

"Yes, Evan? An animal?"

Evan pulled away from the glass and leaned into the open doorway. He pointed at my feet, swung his arm around. "Ants," he said. "Ants, Daddy."

I squinted in the faint light. I stepped up and nudged the box with my toe, twice. Nothing happened. I gave it a good push, swinging the open end around, and instantly a coarse black ball rolled out onto the concrete between my feet. I jumped away, a noise leaking out of me. Not a ball, exactly—a tube, black and churning, breaking apart in tiny, jumping pieces.

"Evan, turn on the kitchen light," I said. I stepped around the seething mass. "Turn it on, Evan." I grasped my shirt at my belly with my other hand. I heard the pop of a switch from inside, and a second later the fluorescent from the kitchen stuttered on.

Hulking black ants, as big as flies—dozens upon dozens. They were into the sausage, of course, everywhere atop it, so thick that I couldn't even see the thing. So many that the sausage rocked beneath them like a boat, seeming to move toward me across the concrete. More ants swarmed over it even as others fell away, and now I saw that ants milled here and there all about the patio, thinning further from the pile. I took two long steps back. I saw, too, a braided black trail that ran along a seam in the concrete, down to the rose of Sharon tree and up over the patio wall.

I squatted, keeping my distance, watching. I pulled the corners of my eyes back, stretching them into focus. The massive ants churned over the sausage, shining. Individuals staggered away, bearing gristly, glistening chunks. Those that left wove between other ants just arriving, or returning. I fancied I could hear the ants ripping into the thing, their mandibles clicking—the wet snicker of vivisection. I couldn't tell for sure, but the sausage looked half-gone, at least. I held my hands against my face and I watched the ants working. I breathed hard through my nose onto my palms. I spotted a single ant weaving toward me. I reached out and flicked a hasty finger at it, lofting it out of sight. A little bile rose in my throat.

"Do something, Daddy."

Evan stood there inside the open doorway, backlit by the kitchen light, his face invisible to me. He leaned out from behind the glass. His shirt hung like a dress. His thick legs looked skinny, and long.

"Like what?" I said.

"Make them go away."

I stood, my knees popping. My feet had gone numb. "Okay, let me think."

I stepped around the ant pile and bent to pick up the box. I grabbed an open flap, taking it lightly between two fingers, and I flung the box over the patio wall, into the side yard. It rustled and thudded into the grass. Crawlies feathered my arm and I shook it, shuddering. I swiped at it with my other hand, and then I perceived more movement across my feet, through the hair on my shins. I minced stupidly to the patio door and in, bending to stare and swat at my legs.

"Did they get you?" Evan asked.

"What? No, no, they won't get me. They don't get you. I just don't want them on me is all." I didn't know that they had been on me. They weren't now, but I could still feel them.

"Can we kill them?"

"I would like to kill them." I closed the patio door and went over to the sink. I rummaged around underneath, where we kept all the sponges and rags, poisons and cleaners. I found spider killer—Evan had a fear— and a plastic bag of mosquito-repellent bracelets. No other bug sprays; nothing I was sure would kill ants. But the big green bucket was under there, cupped beneath the hanging pipes—catching a weak, sporadic leak. I guessed it would hold four gallons or more.

"Here." I slid the bucket out, standing. A handful of pale water circled around the grooves in the bottom. I turned on the water in the sink, shoved the handle all the way over to hot. I ran the water until steam billowed.

"What are you doing, Daddy?"

"I'm gonna drown them. Gonna wash them away."

Evan put his chin on the counter and watched as I filled the bucket. The plastic grew warm and soft as the water rose, and we waited. Evan began chanting something softly under his breath, so low I couldn't make it out. The water got deeper, began to muffle itself, and only then could I hear what Evan was saying: *Go, go, go.* We let the water run. I filled the bucket so high, I couldn't even get it out from under the faucet without spilling some. I sloshed more onto the floor as I made my way slowly across the kitchen, Evan skittering ahead of me.

"Get the door, buddy, okay? Go ahead and open it."

Evan walked the sliding door open solemnly, dropping his head and pushing with both hands, putting his weight into it. I'd seen him do this a hundred times, but for some reason, just then, it caught me right up, watching him do it—a weird kind of ceremony in the poetry of his movement, the sincerity of his labor. I stopped for a second, the bucket dangling warm against my leg, and watched him. He turned to face me. He put his hands on his hips.

"Ready?" I said.

"Ready."

I stepped up to the threshold. I brought the bucket up to my side. I judged that the bucket, full as it was, might weigh as much as Evan himself, but I had no idea how such a thing could be. I held it at my side, panting.

"Heavy," I said.

"Yeah?"

"Oh yeah."

"Will it kill them?"

"No, I don't think so. But they sure won't like it." Outside, the ants were still at work. I could still see the black pile around the sausage link, six feet out. "Okay then," I said.

I hefted the bucket back and threw. It was so heavy that once the water had gone I almost fell into my motion, out onto the patio, following the great bow of water as it slapped monstrously onto the concrete—a huge and startling sound. Water splashed up onto the glass doors, back onto my legs. Sheets of steam bloomed. The water spread like a flame over paper, darking the concrete as it went. The crest of the water hit the sausage link and peeled into a brief standing wave as it broke over the top—scattering the ants, I hoped, blowing them away, though of course I couldn't actually witness such a thing, not from where I stood. The sausage slid and began to tumble across the patio, still caught up in the frontwaters of the little flood. The cluster of paper towels Evan had dropped swirled briefly and was grounded, wet-bottomed. Water curled around the base of the rose of Sharon tree. And then almost immediately the water thinned to nothing—it ran out over the far edge of the patio or was absorbed by the concrete itself, channeled into the seams. I could hardly fathom where it had all gone, so fast. I set the bucket down.

Far out in the wet open, a few feet from the edge, the sausage link sat. The ants were gone, exposing it. Seeing it startled me so much that I just stood there, staring at it, Evan at my side. My stomach turned a little, sinking. What was left, lying out there in the wet, was a ragged chunk the size of Evan's finger, spindly and torn, nearly severed in the middle. It looked pale, much paler than I'd pictured it the night before. Its color and texture looked so foreign to me, given the circumstances—so real—that I thought for a moment that a mistake had been made. A mistake on someone's part. Staring at the thing I even discovered, and could hardly discard the idea, that I could discern parts comprising the imagined whole. Specific parts, I mean, jutting broken from the remains. Bones, touches of skin, the stub of a tail.

"Daddy?" Evan had my shirt in his hand. "Daddy?"

"Go to the couch, Evan." I stepped outside, pulling my shirt out of his grasp. "Go sit on the couch." I waved him away behind my back, not turning to look. Wet, the concrete felt even colder underfoot now, none of the water's warmth sticking. I walked across the patio. Here and there, a few sodden ants staggered. I avoided them. I went to the sausage link and—holding my breath—I bent and picked it up, pinching it between my thumb and finger. It felt much harder than I'd expected, and cold, like a piece of apple. Wetness dripped from it. I held it far from myself. I stepped up to the patio's edge and I flung the thing underhand out into the yard. It spun end over end through the air and dropped into the grass, thirty feet out. It bounced back into sight again, broken in two, the pieces cartwheeling apart even more wildly before falling back into the lawn, swallowed in the pink morning light, in the gray grass.

I turned back to the door. Evan still stood there, his hand in his crotch.

"Evan?" I said, and then he turned and ran, his little penis wobbling.

I went inside. I wiped my feet on the mat. "Evan? Evan?"

"Daddy?" Evan knelt on the couch, peering over the back of it at me, the shoulders of his white shirt shining.

"Are you okay?"

"Why did you do that?"

"Evan, that wasn't really Rafael."

"What?"

"That wasn't really him, not the real Rafael."

"It was just body?" he said.

I went to him. I knelt on the floor in front of him, the couchback between us. My head came to his chin. "No, no. That's not really Rafael at all, Evan. It's . . . it's like pretend." He stared out over the top of me, down the hall, maybe. I looked over my shoulder with him, deeper into the house. I glanced back at the patio. Both of the cats stood there on the threshold, peering out through the open door, their heads bobbing up and down.

"Evan. Evan." He didn't answer me. "I put that there. It's just pretend, I put that there. It's not Rafael, not his body. Evan?"

"Then what was it, Daddy?"

I sighed. "Meat. Just meat. Like from the store." And I thought then that I would have to explain myself, the entire thing—the absurdity of the act, the sausage link. Shame speckled my face, flushing. All the little hairs on my arms stood up and tried to leave me. I tried to muster an explanation as to why things had happened as they had.

But Evan said, "So he didn't die?" He spoke flatly, his face dull with exhaustion, smooth and permeable, his soft gaze still floating somewhere overhead and aside. My chest began to deflate. After moments, watching him still, I discovered that the muscles in my own face were trying to model themselves after his, their strange intelligence burbling under my skin.

"No, he did die. Rafael did die, but that wasn't him. He was gone already. All the way gone."

Evan bent over the couch and into me. He dropped his head into the crook of my neck, dropped his arms around my shoulders. He smelled like sweaty sleep, hung out to bleed into the breeze. He talked into my shoulder. My shirt moved under his mouth and my skin went warm. "He did die?"

"He did die, baby. The real Rafael died and they buried him for us already, for real."

"What did they do?" He lifted his chin and turned his head toward me. Some part of his face brushed my ear. He whispered at me. "What, Daddy?"

"They buried him for us already," I said.

Evan patted my back. He sighed into my ear. "Okay, Daddy." He went on patting me, on and on with both hands in rhythm, a steady beat. After a minute he stopped, and I just kept on holding him. He plucked at my shirtback. He began to hum a loose tune, and after a while that stopped too, and then when a few minutes more had passed, just as I thought he might be asleep again, just as I became aware of how the light in the room had grown, he pulled his head back suddenly, looking me in the face, and he said: "Did they come in the night?"

I brushed my thumb across the corner of his mouth. His earnest eyes were so open and dark that for a moment I fumbled for a fingerhold on where I stood, where the days had led, where Evan had me under his hands. A sliver of something like panic slid through me, cooled me. I held my son. I lifted my head. I thought of answers.

The Lion

SHE SEWS HIM FROM HER DAUGHTER'S BEDSHEETS. THEY ARE camel, and though she has never seen a camel, she has seen the lion at the zoo, and she knows that parts of him are this color. She makes careful, clumsy stitches around the whole childish shape of him, sometimes tugging her red thread too smartly, then fussing back to smooth puckers she's pulled into the cloth. The needle weaves a long path, doubling back often to close impatient gaps, making a scribble of itself. She breathes down onto her work, into her hands. When she is finished, she pulls the lion right side out around his bulging seams and closes him, sews onto him a tail made from her bathrobe sash. She does it all from her chair, stooped over her lap, in the middle of the bright bathroom in the heart of the dark house.

IN THE MORNING, WHEN HER HUSBAND HAS GONE TO WORK, she takes up the lion and folds places for his eyes. She cuts moon shapes from the folds with the curve of her nail scissors. She makes his nostrils, too, and teases out tufts of thread around his ears. Willie the cat comes into the bathroom and makes eights around her ankles. He bats at the bathrobe tail hanging between her knees.

"Wee Willie Winkie runs through the town," she sings to him. She hangs her hand and runs a knuckle up his cheek. He prrumbles and chirps. The sounds are just his size. He pushes his face against her hand again, and when his chin drops she wraps a finger deftly around a whisker, gives a sharp tug. It comes away with a soft *pop* that surprises her. Willie barks and darts to the doorway, where he stops for a moment, blinking and crouching, his anger fuming through his tail. She feels a little something because he looks everywhere but at her. He startles again for no new reason and runs away.

She rolls the whisker between the flats of her fingertips. It is a marvel. She presses the stiff bulb of it into her skin. It is only hair, and what is hair? She remembers the story of an Indian prince who murders his infant nephew by dropping into his milk the thick milk-white whisker of a tiger. She rolls and rolls Willie's whisker, the thin tip flaring. Finally she threads the fat end of it into the muzzle of the lion. She lifts him by his chops, gazing into his face. His eyes are empty, his countenance made more ragged by the lone whisker. But it can't be helped; Willie won't come back now. She holds the lion by the cheeks and examines him. She worries the whisker won't stay. She shakes him once, very gently, like a breeze shakes out sheets, and the whisker drops free, falls into the sink. It lies there. She reaches out and puts her hand on the faucet. Where will the whisker go from here? Maybe it will stick in the pipes, these pipes or someone else's. She runs the water hard. She drapes the lion into her lap and watches the water fight itself down the drain.

IN THE AFTERNOON, SHE MAKES HER DAUGHTER'S BED. SHE uses the dolphin sheets. The sheets do not have dolphins on them— only mottled, oceanic blues—but lying on them meant you could be in the ocean, could be a dolphin. Always a dolphin. Putting the sheets on exhausts her: a new, small ordeal. She cannot reach the far front corner, and so she scoots herself across the bed and back. She does the fitted sheet, flat sheet, pillowcases. She folds the purple velour blanket across the foot of the bed. Willie has come to slap at wrinkles as she works, and when she turns to leave, he swipes at the lion hanging from the back of her chair.

WHEN HER HUSBAND COMES HOME FROM WORK, SHE SITS IN
the front room in her chair, with the lion beside her on the couch. Her
husband pretends not to see. He bends at the waist to kiss her on the
head.

"Good day?" he asks her, going by.

"Yes. I managed."

"Yes?" he says from down the hall.

"Yes. Productive, even."

"Oh yeah?" Maybe he makes a plausible space for her to say how.
The lion curls on the couch. The husband returns, squeezing her shoulder between his fingers and his palm. He takes her by the handles of
her chair and struggles to turn her, keeps trying even though she has set
the brakes. She is not as new at it as he is. He struggles and finally tilts
her, pivots her. Chopping out a laugh, he comes around her to sit on the
couch beside the lion.

"Well, I'm glad you had a good day," he says. "That's great, really
great." He puts his hand on the lion absently, begins to pluck at it. The
lion's drooping eyes fall closed.

"Did you change Lara's sheets?" he asks.

"I'm sorry?"

"Lara's sheets. You changed them?"

She shrugs. "I did laundry."

IN BED AT NIGHT SHE WATCHES THE CURTAINS CURLING LIKE
the toes of waves. Her husband presses against her. He wants her, wants
her to let him, and so she does; she has been waiting for it. He comes up
over her, and she hears her legs being slid across the sheets. He goes
heavy on her. She watches the curtains, practices the feel of her breath
being pushed up and out from her dark parts in bits, and she waits for
him to get close. She doesn't worry. There's no good place for it to go
in there anymore. When he is done, she takes care as he withdraws.
She already has her flat hands beneath her hips, and now she lifts with

her fingers. After her husband rolls back across the bed, she reaches down and finds her knees, spread wider in the dark than she thought. Cradling them, she pulls them up onto her chest, nearly to her chin. She imagines that, below, only heat escapes her. Her husband nuzzles her shoulder like a sick child, wetting her skin. She waits for the sounds of his sleeping, then stretches an arm to the floor. She pulls the lion out from beneath the bed, flat on his back, his haunches splayed. She has already worried the stitches free from his belly, and now she fingers him open. She scoots to the edge of the bed and lowers herself onto the spot, sinking over the lion with her thighs against her breasts. Her triceps burn.

She looks up at the curtains and she imagines slow that she can feel his stuff sliding, passing from her—a tiny mass. She waits until she can't hold herself anymore and then she bends her head to see it, but it is only a dark patch against the lion, no more luminous than her own skin, or the dull shine of curtains, the shadow of her chair nearby. She sits herself back on the bed and reaches down between her feet and rubs the stuff into the fabric where it's fallen, lifts some apart on her fingertips and rubs it around the mouth of the lion's split belly. Before it goes thick, she takes the lion to the bathroom and sews him shut again, her breathing quick and shallow, her fingers going nimble in the night.

LATER SHE HEARS A BREATHY RUSTLE ALONGSIDE THE BED, and she lies on her side with her eyes open, her hands beneath her cheek.

"Shh," she says. "Shh." She listens to her husband sleep.

Willie pads in, his claws snicking through the carpet. She meets his floating eyes where they pause in the doorway, and she knows he makes his quiet, quizzical snuffling. She hears him softly hiss, imagines she sees his needling teeth like torn bits of paper, thinning the dark between them. Her husband turns over, and under the sounds that escape him, sheets rustle. She looks back but sees only rising waterfolds of flannel draped over him into dark. She looks up at the ceiling, back at the door. Willie is gone.

"Shh," she says. "It's okay."

SHE OPENS HER EYES AFTER SHE IS SURE SHE CAN'T HEAR THE car anymore. The lion is beside the bed, his muzzle draped across his paws. "It's morning," she says to him, and she takes him into the kitchen where sunshine lies squared on the counter. He turns his head away as she lays him there, ashamed to be so light. She croons, "Don't trouble yourself." She picks the lint from around his eyes. "You're improving." With long shears she slices into his muzzle, working steadily down the length of it, and he smiles.

SHE SITS IN HER DAUGHTER'S ROOM, FOLDING A PINWHEEL from red paper. It is a school day.

"For your voice," she says to the lion, pooled outside the door. He will not come in, nor has she asked him to. Her hands feel blunted, fingers tired from care, and she pricks herself with the pin. She squeezes a bead of blood from her finger with her thumb, lets it spread beneath the nail, curses to herself. The lion lifts his ears.

At last she gets the petals pinned down, gets the point through the straw and into the cork. She comes to him in the doorway, reaching into his mouth stretched wide, and pins the paper fan to the seams deep in his throat. She imagined it would be harder. She steps back and the lion rolls his jaw, lowering his chin to his chest, a soft, whickering growl rising from inside him. She sees his throat flutter, low down. He rumbles again, twittering low and slow like a monstrous bird.

"Hungry," rasps the lion. When he talks, she can see he is blind. He bumps his whiskerless face against the doorjamb, the wheel of her chair.

SHE IS BY HER DAUGHTER'S BED WHEN HER HUSBAND FINDS her in the night.

"Baby?" The lion makes eights around his legs in the doorway, ice in his eyes.

"Don't come in," she says, but the husband does, stepping away from her lion, pretending not to notice him. The lion stands in the doorway. His new eyes gleam.

"Coming to bed soon?" He bends at the waist beside her.

"Am I?"

"I hope."

"Do you?"

He comes around her, puts his hand on her head as he goes by. "I guess I do," he says, but he says it like he isn't guessing. He turns and sits on the very edge of the bed, his long folding legs trussed beneath himself to the floor.

"You're a dolphin," she says. He stands up again. He walks around her again, back the way he came. He goes to the wall and picks up the Morgan horse from the shelf of plastic animals, lifting him by the head. He makes a sound. "This horse," he says.

"That's Justin Morgan's horse."

"I know." He rubs the horse's nose. "This nose, all worn white."

"That's not for playing with."

"What?"

"That was never for playing with," she says, and she goes to him and grabs him by the wrists and tries to take it. He doesn't fight her but won't let her, and she pulls herself forward almost into him. His face is nearly flat, just lightly troubled, as though he were listening from far away. She peels his hands away from Justin Morgan's horse, and it falls to the carpet between them. An ear snaps off dully into the pile, making a *snick* scarcely louder than the sound of Willie's whisker coming free. The lion paces in the doorway, dragging out a growl like a stick along a fence.

The husband looks at Justin Morgan's horse on the floor, looks toward the ragged, rangy lion rubbing his face against the door frame.

The husband sighs. She knows he will say something strange, and he says, "You can't take all of it. You can't keep it all for yourself."

"What?" she says, not to him but in his direction, and she feels a little sick thinking how much movement there could be toward him that would never reach him. She shakes her head. "What?"

"This, all this." He doesn't gesture around the room; he gestures in at her, at her belly. He sits back on the bed and then he does pluck at the dolphin sheets. "This," he says.

Her head is still shaking. "You say that like there's too little to be selfish about," she says. Her head is shaking and her neck starts to hurt. Her voice comes out squeezing, spreading like blood. She says, "This is all still true." She backs away, backs herself across the room until she bumps against the wall. She closes her eyes.

"Allison," he says—another strange thing for him to say.

She waits. She waits until she hears him get up, hears him walk from the room. She hears the lion's growl slow as he passes. She waits while there is no sound but the creak of her chair, her heart in her neck.

She sits quietly until she hears the lion come in. She thinks she has been waiting for him. He is purring through the paper fan pinned inside his throat. She opens her eyes and watches as he comes over to Justin Morgan's horse, lying on the floor, watches as he works his helpless mouth around it, trying to pick it up. She watches his thin flanks working, his neck drooping, his useless jaws grasping.

"Stop," she tells him, and he lifts his head. The ice is draining from his eyes. Dark rivers run from the sockets down his face. "Let me get you some more," she says.

IN THE NIGHT, THAT NIGHT, SHE HOLDS THE LION'S MOUTH against her sleeping husband's. The husband will not wake for just this. The lion's eyes glitter into her own as she whispers into his ear.

"Don't move," she says. "Let it fill you." And she reaches up and she takes the rind of the husband's ear between her nails, and she squeezes.

She watches his chest rise and fall faster and deeper, like the sea coming up into storm, watches as his struggling sludgy bewilderment blusters out of him slowly. It billows into the lion. She meets the lion's marbled eye and she squeezes harder, wondering with a thrill how hard she can. The husband begins to turn his head, but she holds him and squeezes, grits her teeth. He doesn't come awake until she has drawn blood, and she pulls her hands free just as he is jerking up from the bed. The lion slips away.

"What's wrong?" she says to the husband, before he is fully awake. Her voice sounds like curtains and it surprises her. She talks again to hear it. "What's wrong."

He reaches for his ear. "Something bit me," he says thickly. He feels around his ear, brings back dark on his fingertips. "Oh my god. What the hell?"

She sinks back into her pillow. "Willie was up here," she tells him. "I imagine he scratched you." And she does imagine Willie scratching him, stepping into his ear accidentally on his way across the bed. But she knows how big a lie it is; Willie doesn't come into the bedroom anymore.

SHE FILLS THE LION AGAIN THE NEXT NIGHT, AND THE NEXT after. It becomes her only purposeful routine and she enjoys it, taking the breath of her husband in distress. Often she does not wake him at all, only worries him out of deep sleep and into trouble. She presses her nails against his eyelids while he dreams. She pulls at the short hairs on the back of his neck. She pulls the loose skin of his limp, circumcised penis up around the head, enveloping it, and maybe she will give a twist to the gathered opening of the new little sack she's made there. The lion laughs into the husband's mouth, the melt from his eyes dripping onto the bed as he takes in the troubled air stumbling from the man.

The lion grows large over days, days that are the gathering rumor of weeks passing, maybe months. She sets him to lie in the doorway to her daughter's room, and the husband walks by but does not try to come

in. Sometimes the husband stands in the door when she is in the room
alone, ignoring the lion at his feet.

Other times, she catches the husband looking at the lion. He looks at
him closely, dubiously, as though he were seeing an oddly colored patch
of carpet that might be a stain. They do not like the way the husband
looks at him. She keeps the ice in the lion's eyes, and he is nearly as
large, maybe, as a lion should be, but he has no teeth, and his clawless
great paws only puddle where he steps.

THE HUSBAND CALLS. HE ASKS WHAT SHE NEEDS AT THE
store. She is lying on the couch, the long dwindling length of her belly
pressed against the lion's back.

"Milk," she says into the phone, though she doesn't know that for
sure. She wonders where he is standing now, if he is already at the store
or even standing at all. If he is driving and where. She thinks for a moment she will ask, but instead she tells him, "Grenadine. Peppercorn.
Marshmallows, the little colored ones, okay? And string cheese, get lots
of string cheese."

Quiet comes through the phone. She waits. She smooths the lion's
ears. "Hello?" she says.

"The smoky kind," her husband says suddenly, and a slab of sound
jumps through the phone with him, wind washing over the talkpad, and
a blurb of traffic. She hears a faint sound like a metronome.

"No," she says.

ON A WEDNESDAY, SHE MAKES TEETH FOR THE LION FROM
chicken bones. He has asked for them. She cuts the bones down and
sharpens them, notches them so she can string them into his mouth.
While they dry, he lurks around the kitchen impatiently, his feet pad-
ding across the tile like a child's. She watches him walk, watches the
perpetual melt from his eyes staining his face.

"Come outside while we wait," she tells him, and when they go outside into the sun, the lion crouches in the shade of the garage. It worries

her that he does this. She pulls out her scissors, calls him to her side. While he sits scowling in the sun, she fills his paws with driveway rocks.

A NIGHT COMES WHEN THE HUSBAND RENTS A MOVIE, AND SHE lets him refuse to excuse her from it. In the movie there are serious people, screen-filling faces, the close carnal sounds of talking.

The lion sleeps on the floor by the gas fireplace and she watches him. He is piled there like a fallen thing. His tail does not move. She is surprised to find herself thinking, with some dismay, that his stillness would fail to draw flies in the sun. His ears are like pockets pulled out.

Something happens in the movie. There is sound for it, music maybe or rising speech; she isn't sure. She doesn't look and doesn't think to wonder more until after the husband makes a noise. He makes a noise that she thinks is like the sound of good food going down, but then he reaches for the remote, and the movie sounds drop away. She looks up at the TV. The screen is blank with that blue, that blue. She looks over at the husband and he stares at her, his hands around his head.

"What is it?" she says.

"I think we'll stop there, yeah?"

"Why? What is it?"

He breathes. "You missed it."

"What?" she says, but he doesn't answer. He sinks back into his seat, and she can tell from his flatly pursed face that she has missed something, something that he has given size to; she can't imagine what. She isn't sure she would even try. She watches the husband and grows slowly heavy thinking how it is a novelty to consider him at all, to imagine a wave that has washed over him and not just by. She spends what feels like minutes trying to discern whether what she has missed was something he wanted her to see, or something he didn't. When she finally talks, it is before she is ready, and it is more than she wants to say. She says, "I'm sorry, I was thinking."

The husband lifts his chin, stretches out his jaw without opening his mouth. He puts his hands back around his head. She hears a soft thupping, and she looks over at the lion. His eyes are still closed while his tail curls and slaps across the carpet.

SHE CANNOT GET INTO THE GARAGE FROM THE HOUSE. THERE are three stairs down.

The husband has a white dresser in the garage. She knows that the top of it is pockmarked, and marred by dried pools of paint that have congealed along the outlines of absent obstacles—the straightedge of a board or the machined crescent of a can. Hanging from a shelf overhead, he has babyfood jars filled with washers and nails. The jars are screwed into their lids, and the lids are nailed to the underside of the shelf. They hang there, she thinks, like hives. Like stalled drops of water. There are more lids than jars now.

The lion lies on an angle of green carpet at the bottom of the garage steps while the husband works with glue. She can't see her husband, but she can just see the lion's tail flutter across the carpet below, and she can smell the glue rising up through the open door into the laundry room where she sits. She can see her husband's shadows. The carpet beneath the lion is what's left of what used to be, long ago, the good carpet. Beneath it, she knows, there is a rough and chipped patch on the concrete where her daughter once brought rocks in from outside and crushed them with a hammer. She pounded them into dust. Hoped to find them shinier on the inside. She had to stop because a fragment flew up and into her eye, left an oozy imprint of itself there, fell out again. She had to stop then because she had to be taken to the hospital so she could have a tiny gray seam sewn into the snowy stuff of her eye while she slept.

She hears her husband's voice. She thinks by what he says that he is trying to fix something that's been broken before. She waits for him to fail.

"That should get it," he says. She hears the iron rustle of tools going away.

"Don't you think?" he says. He says, "Yep, yep."

She sees his shadows open like scissors on the floor. The lion's tail flickers as they move across him. "If that doesn't fix it, it's beyond me," the husband says, and his voice grows, she knows, because he has turned away from the white dresser. His shadows scissor together. He comes up the steps and she does not bother to turn away from the door. He almost walks into her.

"What are you doing here?" he says.

"I came to see what you were working on."

"Nothing, really. You must be hungry."

"I'm not," she says, but she is.

THAT NIGHT SHE WAKES UP TO A SOUND LIKE A SHOVEL GOING into gravel. She hears the scrape of it in the garage, again and again. She lifts herself out of bed, makes her way through night-light pools down the hall through the kitchen to the laundry room. The door to the garage is open, and she wheels herself to the threshold, leans into her lap and looks around the door frame, down the stairs.

The scrap of green carpet has been pulled aside. The floor beneath it shines. The lion crouches there with his long back to her, and she sees by the way he moves his head that the noise that has brought her down is the sound of his tongue across the concrete. This tongue must be made of metal, she thinks, and she wonders how it could be. The lion licks the spot beneath the carpet where the jagged rough pits in the concrete still are, and she is certain that they go smooth, like small soft wounds under freshly picked scabs. She sits back in her chair. She listens.

IN ANOTHER NIGHT, IN HER DAUGHTER'S BEDROOM, JUSTIN Morgan's horse stands on the shelf again, very close to exactly back inside its old hoofprints in the dust. His ear is beside him, sheltering its own new impression there. She has made it this way, weeks ago, and her husband has let it be.

She stops in the doorway, sensing that the dry smell of quiet is dampened by a busy dank weight, a thickness that constricts the room. She turns on the light, and the lion is on the bed. His tail twitches and lashes across the sheets, and his sharp new teeth are strung into his mouth with thick black cord. His heavy paws dimple the sheets. The ice is back in his eyes, and he does not blink in the sudden light. She hooks her thumbs around the push rims of her chair, drawing back into the seat. "Here," she says to him, and she pats her lap. She clears her throat. "Here." He gazes at her, a low rustle feathering in the buckle of his jaw. He slaps his tail against the sheets before rising up on all fours, and she almost draws a breath at his looming girth, how he has to look down at her to meet her eyes. He drops heavily to the floor, his paws piling onto the carpet. He comes to her and acts as though he will try to wind between her legs, but he is far too large. Instead he rubs his wet face against the back of her hand. He pushes his face against her so that his lip draws up, and she feels the cold bones of his teeth slide across her skin.

SHE STOPS FEEDING THE LION HER HUSBAND'S BREATH. THE lion does not complain, but he takes to sleeping on the bed between them, and his bulk is thick against her at night. He smells rank, the stench of the chicken bones spilling from his mouth. His ragged seams are swollen like scars, twisted and lividly worn. She begins to dream that he steals her breath while she sleeps, has dreams that a great weight—greater than her belief in her own power to inhale—presses down on her chest, and that the air is stale and close around her mouth. Sometimes she wakes and the lion is always gone, and she almost believes that she can hear him slipping around the bed, that the pinwheel is whickering happily in his throat.

A day comes when she believes she does not see Willie anymore.

"THERE'S A BAD SMELL IN THE HOUSE," HER HUSBAND SAYS to her. The lion is stretched out beneath the coffee table.

"I don't smell it."

"It's terrible." He wrenches up his nose. He becomes an uglier man.

"I don't smell it. I'm here all day."

"Where's Willie?"

"He's around."

"I haven't seen him."

"He's around."

"Well, did he bring something dead home?"

She doesn't answer, and a silence the shape of everything swells into the room.

THE LION STOPS FOLLOWING HER AROUND. SHE BEGINS TO come across him unexpectedly throughout her days and into nights. She finds him curled in the bathtub behind the curtain, pressed ludicrously against the ceiling atop the cabinets in the kitchen, cooling himself in the shade of the garage. She finds him mostly in her daughter's room, never on the bed. She imagines that she hears him jumping down as she approaches, but when she arrives he is alert and cool on the floor. Early one morning she returns from the bathroom and discovers him curving like a blade across the head of the bed while her husband still sleeps. The husband does not snore, exactly, but his mouth hangs open, his thin lips drying, and the suck of his breath sounds like such delicate, ancient work. His folded hand lies against his chin.

"What are you doing?" she says to the lion.

"Gathering," the lion growls.

She skirts around the bed. She leans against her husband and shakes him awake.

"Paul?" she says. "Paul?"

"What?"

"Paul."

"What is it? What's happening?" She imagines she sees the lion blink.

"Take me to the store," she says.

"What? Now?" He sits up in the bed. The lion's tail twitches.

"Yes."

"What do you need at the store?"

"I need to go."

"I'll go," he says, and he is already rising. He is stepping into pants. "You stay here. What are you wanting?"

"No," she says, "no." Her moving face pulls at tight strings in her throat. He zips his pants, sits back on the bed.

"What do you need, Al?"

"No, I could go. We could go, you could take me. I don't know, I know, it's hard." She lifts both of her hands into, onto the thick air, swallows and feels a tug down her arms to her thumbs, and she curls her palms around some heat or cold rising or sinking over the bed between them. Her fingers curl and her thumbs rise. "Why is it like that?" she says, and there is a moment when she says it, a simple clear moment like dreamed falling, when she is sure she means only why her lifted thumbs burn.

Paul puts a hand on her knee, a hand into his hair. "Baby, hey, it's okay. Let me go. Okay? I want to go for you," he says to her. He emphasizes *for*. "What do you need me to bring you?"

She feels her face go flat, like her insides have left it. Her hands fall. Her throat turns to milk. She makes him some names of things she forgets, follows him into the front room, and he bends at the waist to kiss her on the head before he leaves.

When he has gone, she returns to the bedroom. The lion is still there on the bed. She slides from her chair to lie down beside him and he lets his head fall across her shoulder, puts a paw against her ribs.

"Your paw is heavy," she says. She puts her small hand atop it.

He snickers a purr through his throat, flexes his paw. She hears and feels the stones inside grinding, imagines they grate against her ribs, rattling her heart. His hot breaths are in her ear.

"What is that smell?" she says, almost to herself. The bed heaves as he stretches, and she hears the paper fan in his throat crackle as he yawns. His ruined breath makes her eyes water, makes her gut contract.

She hears the mysterious wet lurch of his tongue like a thick shining gritty liquid, hears the hollow shiver of his teeth coming back together. She listens for the door, as if such sounds were discernible. The lion lays his throat across her, pushing her into the pillow, such a hot crushing pleasure, trembling and close.

The Whale Dream

ONCE YOU LIVED WITH A DREAMER. AFTERWARD, ON THE first day you speak since November, she tells you she has dreamed about a whale. She says it is a dream to beat them all, a visitation. She says this as though it were morning over a shared bed. You don't know what to say. You don't say much. You don't question her about the dream. She tells you she has put the dream into words, asks if she can send the dream-in-words to you. She has dreamed you were both in the belly of the whale, she says.

You think you will allow her to send you the dream. You think you will warn her that you will steal it from her, though, take from her the lovely wet fabric of whatever it is she has dreamed, turn it into this very story or something like it. You think the truth is owed, think you can never repay the debt of your ongoing theft. You believe you can hear—even now—the noises made in the busy darks of a body at rest.

Airbag

Two

DORLENE FINDS ME ON THE PORCH. THE STORM DOOR CREAKS
and starts to come open of its own accord, the top window empty.
When it's half-open, Dorlene steps out from behind the bottom panel,
looking right at me. The sun's just under, but there's still a lot of light—
strawberry-yogurt-colored up in the sky but kind of a rosy yellow down
on the lawn. I've been watching it all. Someone's fired up the grill—I
can smell it—and maybe the smoke has rubbed off on me; I'm two cigarettes deeper into my pack. Meanwhile I've hardly eaten a thing.

Dorlene makes a beeline for me. I've still got the swing rocking soft,
but as she comes close I bring it to a stop. The plate's in my lap, and she
comes around the front of me and—figure this—steps right up between
my legs to gander at the food. She actually hooks one arm over the top
of my leg, and as she does it a thrill pulses up into my crotch, my gut. I
hold as still as a deer, feeling her underarm and her ribs pressed against
my thigh.

Dorlene looks the plate over, humming. She takes the biggest red
chip, holding it in both hands. She turns to face the yard, still between
my legs, and starts in on one side of the chip like it's a burger or something. Or maybe more like it's a leaf of lettuce and she's some spry herbi-
vore, having a watchful snack at dusk. It's that rodenty look she has.
I don't move.

Dorlene chews the chip, her little bites rhythmic. Once it's gone she asks me for a cigarette—she mimes it, actually, not a word between us yet—and after she worries her extra tobacco out into a neat pile on the porch and snaps off the filter, we both light one up. Down on the lawn, a girl screams happily. If anyone came into the front hall right now they could see this, me and Dorlene out here on the porch, her between my legs real easy, us both lit up and quiet. But I mostly don't care, and I feel alone here with Dorlene, and we watch the colors go out over the striped fields.

"You seemed like you didn't want to talk," Dorlene says at last. I've no idea if it's even true, but I tell her I guess I didn't. We smoke a while more.

"I met your Tweedy," Dorlene says then. And okay, she's got that voice, but it doesn't sound like she's even *trying* to say Triti's name right. Plus: the way she's phrasing it.

"*My* Triti?" My own voice creaks.

"Oh, you know." She spreads her arms out over the tops of my legs, gesturing out across the farmyard, out over everything in sight, spreading her arms so straight and so far that her elbows almost go backward. Little blue veins, thin as threads, are painted under her skin there. She turns full circle, letting her gesture encompass everything but herself. "All you all. This whole place." What she's heard or what she's divined about Triti, I don't know, but when Dorlene says this to me my throat doubles over on itself and water shimmies up around my vision. "She's sharp," Dorlene goes on, still looking out over the lawn. "Kind of a force—I see what you saw in her. And Mr. Shamblin says she's talented." I nod, my throat still forging a grotesque gravity in my neck. "She's how old? Twenty-four?"

I don't even remember, but that's a year off if it's off at all. I crack my lips and let loose an answer: "Yap."

Dorlene shakes her head. "That's awfully young for you, but I'm guessing you're accustomed to it." I think I'll object to that, but then she says, "She'll be even more formidable when she's older. I'm serious to god."

I laugh, and loosen. It's so hard to imagine Triti being either of those things. "I guess she will," I say.

Dorlene finishes off her cigarette and arcs it out over the edge of the porch. My own's gone dark in my hand, but I hang on to it. Dorlene props an elbow on my knee and taps a finger against her cheek. "Chickens," she says dreamily, out of the blue. She says it like they've just occurred to her as the solution to a problem she's having. "I've been hearing chickens. Roosters, I think." She looks brightly back at me. "Triti has chickens?"

The storm door creaks. I jump a little. Triti herself appears. Even before I see who it is I feel a hitch at being caught out here with Dorlene, us talking the way we are and her standing like she is. But before Triti's even all the way out, Dorlene has slipped from between my knees and moved to the edge of the porch. Another little sweep of warmth surges through the seat of me.

Triti has a plate and one of her omnipresent Nalgene bottles. The thighs of her jeans are still dark with wet. She says, "There you are," without looking specifically at either me or Dorlene. She comes to stand beside the swing. "May I?"

I make more room than I need to, and Triti hesitates, just a bit. When she sits, she sits as far into her end as I've scooched into mine. The swing saws wonkily. She and I start into some clumsy small talk about the abundance of the food and the fineness of the weather and the farm itself. Dorlene watches, leaning against a post, and then says, "Tweedy, how long have you been out here?"

"You mean today?" says Triti, but none of us laugh. She tries the joke because her escape to the farm the summer before last—in the middle of the worst of it all, depending on how you measure it—is a brittle and complicated part of the whole history. I don't know all Triti's reasons myself, but if moving out here was an evacuation, a kind of rescue attempt, no one was saved. The farm was so foreign and removed and unstained compared to town—to the house Lisa still lives in, to my first dingy sublet, to Triti's low long apartment and the tangled blocks around it where I used to hide my car—that coming out here became a woolgathering expedition, a kind of make-believe. And Triti belonged here, so hard and so fast. Her and the farmhouse, the land. The dog. I got swept up. If the farm was an abstract thing that didn't have much to do with the logistical brutalities still happening in town—necessary things, things that mattered—still Triti had this way of putting down roots, spreading bedrock. Because of her, there was a time when the farm felt much more real than anything town would allow. But that was our last lie, I guess—nothing I could have managed on my own—and I think what that lie brought was the end of things. Or that's how I see it. I couldn't say how it is for Triti.

Triti shrugs and pops a piece of ambrosia salad into her mouth with her fingers. "I don't know. Over a year."

"It's far from town. Don't you get lonely?" Dorlene says. *Lonely* comes out like a moan.

Triti swallows. "Well, you know, I think I was looking for lonely." I see her—in a flicker of blankness—ask herself how true that is.

"It suits you."

"Loneliness."

"The farm." Triti goes on eating with her fingers, watching her own process studiously, like she was afraid she'd fail at it. "I thought it would be nice to have neighbors whose houses I couldn't hit with a stone. A driveway used by no one I hadn't invited."

I start to prattle, pushing the flow of talk out and away. I start in about Tom and his near miss with the lighter fluid, but I don't get far.

"Tweedy," Dorlene says, cutting right across me. But all she says is, "I'd like to use the restroom, if that's possible."

A hesitation, a comic and unexpected beat in which Triti and I both—I know it—are considering Dorlene and a toilet for the first time. Triti recovers and gives Dorlene the bathroom spiel. To get to it you have to go through Triti's bedroom itself, a strange consequence of the lay-out and the fact that the upstairs is all but shut down. Dorlene listens like she's interviewing Triti for a job, and Triti ends up nattering on a sentence or two too long. She apologizes to Dorlene—for the architecture of the house, the nonexistent messiness of her room, the iron stains in the toilet bowl. Dorlene listens until she's done and curtsies as she thanks her. We watch Dorlene across the porch. When she reaches the door we—the both of us—look deferentially away.

Triti waits for a long ten count after the door bangs closed. I'm not sure how long I'd have waited—maybe the whole time—but Triti leans over my plate. "So, what's all this about? Is that tabouli? You're trying to impress someone." She says this like Dorlene hasn't just been out here between my legs, like she hasn't been waiting for her to get out of earshot.

"Dorlene asked me to get her some food."

"Ah."

"Don't say ah."

We sit there. I've got one of her cookies on my plate, and I know she knows it. But she points instead to the red chips, all but untouched. "Do you even know what those are?"

"I thought they were sweet potatoes."

"They're beets."

Beet chips, for crying out loud. Honestly, I wasn't even aware this was a thing you could do. Suddenly they look very red to me, blood-red, like they were made of flesh or something. I pinch one; it feels like vellum. I think about the sound of Dorlene's nibbling. It's possible, I think, that she didn't know what they were either. "Did you make them?"

"Susan made them."

"Fat Susan?"

"I don't know why we have to call her Fat Susan. There's only one Susan."

"I think one of the Gottlieb girls is a Susan."

"None of the Gottlieb girls made beet chips," says Triti.

"You don't know that," I tell her.

Triti has some of the yellow gristly stuff on her plate. She pokes it with a fork and makes a face. I ask her what it is.

"I thought it was potatoes." She points at the slab of the stuff on my plate. "What did you think it was?"

"I didn't. There was this girl standing there, and I—"

She cuts me off with a hum, deep and vocal. I wait for her to start in. "I'm sorry," she says, "I'm savoring. These are the words that explain everything. Your whole life, maybe? *There was this girl*. . . . I think maybe none of the details that come after that even matter." She pauses, thinks. "I'm not trying to be mean."

And she isn't. I consider flipping the yellow crud out into the lawn.

Triti leans out to look closely at me. I realize we've gotten the swing going again without me realizing it, just a little. Her hair hangs from her cocked head, swaying slightly, pink on the inside. "I'm sorry," she says again. An apology this time. "I'm not complaining. I was that girl once."

"The girl who talked me into crud?"

"Is that what we're saying?"

"I'm not." Out ahead of us, down by the fringe of the corn, Lord Jim goes by slow. He slips back into the cornrows now and again, his long body weaving through the stalks, becoming a procession of ghosts. "There's that dog," I say.

"*Aroof,*" Triti calls out, thrusting and snapping her jaw. It's not very loud, but it carries like a thrown thing. This is something she does. "*Barooo-roff.*" Lord Jim turns his head to look at her, not even slowing.

"He's getting old, right?" I say. "For a big dog."

"He's in his prime," she declares, still watching him. A few of the kids down there move through the dusk to intercept him, the swayback girl among them. The dog stops for them like a patient trolley, wagging faintly and staring straight ahead, panting. They bustle around him, giddy at his very presence, touching him and crooning. "He's a good dog," Triti says. A minute or two on, Jim's admirers—admitting to themselves the stoic detachment I can see in the dog even from here—step away. After a beat he plows into motion, picking up his patrol again as though nothing had interrupted him. The swayback girl laughs throatily.

"God, that dog's huge," I say.

"You never liked him."

I open my mouth to object, but if I'm honest she's almost right. And listen, I grew up with dogs, still consider myself a dog person—even though with Lisa it was the cats. But Jim has always made me nervous. I think *nervous* is the right word. He's pony sized, first of all, but that's not the main thing. I've tried describing this to Triti before, and so with practice I can say it's Jim's indifference that makes me tense, his particular brand of it: massive and vigilant. If there is such a thing. Like he was with those kids just now, what Triti takes for gentle and I call ominous. Lord Jim doesn't, for example, ever really look at you. Not directly. He comes up beside you with that impossible head, his mouth cracked, panting just a little no matter what the heat, and he fixes his gaze off somewhere else, on some middle distance, maybe fixing on the property lines he's forever ranging. But the whole while, you know he's on to you. His awareness rolls off him like armor, or like a threat. Or like both of those things—like a ward. Maybe it's just me, but because of his size, and because the whole farmyard is so totally his territory—more than it could ever be Tom's, or even Triti's, or anyone's—when Jim moves around the property he moves with the blindly implacable confidence of a ship, and you get the sense that your presence is irrelevant to his passage. Or it's more like, his approach is a function of his own gravity, and it's *you* who is drifting into *his* path, but he is too polite to mention it. He is just quietly and massively there.

Triti would say that what I see in Lord Jim is a matter of him being a herding dog. "He's herding you," she says, all the time. "He's a herder." And she would maybe know, because she's one herself. One time last spring, when we were out here at the farm alone, we went out into the yard in the middle of the night naked. Because we could, you know. The grass was hard and cold and caked to the lumpy ground like baby hair. Triti shone. And just as we were lying down in the grass together, under the wide moon that had led us out to do exactly this thing, Lord Jim came up from nowhere, glowing like something celestial himself, and he came right up beside us, *above* us both, so close that you could feel his heat and his breath and his stink. I was so aware I was naked. I felt like a woman must feel.

But Triti got up on her bare feet and she leaned into him, sinking her hands into his fur, muscling him away. She steered him up to the house, talking to him, repeating his name and saying stuff to him that seemed to matter. She took him up the back steps and locked him in the porch—a spectacle in its own right, since he wasn't allowed in the house. And then Triti came back down to me in the yard and got me going again. She got on me. She closed her eyes and lifted her chin and when I rolled her over onto the stony earth she lay there and watched me hard like I was all the reasons she could even begin to spread herself in the first place. Like this was the only lesson I'd ever need. The whole time, Jim stood in the back porch like a horse in a stable, looking out but not at us, outsized and patient there in that airlock, and the branches moved over the moon.

"He's just different than dogs I've had," I say to Triti now, here and now, here beside me on this swing.

"That's because he has a job. You never gave your dogs jobs. Probably they had weak character because of it."

"Yeah, well," I say, "it's either them or me."

Triti sighs. Jim has passed out of sight down below. The kids wander goofily off, too, and neither of us makes the jokes we ought to about the way they are. As we watch them the thought returns to me, as it sometimes does, that they're about Triti's age. I wonder if she ever thinks of it.

Dorlene's taking a long time. I flash stupidly across the worry of her falling into the toilet, which is uncomfortably high even for me. I look back through the window at Triti's bedroom door.

"I know what you're thinking," Triti says.

"That means you're thinking it too."

"Only via you."

"I doubt that."

"You like her."

I shrug. "She's bright."

Triti starts to laugh. "Oh my god, you *like* her like her." I start to prickle, but Triti steps right back in and sort of saves me. "You all do. Fucking boys."

A shape appears in the screen door, hovering. The porch light fires up, blinding us, and then goes dark again. Ernest's voice slides out to us. "Oops. Private party?" he says. The sound and the sight of him is like a car in a forest.

"Not anymore," Triti tells him.

Ernest comes out and takes a seat on the edge of the porch, leaning back against one of the posts. He's toting a wineglass half-filled with a precariously tilting red that looks almost black in this light.

"Are you swooning too?" Triti asks him.

"Who isn't?" he says.

"I'm not."

Ernest chuckles. "Right."

"I thought she would be taller. I thought Tom was exaggerating."

I swing my head at her. "You *knew*?"

"Oh, right. God, he didn't tell you. I forgot."

Ernest starts to laugh and then so does Triti.

"You knew too?" I say to Ernest.

He lays out his hands. "I never claimed not to," he says, and the sense I had earlier about this all being some joke comes barreling back over me.

"Did you think she would be taller?" Triti says to Ernest.

"I saw pictures."

"So did I."

"Didn't do her justice."

"No."

Ernest says, "Tom's words to me were: *you could fit her in a carry-on.*"

"I think I could," says Triti.

"But he also said—what was it?—*but you'd be the one that felt like luggage?*"

"Hm," Triti says.

"Jesus Christ," I say.

And right then Dorlene's voice steps out of the window, from right behind me and Triti. It grips us like we were children. Even Ernest goes stiff. "David," the voice says, and it's like it's not even asking—I mean, it's naming me like I'm a fact. But it's a sad voice. Or not sad—resigned, maybe.

I turn. She's backlit now that the dark has begun to settle in, her nose and brow gray behind the screen, her fingers up on the windowsill under her chin.

"Hey," I say.

Dorlene sighs. I hear her feet scuffle on the wooden floor, and I imagine she's on her tiptoes. "David," she coos, "I'm so sorry, but I wonder if we couldn't get my bag from your car. I'm needing it, I'm afraid. Ernest, Tweedy, I'm sorry. Would this moment be all right?"

And suddenly we're all scrambling, throwing politenesses and alacrity at Dorlene. Triti and I get up out of the swing at not quite the same moment, sending it reeling. It bangs back into us both at the knees, me and then her. Somehow we all end up going inside. We head over to Dorlene like suppliants, and that's how she receives us, watching the three of us approach with her head slightly cocked and her chin high. She is flawlessly calm, regal.

"I didn't mean to summon the bunch," she says. Ernest seems surprised to be here—his eyebrows shoot up at the word *summon.*

"I want to apologize," Triti says. "I feel bad because we were talking about you and I think you might've heard us."

Dorlene sighs, a cartoon bird. "You're all so funny." She reaches out and lays a hand on one of the faded wet patches barely visible now on

Triti's jeans, right at eye level, and she rubs her hand across it, back and forth, fast and hard. Triti's thigh shimmies. Her boobs jiggle. Dorlene leans into it, her hand making a sound like a tiny zipper being worked up and down.

"Ow," Triti says.

Dorlene pulls her hand away. She smells it, delicately. "You're damp. Mr. Shamblin took all your towels."

"Yes," says Triti. "He did." And anyone can see that Dorlene's thrown her.

Dorlene looks at me. "David," she says again, like I'm hers, and she turns.

I follow her through the dining room, where a handful of people mill with plates. Through the kitchen, nearly empty now. Out on the back steps, Dorlene has to turn sideways, toddler-style, to navigate the short steep flight of peeling wooden stairs. We're outside before I know it, and almost everyone's here, getting what they want from the grill. The smell of meat climbs and clings inside my nose, but for some reason I'm not interested. I wonder if Dorlene is hungry—she's eaten almost nothing. I wonder if I ought to get her something or at least offer, but almost before we've touched ground, Bob Everitt totters up to us beaming, the stub of a bratwurst in his hand.

"You're just in time for the show," he says to us.

"The show," I say deadpan, just as Dorlene says, "Is there to be a show, Mr. Everitt?"

Bob turns right to her, ignoring me. He glances over his shoulder. "Tom's still trying to light that fire. They've escalated to gasoline."

Dorlene starts to cuss her way into an elegant complaint, but I don't stay to hear it. I go right on down the hill, into the half-dark, down to where Tom's silhouette is crossing the yard from the garage, heading for the brushpile, the shadows of kids all around him like rats. They're ribbing him and he's loving it, giving it back before it's even delivered, his voice bounding merrily up toward me. The big red gas can hangs from his hand, the yellow spout glowing.

"Oh good," he says when he sees me. "You're here to watch too. Everyone's eager to see me die."

"Gasoline," I say.

"It's under control." A fresh round of joshing erupts between him and the kids.

I say, "I don't think this is a good idea."

But he just shrugs and says, "Ideas are for pussies." He wades in and starts spritzing gas on the pile, like he's watering a bed of flowers. Sticks snap under his feet. He stumbles a little. All around him, down in the midst of the failed fire, bits of ember still glow, and here and there tiny blurts of flame shiver.

"You and Dorlene seem to be getting on well," he says. "Up on the porch and all." He waves his free hand at me. "Don't get me wrong, I'm not—"

The world lights up. Right around his legs a huge gout of flame flares, rearing high up over his head in a flash. It turns the twilight black and orange, far bigger than the fireball from before—and louder, a roar instead of a tear. Tom all but disappears inside it. A push of hot air hits me all over my front, harsh up under my eyebrows for some reason. I make a little sound, I don't know what, one of those little surprise noises. Everyone else does the same, all those little sounds, some of them loud. A girl further up by the house shrieks. Back behind me somewhere, Dorlene cries, "See, oh!"

Tom steps out of the flame. He's not on fire, but he's still right up in the edges of it. He's hunched over, his shoulders tucked sheepishly up around his cheeks, into his beard. The fire shrinks but goes on roaring, standing man-high, the shape of a haystack, gray smoke blooming up into the twilight. I can see the terse smile on Tom's face as he steps away, and the crowd noises behind me swell—exhalations and people saying *oh my god* and stuff like that, laughing. Tom sidles away, still bent. He looks back at the burning brush. He feels his beard, his eyebrows. The blaze lights up his glasses from where I stand. But he's got the gas can in his hand still. From the mouth of it, a little leaf of fire flutters.

"Hey—hey," I say. I'm the first to speak. I take a step back. "Tom, the can."

"Drop it! Drop it!" somebody calls from back by the house, and Tom glances down at the can. The flame, like an orange thumb, seems to fatten as he turns, coming right out of the spout, and for a second it looks like it'll sputter out, but it doesn't. Tom doesn't even seem to notice, but he drops the can at his feet, real casual, not even seeming to watch it drop, like he is tossing his keys onto a table. And then, still turning—all of this in one big turn away from the fire still petering out in the pile of wet brush—he keeps walking off kind of slow. He makes his way toward me. The can smokes in the grass behind him.

"Back up, back up," he says, palming his hands at the air between him and me.

"Is there still gas in there?" I say.

"Let's just back up."

"Is there gas in there?"

Tom shrugs, but it's one of those coy shrugs, like he knows but doesn't want to say. Which could mean either thing. We walk backward, watching the can. And then suddenly Dorlene's between us, walking forward up the slope with us. Something about her posture, her hunched shoulders and her bent little neck, makes her seem like a tiny draft animal, like she is pulling Tom and me implacably uphill in her wake. She shakes her head at the ground.

"Mr. Shamblin," she says. "I don't believe I'll allow such a thing again."

We back up against the driveway. Ernest meets us there, his shoes grinding in the gravel. Further down the house Triti's silhouette stands alone at the front porch, halfway out on the steps, arms crossed beneath breasts. Even in this meager twilight her shape is as recognizable as the sound of her voice, and it doesn't matter that I can't quite make out her face—I know it is firm and watchful, as peacefully worried as a mother.

"You think it will explode?" Tom says to me.

"I wasn't expecting any explosions when I came here," says Dorlene.

"Gas explodes, right?" I say, though I have no idea how all that really works. "How much gas is in there?"

"Enough," Tom says, and he starts ambling away to the left. He starts off on a big circle around the can.

"Mr. Shamblin," Dorlene says. She stays by my side, though.

Ernest taps his lips, swirls his wine. "We should keep back. It's gonna go."

"It is?"

"Oh yeah. When enough air gets sucked in and the ratio of oxygen is right."

"Oxygen to what?"

"Fuel, man. Fuel." But somehow when he says this I know it's not going to go, almost *because* he says it, like him saying it is itself a safety measure.

Something tugs at my jacket. Dorlene is pulling the cigarettes from my pocket—or putting them back, rather; she already has one in her hand.

"You're almost out," she says, looking up at me.

"There's another pack in the car."

"I know," she says, but there's no way she could. She begins to wring the tobacco from her cigarette. She watches the can, burning like a candle down below. Tom makes a quarter circle around the can and comes back. The brushpile itself has gone dark and smoldering again. He stands with us, looking out at the can, his arms crossed over the top of his belly. Some tool down below shouts out something about Prometheus.

Tom says, "You know, what I should've done is thrown it into the pile. The can. Once it was on fire. That would've done it."

"You didn't really throw it at all," says Ernest.

A few seconds later Tom says, "I can't believe that brush didn't catch. That was a big fireball."

Ernest says, "Bigger than you."

And then a minute later: "That mower's got a plow attachment. I bet I could push that thing in there."

Dorlene jabs at him with the glowing point of her cigarette. "Mr. Shamblin, if you try that I swear I will physically fucking stop you, I'm serious to god." And that is a thing I would like to see. I can picture Tom on his riding mower, that old yellow thing barely big enough for him, and Dorlene standing out on the lawn in her plaid autumn dress, blocking the way, the whole thing a set piece, a tiny Tiananmen Square.

I look down at Dorlene, sure she would do it, and I can't help thinking to myself in this light, with a bit of smoke drifting between us, how beautiful she is. A sound leaks out of me, a stray fragment of a throaty hum.

Dorlene looks up at me, right into this squeezed-off sound, these thoughts. Her eyes are calm and appraising. She sips her cigarette, lighting her face. I feel utterly seen. Meanwhile Tom and Ernest are discussing, in low tones, the possibilities of the mower plan.

"My bag," Dorlene says.

"Right."

"Walk me down?"

"Okay."

And just like that we leave them there, the gas can still fuming. As we walk, it occurs to me that I don't know where Dorlene is staying tonight. I wonder if she's staying here in the farmhouse, somehow. I veer toward the jumble of cars, trying to summon up the right tone of indifference with which to ask about her plans, but before I can speak Dorlene says, "No, not that way," and she keeps walking straight ahead, down toward the outbuildings past the back elbow of the drive.

"I thought you needed your bag," I say, angling alongside her.

"I don't, David, I'm sorry." She keeps on heading back toward the dark.

I almost stop then. I almost don't go. Not so much because of what she's saying or doing—because I'm not sure of the truth of that, not yet—but because of what it turns me into, what I can't help thinking. I don't even have the gauge to measure my readiness for this, and the fact that I'm fumbling for one makes a slice of me feel old. The rest of my mind is puppies. I follow Dorlene like a stranger. I keep my steps small. We cross the drive back by the cars, passing through the buzzing orange glare of the farm's single sodium light, high overhead on the utility pole. We don't look back, either of us. She leads us down to the deepest part of the yard, out where no one else is. Me this man, her this woman. We round the corncrib into darkness. We hit upon the wide path Tom keeps mowed through the weeds, a circuit that makes the rounds to the outbuildings—the corncrib, the pigshack, the dairy barn with its high floors of compacted manure, the old barn collapsing picturesquely, the machine shed prim and modern and out of place. All of it unused. We've left behind whatever warmth was in the air up by the house, a thing I discover and realize I've forgotten about this place—the way the cool air pools in the belly of the back lawn in the after-summer evenings.

No one can see us now. We walk quiet halfway around the mown loop before Dorlene stops by the big metal water trough.

"What is this?" Dorlene says, and I think it's an ignorance until I understand: she can't see over the lip, can't see the water, black and textured and still inside. The water's half-covered in rotten wooden planks that Tom is always threatening to replace. I tell her what it is and she raps a knuckle against the side, light as a twig against a window. It sounds like stone.

Dorlene looks all around us, out at the lightless fields in three directions. When the property went up for sale, Tom took the house while a neighboring farmer took the fields all around, and so the place feels like a promontory out over alien spaces. We're deep down in that territory now.

Dorlene tilts her face to the sky. It makes me feel giant, so I look up too. Westward, blue twilight still stains the black, but the stars are already out with a force they could never muster in town, and I know that later the Milky Way itself—the actual visible thing—will blaze from one horizon to the other, letting us know just exactly where we are. It's a spectacle that would make anyone feel small, a scale-crushing sight, but I can't make it out just yet.

"Tell me about Triti," Dorlene says.

I breathe. The words jangle me, derail me, though I can work them into the tumble of thoughts I've been riding if I try—this could be a formality, of sorts. I stand there and think it through, but the more I try to imagine a way to begin, the more impossible an answer feels. There is no telling that could mean anything to anyone else, certainly not Dorlene. A thousand little stories I tell myself, really, messy and disobedient, each one an attempt to wrangle what happened into an overall shape I could encounter, could wrestle to the ground or put on a shelf or kill or own outright. And these are wordless stories, too, drawn around the relative moving positions of the relevant players. Meanwhile all of it shifts and rearranges itself restlessly as the events themselves drift further from where I now am, at any given moment. And so to tell it, to speak any one version of what happened—that would mean pretending that this one story was more true, or more meaningful, or more revealing than all the other stories I might tell. And I don't mean the facts, because there are no facts. If there's an account that's even close to true, I don't know who knows it. It would be an elected truth. And if I can't even claim the silent sculpted stories in my head I sure won't claim anything that I drag out now and beat solid beneath the stars for Dorlene.

I look down at her. She is frowning, an expression that slides a needle up into my heart. I tell her, "I can't."

After a minute Dorlene nods. "Well, that's fine, David," she says, and somehow the way she says it makes me feel like the two words I've chosen to say have told her more than anything else I might've given up.

And so I tell her about Lisa. Not about anything that happened, but just about how things were. I don't know why I do it—I'm just here at the farm, out among all these owned abandoned buildings, trying to de-scribe for this tiny woman, this miracle of a person, the jagged growing

chasm around which Lisa and I at some point began to circle. I talk
through our last cigarettes, and well on past that, and Dorlene just listens. She doesn't speak. She doesn't even make any listening sounds—
not a *yeah* or an *oh* or even a hum. I tell her things I haven't told anyone,
like how the shape of Lisa's panties lying on top of the laundry used to
make me sick, a sensation I can't even imagine anymore. I talk until I
say, "I don't know." I say it two times, three times.

Quick into the quiet that follows, I'm wishing I had more cigarettes.
The voices up by the house seem a mile away at least. Finally Dorlene
says my name. She holds her arms up toward me. "Here," she says, but
I have no idea what she means. She wiggles her fingers at me, waving
me in. "Here."

I drop into a crouch. I've got no idea if it's what she wants, but she
wraps her thin arms around my neck like rope. She puts her head on my
shoulder, buries her throat in mine. I put my arms around her, easy at
first but a little harder when I feel how unfragile she is. I wrap myself
around her so completely that my hands come back around to touch
my own sides. She smells like fruit and bark. Her hair on my cheek
and neck is coarse and thick. She tightens her grip and I wrap her up in
return, pulling her so close that at last I understand I've lifted her from
the ground, that one arm is crushing our chests together and the other
has pulled her pelvis and her thighs up into my belly, her legs between
my own. Her legs strain toward me, stiff, the tops of her feet curled firm
against the undersides of my thighs.

I drop onto my knees, my legs spreading. And just like that I get am-
bushed by the vague thoughts that had me going as we came down. I get
huge inside my pants. It happens in an instant, dizzying me. I loosen my
grip on her and arch my back awkwardly to get away from the press of
her shins into my crotch, but she tightens her grip around my neck and
worms her body into mine. I know she can feel me. Her face shifts into
the crook of my shoulder. I feel like a fucking flashlight down there, not
even me at all, an unbelievable heft and pressure—hell, if conditions were

different I'd like to take a look at what I've done. I arch over Dorlene, frozen, my back straining against all the weight of this embrace.

Dorlene lets go. Her body goes slack and her arms leave my neck. She drifts right through my grasp like water and alights on the ground, her hands on my shoulders and her eyes into mine. My own hands come to rest on her hips, and I've got no idea at all what to do with them. My knees complain, but I stay down if for no other reason than I'm too embarrassed to straighten.

She arches toward me. "It's okay." Her words are like bubbles. Her breath blooms around my face. "It's okay."

I want to swallow her, put her inside me. I squeeze the horns of her hips and feel the sure, answering bone beneath her flesh. I want to wear her like a puppet, hollow her out like eggshell. She lays a hand against my cheek, her fingertips on my skin the most novel thing I have felt in adulthood, I swear, and what wouldn't I do for this? What wouldn't I do?

Dorlene steps back. My hands fall from her hips and onto my legs. She bends down, her eyes on me still, and she reaches with one hand up under her dress. As she straightens she lifts up the hem, her hand traveling up the space between her legs until it stops at the top of them, the front of her dress all bunched around her wrist—hiding her there still, but exposing her legs to their roots. She's barefoot; I have no idea when or how that happened. Her legs are white and longer than I thought they would be. They are tiny and fatless, the muscle of her thighs like plastic. She works her hand gently, works her hips around her hand too, looking down at herself thoughtfully. And for a moment, in a way—I don't think I'm exaggerating—it's the most excruciatingly spectacular thing I've ever seen, her out here like this with all these dark buildings standing over us and the grass all around and the sky overhead.

But then, for no reason I can name and all at once, I lose everything. I mean all of it. Every bit of urgency in me goes silent and soft. Maybe it's the sight of so much of her skin, the imagined body revealed; or maybe it's the way she's working her hips and the sensation that she shouldn't know how to do this thing. Maybe it's that I want so badly to know what any of these approaching acts would *be* with Dorlene, because they seem literally fantastic. Or maybe it's because when the actual mechanics surface in my mind—the simple act of kissing, to say the least—I can't quite tune my urgent body to the choreography her strange machine would have to require, and I just stall out. I don't know. I'm inventing things. All I know is I can't understand what's happening to me and I can't make it stop. Something in my vision and in my skin and in my muscle has lurched sideways, and for several long seconds that I can't escape, Dorlene looks like just what she is. Like just what she is and no more: this little thing.

Dorlene steps back into me, thighs still bared. I tense. I realize I'm holding my breath. I turn my head slightly away, and I work to keep my face from wrinkling in distaste. Dorlene comes right up to me, straddling one of my legs. The lifted curtain of her dress grazes over me. One of her bare legs touches my arm, cold as dirt.

I raise my other hand. *Wait,* I am about to say, but before I can say it she's gone. She's off me and turned away, her dress fallen back into place. She stands still and pert, like a lawn ornament. She's turned, staring out and away into the long grass.

"What is it?" I say. I sit up, craning my neck, following her gaze toward the machine shed thirty yards beyond. I can't see anything.

After a long pause she speaks, sounding like a songbird, a dove: "Got spooked." She holds her pose a beat longer, and then she flits into motion, turning and heading back up toward the house, drifting across the dark like a spirit.

I scramble to my feet. I straighten to my full height, turning, knowing what I will see out in the weeds, out by the shed. But I don't. Instead I see nothing. I don't hear anything either, just the people noises from up at the house and the gentle ocean sounds of the breeze through the corn buried out there in the dark. And it's only then that I suspect there wasn't anything to see.

I go after Dorlene. I say her name. I nearly catch her, a dozen yards down the mown path, but then I see how slow she's moving, and I fall in behind her. She plucks long stems from the weeds as she goes—looping them around her hand and heaving back bodily till they snap. She pulls off three or four stalks of that thin weedy stuff that looks like wheat up top, a drooping horse tail, and she turns to walk backward, gathering the stalks in one hand, watching them and me. I imagine her face is rapt with mischief, devilish. Then real quick she slides the other hand up the stalks, popping the seeds loose with her thumb like an explosion, like fireworks.

"Boo!" she says. The seeds shower down around her. She lets the stripped stalks fall and turns back, walking on.

She's trying to make me think she knows who spooked who, I can see that—I think I can—and I don't appreciate it much because that's not how it is. It's that things are complicated. "It's not like that," I tell her.

"I don't know what you mean."

"I think you do."

"I'm certain I don't, but David—I'd rather us not overestimate the importance of the occasion."

I chew on that. I go on following. "Well," I say, "that's good advice I didn't need."

After a few silent steps she laughs, her voice pealing out over the lawn, coming from everywhere—not a snide laugh, I'd bet my life not, but a laugh of delight. And I guess I've said the thing that has made it all right. I laugh with her, still following, and our laughing spreads around us like a thing I'm wading through. I sink myself in this queer relief that doesn't have a name and I think we'll go back to the house and it'll be fine.

And then movement catches my eye. Out in the dark we were considering just a minute ago. The sight makes me stop, makes my head snap and my heart dive but it isn't Triti at all, of course it isn't. It's Lord Jim. His great white shape sails slow through the long grass straight toward us. He moves like a planet. I know he sees me.

I move forward again, lengthening my step, my pulse suddenly pounding. "Dorlene," I say again, coming up beside her. She's stopped laughing. I know she can't see the dog—the grass along the path is too high—but without a word she reaches up and slips her tiny hand into mine. She smiles up at me. She walks us on—or maybe I do it myself, I don't know. All I know is that the two of us and the dog are angling in toward each other. He'll emerge from the grass on Dorlene's side. And I can't tell you what this does to me, this moment, this triangle—me seeing the dog and her not, her making this gesture in just this instant, the bend of her back, the shape and pull of her tiny hand from below, the great dog limping through the tiger-long grass to meet us. I can see his eyes now. I squeeze Dorlene's hand, very gently, thinking how wrongly placed her thumb is, how wrong it has to be. She squeezes me back as best she can, a pinch. The dog's approach has grown so loud that I can't figure how she doesn't hear it. She takes in a breath to speak.

And then he arrives. He steps out of the weeds and into the mown path, practically into Dorlene's face, and there it is—the sight I'd imagined earlier. We all three stop. Dorlene turns to wood. Her hand leaves mine. Jim's monstrous, the kind of dog whose size makes you a little breathless whether you feel the twinge of fear or not. He looms over Dorlene by several inches, looking like some great steer or something—I don't know, like an impossible bear or some terrible beast. His head alone is practically the size of Dorlene's whole torso. He stands there, huffing, giving Dorlene his glassy, sideways gaze. It's pretty clear from where I stand that it's Dorlene who's brought him to a halt. I wait for something to happen, and when nothing immediately does I recognize that I'm waiting for Dorlene to make some move. To speak or act. But she is as frozen as a fencepost. Jim just huffs and huffs, his head bobbing slightly.

I step around between Jim and Dorlene. I don't know what I'm doing. I say Jim's name. I lean in and take his head in my hands. His jowls are coarse and wet and cold, and holding his head is like holding a huge and dense wad of damp, forgotten rags. It smells like that, too, something hot and thick and alive with filth. He goes on huffing and rolls his eyes away from me, past me.

I've no more got him than a swimmer has the sea. I can't think of anything to say to him so I just keep greeting him, saying his name, saying, "Hey, Jim, what's up? Hey, Jim. Hey, hey," and trying to look him in the eye. He doesn't pull away, but he bucks and rolls his head in my hands. He's not letting me block his view of Dorlene. And I don't know how I feel it, but I sense something curdling up in him, some energy or intent gathering, maybe made even worse by the harassment I'm handing out. My balls huddle together. I slide my hand through the yeti fur on his neck, feeling for his collar. I dig with my fingers. I scratch down to the skin before I admit to myself that the collar isn't there.

Panic vomits up inside me. Jim rears back hard and wrenches himself free, thin bundles of white hair coming loose between my fingers. He surges forward, bulling me aside. A slug of gruff sound rumbles up out of his throat, a deep and jowly half-bark, like a shovelful of rocks hitting the ground. He chucks this sound at Dorlene and steps right up against her, stiff-legged. He tucks his jaw against his chest, lowering his snout to snuffle loudly and alertly around her neck. I can't even see Dorlene behind his bulk. I reach for the dog. I am still saying his name—*Jim, hey, Jim, Jim.*

And then I'm not the only one. Triti's here, suddenly present, trotting heavy and low and calling the dog's name and pounding her hands together between her knees. She looks like an animal herself. I think she will slow but she doesn't—an instant after I'm even aware she's here she's up into the dog's shoulder, shoving him aside with a strength that's only partly muscle. The dog barrels into my knees, knocking me back. Jim actually turns and snaps at Triti as they stumble by me, but she grabs him by the scruff the way you'd grab a cat, and somehow she leverages him to the ground, her momentum carrying them both into the long grass and down. In the darkness, in the weeds, she's just a dark shape over the big shining body of the dog but I can hear her talking to him still, her tone light and conversational, at utter odds with what she's just done—she sounds as though she's making plans to take him to a movie he might enjoy, or asking him how his day was. He's only down for a second, torquing gracelessly to his feet again like a horse, but once he's up he just stands there. Triti is right with him.

"I'm sorry," she says, lifting her voice. "She's freaking him out."

I've forgotten Dorlene, but she's gone nowhere. I step over to her and crouch down in front of her. She doesn't see me. She breathes the tiniest shallow breaths, each one swift and thimble-sized but far apart, like a dying fish. "Dorlene," I say. "Are you okay?" She's made fists deep into the fabric of her dress, so that the hem of it is daintily raised, as though she were about to walk through wet. I catch the acrid scent that's steaming off her—she's pissed herself. I reach out and grip her gently by the back of her neck, embarassed by the violent size of my hand. Her neck is slick, and it takes me a moment to realize that it's the dog's saliva. "Dorlene. Hey. Dorlene."

Her breath goes quiet. She looks down at her feet. Her hands slowly loosen and she wipes at her throat, her neck, her chest. She ducks her way out from under my touch and starts to walk away, her legs stiff and awkward because of the pee. It makes her look more doll-like than ever. She heads toward the cars, tottering slow, not looking back, and I swear a little disfigured bolt of laughter threatens to punch its way out of me as I watch her go. My stomach buckles as I choke it down.

Triti has her eyes on me. Her frown is deep and old.

"She needs help," I tell her. "Girl help. I think she wet herself."

"I need to get the dog away first. Come with me." She says that, but then she doesn't actually need me. It makes me think there's something I'm supposed to be doing that I'm not as she claps in the dog's face and walks backward, calling him. He follows her—not eager, never eager, but inevitable—like some great toy boat on a string. I glance up the slope for Dorlene but don't see her. I follow Triti as she leads the dog to the corncrib with its slotted walls, around to the door. She steps right inside, sliding apart in the origami shadows of the place. She keeps calling Jim's name from in there. The dog hesitates at the threshold, swinging his mammoth head back in my direction, but at last he steps through. Triti pops back out and closes the rickety door behind him. She lifts the door on its hinges a bit and wedges it tight. I figure Jim will object, that he will just plow his way out, but of course he doesn't. This is the dog everyone knows, even me: he walks to the door and stands there, sideways, his white mass cut into stripes by the wide horizontal slits in the walls. I see his eye, bobbing slightly as he pants. Otherwise he doesn't move.

We stand there a minute. Dorlene's long gone and I can hardly see Triti. She is caught in a shadow. I can see her arms, mostly, just her arms. And so I can't tell exactly where she's looking when she says: "This is what you get."

Opinion of Person

THE CAT WAS INTO THE CURTAINS; HIS GODDAMN CLAWS were pricking and popping. Even from the bed, Julie could see the new little starholes he was making in the cloth. The fabric swung as Rory's shadow twitched, high up between the sheers and drapes where he was hanging. Julie waited for him to fall. "You'll die, you dumb animal," she said.

Julie listened for sounds further out in the apartment. The clock said 9:17, which meant, probably, that Ed would already be gone. The air over the bed was freezing and thin. Julie lifted the hem of the blanket, pressed it against her lip, made it the world's largest mustache. She held it there, breathed in through her mouth, out through her nose. The cat's damn claws pricked and snagged.

Water ran in the bathroom. Shad was awake. He belched sonorously, shut the water off, said, to himself, "Shad, you fuck," and the medicine cabinet opened and closed. Julie listened close through several quiet seconds and then startled at the sudden plunge of piss into the toilet. Rory fell down from the long window, landing heavily on the floor, his feet gathering and mincing, prissy little things. He meowed like answers were owed him.

Julie rolled onto her face beneath the blanket, spread her legs and elbows, opened her eyes into the sheets and listened to the sound of Shad peeing. Right now, she thought, his cock is in his hand. He peed and peed. If only she'd been counting. Shad said, plenty loud enough for her to hear, "Oh my Christ." Such a heavy sound he made, and why was that true—that a man's piss always sounded so heavy? Their streams were so thin. When Ed peed it was precise, braided almost, arcing into the water.

"My pee has no arc," she said into the sheets, and she smelled them and thought of Ed's long, thin cock, with its own arc, long and thin especially when it was hard, and pale—a strange animal bone. All of him so smooth and nearly hairless, so eager and certain. The toilet flushed. Rory ran from the room.

Julie got up and put on a pair of Ed's boxers, yesterday's shirt. Her boobs were freezing. She checked their sag with her hands, hefting and dropping them, feeling the sad little peas of her huddled nipples with her thumbs. She thought briefly of a bra and decided she could go without. She stepped onto the floor vent, but the air coming out was vacantly cold, the product of some strange cycle the furnace here had. Ed's socks were laid out on the grate, flat and crisp.

She lifted her chin and called out, loud, "Is Ed gone?"

Shad's big voice barreled back, like he was the walls. "He is."

"Are you dressed?"

There was a long pause. She could hear the TV talking low. Shad said, "I am."

Julie went down the hall. Shad stood out there in the living room with his back to her, nearly filling the space between the couch and the wall. He wore tentish tan shorts and a long red shirt. He was watching a preacher on TV.

"Hey," Julie said.

"Christians," Shad said flatly, gesturing with the remote. He didn't turn around. The preacher talked into his microphone, marched across a big black stage, a phone number beneath him on the screen.

Julie went to the bathroom. It stank of damp air and boy products—cloying and vigorously ambiguous scents. She checked the toilet seat before she sat down. She left water running in the sink while she peed, and while she peed, she bent and watched herself go, holding her pubic hair down with her hand. She peed until she became aware that she was counting, and when she got to eleven she cut off her stream. She held that muscle, felt it quiver, tried to feel, again, what it was connected to and where. She held it until she could imagine she no longer needed to pee, and then she let it go again. A queer little twinge of pain passed as her pee fell again, rudely, in a shower.

Afterward, she pulled up her panties, Ed's boxers. She didn't wash her hands. She watched her arms as she put her hair up in the mirror.

Shad was still standing in the same place, watching the preacher on TV. He said, "Who answers if you call that number?"

"I don't know."

"Those phones are somewhere. People answer."

"Yeah, I don't know, Shad."

He lifted a thick arm at the TV. "Christians, sure. But I mean besides Christians. I mean who by name. It would be someone. It would be what someone was doing, right that second. It's strange."

"Very strange," Julie said. She was so fucking freezing. Her nipples were so hard they felt like little injuries. She cupped them, felt them sink into the soft sag of her breasts.

"Bruce, Mary Ellen, Connie," said Shad. "Earl."

"Call them," Julie said. "Was Ed late for work?"

"I don't know. Did you hear back about the thing? The job?"

Julie sighed. "It's Sunday."

"Oh, right."

"It's the weekend."

Shad nodded. "I can see you in the TV."

Julie looked down at herself. She flexed her hands, drew her arms in closer around her body. "Well, I'm freezing, what do you expect? I'm just freezing. Why is it so goddamn cold in here?"

The TV preacher had his hand on the shoulder of a little girl planted on the stage. He leaned over her, looked out at the audience. "This is God's house, right here," he said to them.

"I can't see you *that* well, Julie," said Shad.

Julie went into the kitchen, drank orange juice from the carton, listened to TV sounds rolling in through the breakfast-bar window. Rory the cat sat on the counter, licking the wooden handle of a knife that was sunk deep into a whole pineapple. His eyes were closed. The pineapple rocked.

"Hey," she said to the cat. *"Ffft."*

"Connie is short for Constance, did you know that?" Shad said from the other room.

"Yeah, people know that, Shad."

"There's no name like that for men, you know?'

"Constantine," she said. She took a big drink of orange juice, let it sit in her mouth. She waited for a burning sensation. Maybe if she left the orange juice in her mouth long enough, it would burn a hole out down through the entire soft bottom of her jaw. That would be a shock. What would you do for such a person, or think? She imagined the breeze coming in through there. She watched the stupid cat and she waited for her mouth to begin to burn, but all that happened was the opposite of burning. Her mouth acclimating to the juice, or the juice to her. She held it.

"Conrad," said Shad from the other room.

Rory worked his tongue hard, up near the base of the knife's handle, where it was close against the pineapple's skin. He had his head turned almost upside down, one little paw up off the counter, bobbing in time with his licks. She could hear his soft licks, hated them. She couldn't tell how much of the blade was bared down there. The pineapple thudded and rustled as it rocked. Julie opened her mouth. She could feel the juice pooling, lapping against her bottom lip.

"Rory," she tried to say, but it came out *"Woewee."* She moved closer to the counter. The stupid cat was giving her an ear, but he just licked and licked. She stood right over him. She'd make sure she got some on the back of his head—he'd hate that. What a curse to be made so fussy but to be given no hands. She leaned over him and spat.

Rory instantly became a cartoon—he seemed to start to scramble even before the juice hit him, maybe from the sound squirting stupidly from her. He hit the floor skittering, out of there, a dark patch down his back.

Julie wiped her chin, cleaned up the dribbles of juice on the counter, the floor. She wiped the handle of the knife, dabbed the pineapple dry. She turned the pineapple around to see if the tip of the knife came out the other side, but couldn't see it. She ran her finger over the spot, wondering with a thrill if she would be pricked.

She took the orange juice carton into the living room. Shad had his body folded and slumped complexly into one corner of the couch. She took the other end. A man on TV talked about bicycling in Prague.

Shad had a little smudge of white stuff in the corner of his mouth. Julie didn't tell him—because he would care, but only barely. The big red shirt he wore was one she'd never seen, tight and long and red, with yellow print on the front, like the top half of a pair of long johns, or more like a nightshirt, meant to go to the knees. It was long enough for him—like a regular shirt—but it wasn't wide enough. The yellow on the front was a dog's head, like a Goofy or a Pluto head, stenciled on, cheap and peeling. The dog had his head sticking out of a yellow circle, and his square teeth were out, and around his mouth bent lines made it look like he had a hold on the shirt in his teeth, but it only sort of did, and in big curving yellow letters over the dog it said FETCH-N-WARE.

"Where'd you get that shirt?" Julie said.

"Ed," said Shad, staring at the TV.

"I've never seen it before."

"You will now. It's my favorite shirt now."

"It's freezing in here. Why's it always freezing here?"

"I turned the heat up," Shad said. They listened to the man on TV talk about the famousness of the french fries they make in Belgium. The man stood beside a food cart near a park. In the background, old men played chess. "The Pope died again."

"I know."

"It's weird how that happens. That whole thing."

Julie set the carton on the floor. "Is that your pineapple? In the kitchen?"

"Yeah, I thought I might eat that."

"That damn cat," she said. "He's up on the counter, he doesn't even care. He was licking that knife."

"What knife?"

"It's Ed that lets him up there. He says he doesn't, but he does."

Shad shook his head. "That cat. Rory. I hate that cat."

"He walks in his own toilet," Julie said, and Shad nodded heavily.

They watched TV. Shad changed the channels. He stopped on an old woman doing yoga on a dark volcanic seashore. After a while he said, "She's totally hot. This chick? I mean for what, like sixty? For sixty she's smoking. That yoga, that's for real."

Julie folded one arm across her chest and tucked her legs in. She watched the woman move her strange body, her too-high pelvis and her too-bent back giving her away, despite all the meaty leanness between her joints.

Shad tilted his head toward her, his thick face buckled around an awkward crimp of concern. "I didn't mean anything by that, Julie."

Julie felt herself flush. "Well, I'm not sixty."

"Fuck, I know that."

"I'm closer to your age than hers."

"I know." The woman on TV talked to them about what she was doing. The camera switched to a close-up of her face. Her hair was pulled back severely, held back in an arcane and impenetrable bun, her face like wicker.

Julie watched Shad watch the woman. She considered his sturdy neck, his deep shoulders. His torso uniformly broad but bellyless beneath the red shirt, looking pliably dense, monolithic and rubbery, like the body of some marine mammal. His heavy, hairy legs were spread, his hands hanging between them, the muscled curve of his thigh into his knee the most textured shape beneath the surface of his skin. "You should do yoga, Shad."

"Fuck that."

"You should lose weight."

"Oh my god."

"I mean, you're not exactly fat, not really, but you could be smaller."

"I am very large," said Shad.

"Yoga's good for you. I do yoga. And you should eat that pineapple. Fruit, you know. Your body needs that. You guys don't have anything decent to eat around here."

"I was gonna eat that pineapple."

"Your body knows you need it."

"My body."

"You should listen to your body." The yoga woman stretched into a bend that made her crotch bulge. Her ass disappeared and the fabric of her leotard went taut across the mound between her thighs. She talked all the while. "Jesus Christ," Julie said.

"Vulvular," said Shad. He changed the channel to a shrill cartoon drawn with thick lines. The kids had big heads, crazy jaws. He switched again, landed in a courtroom drama that was just going to commercial. "Julie Julie," he said. "You and that Ed." He got up. The dynamics of the couch changed. He went into the kitchen. The TV began to meander through an advertisement for a Teddy Roosevelt coin.

The refrigerator came open. "There's no juice," said Shad.

"I have orange juice out here." Julie picked up the carton.

"You took my juice?"

Julie froze, her mouth open indignantly. "It's mine, Shad. I bought this juice."

"You're buying juice now?"

"I brought it over here, for myself."

Shad leaned over the breakfast bar. "Anyway, fuck that, I bought that juice."

"You don't even drink juice."

"I drink orange juice. That's why I bought it. Man, are you drinking from the container?"

"You didn't buy this, but get a cup, good lord."

"Yeah, I'll get two cups. Drinking from the carton, you're some girl," he said, and when he said that, a flush curled out of her belly and lit her arms. Shad dug into the dishes in the drain board, made them rattle and shift. Julie examined the carton, wondered if it was hers after all.

Shad said, in the kitchen, softly to himself, "Oh man, killed my pineapple." He came back out and took the carton. He poured them both juice in the little green cups.

Shad drank his juice. They watched TV. Shad put a red corduroy pillow across his belly and Julie didn't tell him it just made him look fatter. A single hair jutted out from the mat of his eyebrow, terribly long—long enough to be a queasy curiosity—and it rose in a jagged curl back to touch his forehead about an inch up. What a hair, Julie thought, and she itched to pluck it. A commercial for detergent came on. Shad pointed at it and said, "Time and color enhanced."

"What's that?"

"It said that—at the bottom. Time and color enhanced."

"That means nothing to me."

"They had to say it. They enhanced those."

"Time, they enhanced time."

"Yeah. Made it go faster." He lowered a finger at her. "Which is only occasionally an enhancement."

"You don't even know," Julie told him.

A car commercial came on. A black car glided around the curves of a silvering, snake-shaped road. "I feel a little weird about it," she said. "I didn't really notice the enhancement. Did you?"

Shad shook his head. "That's because it's all enhanced. You're numb to it, man."

Julie pointed to the TV. "Professional driver. Closed course."
"They always say that," Shad said. "It's not very dissuasive." He
scratched his nose. He said, "I wonder what professional drivers do for
a living."

"This, I guess."

Shad looked over at her. He gestured between the two of them.
"This," he said.

Julie clucked her tongue, lifted her eyes. "Yes, Shad, this."

"With each other or with you?"

"With me, of course."

They watched TV. "I don't even know what this is. I don't even know
what you're doing here," said Shad.

"There are a lot of car commercials, is what I meant," said Julie after
a while.

Shad switched to a news channel. Julie waited for the newspeople
to talk about the Pope, but no one did. They talked about the recovery.
They talked about gas prices. They briefly showed a beautiful young
woman in a long green skirt pumping gas. She wore sunglasses, held her
hand against her cocked hip, watched the pump. She had her ponytail
pulled forward over her shoulder. She was far away.

Julie took her hair down, put it up again. Shad changed the channel.
A commercial ended and another began, a juice one. They watched the
bottom of the screen.

"I might make some Jell-O later," Shad said.

"Are you hungry?"

"I am."

"Make it now. It'll be ready later."

"I'm not up for that just yet. You would think it's like making Kool-
Aid or something, but it isn't. The stove and all."

"You know you can't put pineapple in Jell-O."

"I wasn't considering it."

"I'm just saying. It won't set if you do."

"I think I've heard that. People say that."

"It's true," Julie said. "And not just any pineapple, only fresh pineapple. Canned pineapple is fine, but not fresh."

"Now why in the fucking world would that be?"

"It's something in the pineapple. But when they pasteurize it, it goes away. When they can it."

Shad reached for his cup. The pillow slid to the floor.

"Call fucking Jell-O, they'll tell you," Julie told him.

"Just pineapple."

"That's right."

"Now how would you know something like that, Julie?"

"I've just always known it," Julie said.

A commercial for pills came on. The TV didn't say what the pills were for.

"Results may vary," Julie read.

"They must, necessarily," said Shad. He set his juice down and gathered the red pillow into his lap again.

Julie said, "I think Ed worries that something is going on between us. Or, I guess, that it could."

Shad squinted. "What?"

"You and me," Julie said. "Each other, I mean. I think he worries about us."

Shad began to nod rhythmically at the TV. "You and me. You."

Julie said, "That pillow doesn't make you not look fat, you know."

"So what did he say?"

"Nothing. He didn't say anything."

"You just get the feeling."

"Sometimes. I have."

"You're like twice my age."

"I'm twice Ed's age."

"You're hot, though."

Julie shrugged.

"Not just for your age."

"I know what you meant, Shad. Thank you." She scratched at the backs of her thighs.

"I wonder if he said something," Shad said.

"You can wonder," said Julie. She put her fists into her crotch, closed her knees around her elbows. Shad flipped through the channels.

They came into the thick of an infomercial, where a tan woman talked to them through the camera, through wires—through the deft mysteries of magnetism, or light—into the air, out of the TV. She said this was the greatest moneymaking opportunity available to the average American today. The simple answer to difficult times. Behind her a swimming pool gleamed. Fine print at the bottom of the screen said: *Extraordinary claims, individual experience not guaranteed.* They watched the woman. Her teeth were magnificent.

"The world is full of desperate, right, Julie?" said Shad, and he laughed and he laughed, and he pushed buttons on the remote, and the TV flashed and blurted.

The TV began to talk to them about lions. On screen, lions slunk across a lion-colored plain, lounged blandly on rocks. A narrator mentioned their deadliness. Shad put the remote down. Julie read from the back of the orange juice carton.

"Folate," she read aloud. "Thiamine."

"Riboflavin," Shad said without looking.

"There are no ingredients here. No ingredients at all. Only nutrition facts."

"It's juice," said Shad. "One hundred percent."

The TV told them about an ongoing situation with the lions, how poor people were fleeing hopefully from some miserable African country to some slightly less miserable one, crossing a wide savanna park there on their exodus. But occasionally in their search for prosperity—or security, it wasn't clear—some of them were eaten by lions on the way.

"Oh, man," said Shad.

A deeply shining black man in khakis stood and talked to the camera, his musical English sharp and sludgy in strange places, and he said that they found about seven kills a month in the park—would-be refugees from that other country. But when he said *kill* he mostly meant just evidence of a kill, because they might only find a shoe, or a jagged scrap of bloodied fabric. And when he said they found about seven kills a month he meant that was all they found, and the park was very large and the rangers were few, and anyway how would you know to look? These people who were crossing the park in the night, no one would tell you if they had gone missing. These people, the black man said, they want to be missing.

"And then the lion, she comes," the man said, and he slapped one flat palm off the other into the air, off the edge of the TV screen.

Julie got up and went down the hall into the bathroom. She closed the door behind her. The fan came on. Shad lay down on the couch. He propped his elbow up in Julie's warm depression. He listened toward the bathroom but there was nothing to hear. The clock said 10:52, and he tried to gauge what Ed would be doing at work now, and how likely he might be to come home for lunch, even though he never did. Shad watched the show about lions. He thought about Julie in the bathroom. After a while, commercials came on, and he read the small print: *While supplies last. Use as directed. Serving suggestion.* When the lion show came back on, he flipped to other channels. He went back to the moneymaking infomercial, in which a mustached, middle-aged man in an ornate sweater was just beginning to talk animatedly to some entity off-camera. After a few moments, below the man, the screen read: *Opinion of person.* Shad sat up. He turned the volume all the way down.

Shad turned his head, kept his eyes on the TV. "Opinion of person," he called down the hall.

Julie's voice came back, singsongy and muffled, unintelligible.

Shad sat on the couch and watched the person on TV with the sound still down. The person gesticulated and smiled. He made a broad, circular gesture up into the air around himself, as though he were referencing the world, or everything available to himself, or something that had ascended, or would descend. The person made a gesture that involved laying both his hands on his belly. Shad tried to read his lips. He watched the shapes his mustache made. The person's eyes were small, wide set. And then the person sat back in his seat, stopped talking, a look of completion on his face—or not just his face, but around his whole head, his shoulders, his chest. Something in his high-chinned slouch looked so proprietary, so smug. The camera lingered on him an awkward moment too long, and then the scene switched to an empty studio somewhere. Microphones hung from the ceiling.

Shad tried to mimic the person, settling back into the couch, arching his neck and making his shoulders as heavy as they could go. He exhaled. He let his eyes unfocus on a specific point over the TV set. He sighed audibly. Down the hall, the toilet flushed.

Shad flipped back to the lion show and went into the kitchen. He pulled an open tube of flavorless crackers from a box, took them back to the living room, sat down on Julie's side of the couch. He ate the crackers one by one, putting them whole into his mouth salty side down. He turned the volume back up on the TV. And now he saw that the show wasn't just about lions, it was about big cats in general. There were interviews with a number of people who had been attacked by the animals: lions, yes, but leopards, tigers, cheetahs. An account was given by a man, a trainer, who had been attacked by a captive tiger he'd known for years. He described how the tiger had him in its jaws and was shaking him, trying to shake him, basically, to death. And the man's leg was ripped open, and muscle was being torn from his bone, and his leg nearly came off entirely, but the man said he felt no pain while it was happening. Just a kind of calmness, a surrender, or like a peace. And he was saved by another trainer but he almost lost that leg, and he still walked funny.

After that a French man came on and he spoke in French, but a voice-over was translating for him, and he talked about how that phenomenon is often described by survivors of big-cat attacks—a calmness, a ludicrous absence of pain—and how naturalists have observed the same behavior from prey in the wild when a lion or a tiger has a hold of them: a kind of peacefulness, a seeming resignation.

And then the French man kept talking, and the voice-over translated for him: "And maybe this is God: that prey, in its final moment of discovery, would be asked to have faith in the futility of resisting a predator so lavishly designed."

"Oh fuck," Shad said, and he sat on the couch and listened to the rumble of his bones tingling.

The toilet flushed again. Water ran loudly. On TV, a man showed off a huge and gruesome scar on his inner thigh. It looked like cabbage. Julie came out of the bathroom. She slid into Ed's bedroom, rustled around, came back out. She had pajama pants on. Her ponytail was pulled forward over one shoulder and was wet at the end.

"That cat is fucked up somehow," she said.

"This guy just said the most incredible thing."

"This guy?"

"No, no, this other guy. A French guy. About, about the tigers and stuff. The lions. They, like, grab you in their mouths, and they're so goddamn strong and there's nothing you can do and you know it, and you go into this sort of trance, and you don't feel any pain. Even though he's shaking you, you know, tearing the muscle off your bones. You just like surrender. And he said, this guy said, maybe that's what God is."

Julie stood there, watching the TV. A woman was holding a leopard pelt in both hands. Julie scratched her chest. Her boobs shimmied.

"What's this now?" she said. She walked around the table, curled into the other end of the couch. A soft wave of soap smell drifted briefly over Shad. "What's this?"

"Yes."

"What's God? The lion is God? The tiger?"

Shad said, "No, no, it's not about the lion. It's not about the lion or the tiger at all. Or the animal, the person. It's the—" and he tried to cup a shape in his hands. He shook his head.

"That cat is all messed up," said Julie. "That Rory."

"You should've heard it," Shad said.

"He's got some stuff all over him. Some sticky gunk, all up on his head. I don't know."

Shad rubbed his chin. "What, like glue?"

"I don't know, some sticky wet crap. Look, there he is." Rory stumbled into the room. He was dying, it seemed, on the verge of collapse, allergic or epileptic, maybe, some devastating neurological spell—but he was only staggering into a bath. He sank against the wall, already licking his side, his back legs out, stiff like skis. There was a dark shiny stain on his fur, all down his back and head. He licked and licked. He held his eyes closed. The dark patch was smoothly curled in places, where he'd been working.

"What should I do?" Shad said.

"I don't know. Nothing."

"I hate that cat."

Julie said, "I heard about this lion once, there was this lion, and he had killed about fifty people. Somewhere over in Africa. It was the deadliest lion ever. And they finally caught him, the people caught him and killed him—I think it was a him—and they found out one of his teeth was all cracked. All busted up and fucked up, terrible, and they think he must've been in terrible pain. Toothache, I mean. And that's why he was eating people, they think, because apparently people are like butter compared to, like, water buffalo."

Julie's cell phone rang from the bedroom, shrill and tinkling, once, twice.

"That's you," Shad said.

"I'm aware."

Julie held her elbows in her hands. She stared at the TV, her smooth forearms like wood. There was tapering meat beneath skin there. Shad made fists, rolling the tendons in the long thick bellies of his wrists. He fingered and smoothed the nearly empty tube of crackers in his crotch.

"Toothache," Julie said, and she held her hand up, and she held her index finger and her thumb apart in what was, Shad knew, her best approximation of lion tooth size. Julie looked at her own hand as she did it, her head slightly cocked, her lips parted. Shad reached deeper into his lap and snapped the remaining stack of crackers into halves, quarters, crumbs, inside the plastic tube. Julie turned to him on the couch, her long legs all up underneath, Indian-style.

"And, yes, okay, you might say there's no excuse for the first one," she said. "Because how would he have known, right? About the softness of people. But people are easy to catch, of course. For lions. And maybe that first person was especially soft. The softest, creamiest person in the village. Somebody old, or young." Julie chewed on nothing, made smacking noises in her wet mouth. She made the vaguest little bent-finger claws with her little lifted hands. "And that lion had never had such good food before, but all the rest of the people after that were never as creamy, as tender, and he just kept trying and trying, but no other villager was as good. As gristle-free as the first." She dropped her arms into her lap. She pulled her collar out, glanced down into her shirtfront, let her collar snap back. She said, "I'm just saying, we don't know."

Rory washed himself against the wall.

Shad said, "What is gristle, anyway? Is it bone or isn't it? Gristle. Gristle."

"I wonder how it would be if the Pope was attacked by a tiger," Julie said. "What he would think, or do. How he would taste."

"Anyway, I think you made that up. All of that."

"If Rory was a tiger, how big would the Pope be?"

Shad looked over at Rory. Rory wet a paw and drew it over his head, down to his mouth again and back, over and over, a smooth oval, cleaning himself. The fur on his head stuck up like dead grass. Julie clucked at him, but he paid no mind.

Shad surged forward on the couch. "Scram, you fuckhole!" he yelled. The couch tipped up, rocked. Julie threw her arms out. Rory flickered instantly up onto all fours, strung with tension, ears and eyes. He stared at Julie. "Get the fuck out!" Shad shouted, his neck swelling with effort, and then Rory was gone, his paws crackling through the carpet. The couch fell back on its feet.

"Fucking Christ, Shad."

Shad worked the remote. He went to the channel where they tell you about all the other channels.

"I mean, goddamn lord," Julie said to him.

The landline rang. Shad said, "What the hell was that stuff? What do we even have around here that's like that?" He smoothed his eyebrows down. The phone was ringing. "Are you getting that or what?"

"I'm in the bathroom."

"And where the fuck am I?"

"I don't know, you're just being Shad, Shad."

The phone stopped ringing. The answering machine clicked and droned on the counter, gave its long beep. There was a pause and then Ed's voice came through, like it was coming through paper. It sounded like Ed's voice, but it was so high, so canned.

"O-o-o-o-kay," said the voice. Shad flipped through the channels. A clumsy, heavy sound of disconnection came through the answering machine.

The answering machine said, "Sunday. Four. Thirteen. A.M."

They watched TV. A couple was cooking, a woman washed a car. A crowd gathered outdoors.

"It smells like cat piss right here," Julie said after a while.

"Where, the couch?"

"Maybe. I don't know. I keep smelling it. This whole apartment." She sat up. She drew up her nose, drawing in thread after thread of air, letting it out through her mouth. "I think I do."

"It's the couch."

"I don't know. See, now I think I can't smell it."

Shad lifted his face into the air and sniffed. "That cat. I wish he would get rid of that thing."

"Do you smell it?"

"No. Maybe. That cat pisses on stuff, I know it."

Julie sat back down, facing Shad. "There, there it is. I think it is the couch. Or I don't know."

"That fucking cat. I wish he would get rid of it."

"Why am I even here?"

"I don't know."

"I'm old enough to be your mother."

"I know it."

"You could have come out of me."

Shad pushed buttons on the remote.

"Think about it," Julie said, and she laid her hand inside her lap, her fingers curled around her inner thighs, her thumbs angled out to frame the rounded V between her legs. She lowered her chin. She pressed her knees out and down, away from one another. "Think about it. You could have come out of me."

Momentary

I SHOULD MENTION: SOMETIMES IN THE HOSPITAL WHEN I AM
wandering heavy around my sleep, I think about all the beautiful sheltering trees in my neighborhood at home, and the spastic indecision of
squirrels in the road.

HERE IS CELIA STANDING AT THE KITCHEN COUNTER, LOOKING
out our window there, or down at the knife like a needle in her hand.
She is sewing a tomato into pieces. The knife is one of our big television knives, forked at the end and mouthed with menacing, ornate
serrations. The tomato came from the garden. The sound of the blade
across the counter comes like scratching at the door, and as Celia makes
it she looks out at the sideyard, down at her work. The knife is so fine
the tomato barely bleeds, and my question is whether you could ever
hear the sound of that flesh being torn gently apart beneath the scratch
of the knifetip across the countertop.

The woman outside my room owns a soft busy sound herself. She
makes it in the hallway and I wake to it in the morning; she always rises
before me. It's a small sound she makes, but it fills the room like the
breathless voice of an insect, whirring. It reminds me of Celia's toothed
knife being dragged lightly and quickly down off the edge of a cutting
board, over the soft buried bone of meat.

I get up quiet and I go to the door. The woman outside my room is there. Her hair hangs in blinders, and I can't see her face. She stares down onto her hands together below her belly. They curl into a cloven shape, her fingers bent over deep, nuzzling one another at the nails. She works her hands back and forth swiftly and they blur in a little safe space there barely larger than themselves, like they are busy making fire. The faces of her nails slide across one another, whisper and click, seem to hum. The sound is trickling down around her feet, feathering through my door.

I drift back, let my bed pull me back in. As I settle there, the sound the woman makes stops just for a moment, starts again. Celia doesn't set the knife down until her tomato is diced into pieces smaller than fingernails. A small pool of seeded pulp stains the striped countertop. I wonder how close any single piece of tomato has come to a cube now, and what shapes it shed to become that way.

CELIA HAS A STORY SCAR, ONE THAT HAS A SIMPLICITY I ENVY. I never tire of hearing her tell the story to people; I tell it myself when I can. I tell it to Theresa in the hospital, in the common area where she has been sent by Dr. Lane to listen to me: how when Celia was very young she had two of those cheap swingsets in her yard, two swingsets back-to-back, and one day when she was about six she was swinging very high, crazy high I imagine, I imagine high enough that you could feel the feet of the swingset lurching just up off the ground—this sensation, in fact, was her motive. And a neighbor boy was on a swing behind her, I don't remember his name, and as she describes it I have this very vivid picture—silhouetted against the sky—of the point between the two swingsets where two robustly moving swings could nearly meet in the middle, high off the ground. On that day the meat of her hanging calf met the squared bolt protruding from the side of the boy's swing, and the bolt was driven through her skin just in that instant. Or maybe: her skin was driven down over the bolt. It doesn't matter, really, because it's at this point in the story, when Celia is telling it, that she always makes the earnest gesture that mimics the two swings coming apart—

her drawn-flat hands sweeping out and down to the sides. She says she remembers looking down into the grass, seeing a piece of her flesh there. She calls it a chunk.

And now after all this time a delicate drop-shaped patch the size of a mouse decorates her leg, like a patch of oil on water, and I find it a miracle that you can see one or two thread-sized veins running through it. If you were to press your thumb lightly against it, you would find that it feels like the skin on top of pudding. It gives, I'm not sure how much. I don't like to touch it, or I love to. I can scarcely bear to think of it.

I tell Dr. Lane this story, too, early on. Who knows what he'll make of it. Probably he thinks it doesn't apply to my situation, because the accomplishment itself—Celia's injury—was so improbably orchestrated that it had to have been an accident. In this sense, he doesn't appreciate me.

I AM MADE TO MANUFACTURE WORDS HERE, MOSTLY FOR Theresa. Dr. Lane sends her to me—banking, I think, on Theresa's sturdy brand of bovine maternalism. And I do talk to her. I tell her she should think of my experience as something akin to the slight, understandable slipping of barely imperfect gears, that I was unlucky in a way, encountering an instant of lost traction under unfortunate circumstances. Circumstances, you understand, bloated with potential. Theresa listens to me talk. We sit together in the common area, and Theresa has a way of angling herself against the table, of looking around the room, of humming in a warmly distant monotone that makes it seem as though we are out together at leisure, talking our way lazily out of lunch, meeting for the first time or the thousandth. She is very intelligent, a constant surprise; I weigh all my words with her like a druggist—the same as she and Dr. Lane do for me. I tell her things she should know, how for instance you might find yourself at the kitchen counter with a long perfect knife in your hand, and how it seems such a deadly thing, and how your soft belly is right there, such a soft and vital thing, and how it would take so little. So little time, so little effort, maybe just a lack of effort. I describe the laughable relief of putting the knife down, walking away. Theresa hums and she makes her faint nod which is not a yes. She is devastatingly unattractive, strictly utilitarian. Like burlap.

I say to her, "It seemed like such a danger, you know? More than danger: a threat. To even be there like that. It was like I'd armed myself, and it was a thrill—suspecting I was someone I couldn't trust." I hold up my good hand. "Not a nice thrill, though. I was pretty scared. A thrill like falling in the dark." I stop talking. Theresa sits in her implacable plastic chair.

"It happened fast," I tell her.

She blinks at me. She points vaguely at my arm, her finger circling as she points. Her voice is always sure, I love and hate her voice, and she says, "This didn't happen to you, James. You did it." She dips her head as though she is giving me another nod, and maybe she means it as a prod—in the way, for example, you would urge a child into water.

"Hm," I say.

Theresa scratches her nose. "I mean, god," she says. "You did this to yourself, James." She emphasizes *did this*. She says it like you would say *cancer*. The rest of the sentence is warm.

I slide my forearms on the table. I make them as symmetrical as I can. I should mention: I am missing my left hand, and what Theresa means when she talks to me now is that there was an accident in which I cut it off. Or, at least, this is close to what she means. I spread the fingers of my other hand carefully, until they hurt. I see that my bandages need to be changed. Theresa is very homely, did I say that? I shake my head at her. "You keep saying that," I say.

She sighs. "Well, James." She looks around the room.

I'm never sure we should speak to each other this way. There is something of an impropriety about our talks, I'm sure I don't imagine it. She must sense it too, because we always work our way into silence. And there are things I would like to tell Theresa. Details that might interest her. Maybe, for example, she would like to hear about how I recall shouting for Celia, and how Celia finds me in the grass going black, and how her face comes rushing in and swims away at the same time. How I remember that last turgid look on Celia's face, like something detonating powerfully in a stubborn steel box. How she says nothing, but her hands are busy and sure. Maybe I could describe for Theresa how my skin surrounds me, toiling to become new, or why I am conscious that every hair is oldest at the tip, or what I feel about water's way of delivering weight. But by the time I can muster these thoughts, I am back in the doorway of my room. When I go in, the woman outside says what she says: "Oh, you're *that* one." I tell her what I always tell her, which is that I might be.

The lights go down. The woman outside my room reassures me, frightens me. My nights here are long and perversely private, here where people are so unabashedly preoccupied with their own obsessions, and I wait to re-emerge into morning, myself or something like it. Here is myself, my bed here, and sometimes the woman outside my room and always the hours before I wake, myself. At home Celia saves our plastic grocery bags, keeps them in a cloth tube that hangs on the refrigerator, elastic openings at both ends. You push the bags in through the top and pull them out the bottom when you need them. The tube bulges, crinkles. I tell Celia: it's like a little time machine.

"What?" she says.

"The thing, the tube. The bags," I say.

"I have no idea what you're talking about."

"The bags, you put a bag in the top and the same kind of bag comes out the bottom, but really it's a different bag. A bag from the past. Like maybe the bag you brought ice cream home in six months ago."

She frowns. She is looking up over my head, around me at the walls or the ceiling maybe. She says, "I don't keep those bags. They get wet."

I think myself light as a feather stiff as a board. I try to imagine my bed into motion, into flight, into any gentle rocking, but it's hard because my hand itches terribly. That hand. I don't mean the wound itches, although it does—I mean past that, further from me. It happens to me sometimes. The itch is always specific, fascinating. Sometimes it's a desperate hot irritation, jumping up between two fingers, or just an insectlike disturbance on the back of my hand, but right now it's a deep pulsing jangle that slowly swells in the fat of my palm where the thumb roots, just southwest of where that last curving crease would be. That palm line, I don't know the name. I check my other hand to be sure of the geography.

It's not surprising, of course, that so cruel a trick could be played on me, but it keeps me awake. The hospital is otherwise very quiet. As far as I know, others sleep. I lie in bed, and I try to scratch my itch along the same stream of thought that makes it rise in the first place; sometimes I can. I could mention too: sometimes with my left arm I still reach up unthinking in the dark for my hair, or to smooth my eyebrow or pick at the corner of my mouth, and just as the expected moment of contact passes I get a chill I can't really describe; maybe it's like a ghost passing through my face. Or sometimes, horribly: my face is the ghost. Or one and then, quickly, the other. Confusion burbles thickly then, heavy inside me like a desperate, symptomless sickness. I tell myself it's a problem of perspective.

The fold of bedsheet I rub between my fingers is slick and thin, not like the flannel sheets on our bed at home. Those sheets at home, I like them; they have always been thick and warm, the bed's own pajamas, but you can't run them between your fingers like I am doing now. And anyway I don't sleep any better on them, I don't know why.

It's not that Celia is always there; she is an adversarial sleeper, but I don't mind. She takes, for example, the shape of a lowercase *h* across the bed, and I become an *r*. I understand that she needs this; there are rumors of the trouble her back gives her. After she's asleep, she stretches her long smooth slender thigh out into my part of the bed, holds her knee there just where I would lie, and it means there isn't much room for me but I don't mind. I wouldn't ever want her to know about it. I never sleep much anyway, and furthermore it seems like a vivid element of our romance—that I would keep a secret from her about herself, I mean.

Sometimes at night I get up, get away from her, go to the bathroom and fill the tub in the dark. In that kind of total dark you can only get in windowless, appliance-free rooms. There's a night-light, but the bulb is forever burnt out. The tub fills in the dark; the faucet becomes too hot to touch. The tub makes its intestinal sounds, the sinking pitch of fallen water rising. I try to gauge how near to the top the water comes, using only my hand because that's all I have, and I marvel to imagine what lies my fingertips tell me as they reach down, stretching into the heat rising thick, into the water more hot than wet, or maybe they haven't reached the water yet, or maybe they have been in water all along. You think your fingers will know, that they would never lie to you about the difference between water and air, but they are dumb. More than half mute from all their listening. Too vigilant to engage in gossip.

So I slip into the tub, into the watered dark, into warmth like skin. I go under until even my mouth is under, water sleeping around the feet of my nose. I pretend that I exhale so softly that I make no ripples. I rock my head back and forth, let the water come conducting into my ears, listen to the faraway pipe sounds, the sounds of myself against the porcelain, the sounds of blood bringing breath to my eardrums. Mostly I lie still, mostly water myself. Something like sleep comes to me, or maybe I am being taught that time runs differently through water, like light.

Celia keeps a supply of tiny paper cups on the sink for rinsing. The stack dwindles, recovers; disappears, returns: a lineage of tame mushrooms. I never use the cups; they seem so trivial. And they hold no more water than I could gather in my hands anyway. But sometimes before I get into the bath at night, I find a cup in the dark and I draw icy water from the tap—just enough to set the cup floating upright in the tub. And when I'm in there in the dark, the cup floats around on the quiet currents made by my breathing, or by the thermostatic emergence and submersion of my feet, and it comes near some island of my body— unseen, broadcast first by the tiny chilled cloud it makes around itself—

bumps against me and drifts away. At a certain distance from myself, I can no longer feel that the cup is there, a distance that grows small as the water inside the cup warms. I am able to imagine, eventually, that the cup disappears, or is somehow contained.

I don't sleep. Because of it I learn something valuable about myself. My itch has subsided, and I lie awake, composed now, my arm beside me on the sheets, and by trying very hard, very quiet, by believing that I can, I begin to hear the quiet electric talk, streaming through the deep flesh of my arm, that forever asks my absent fingernails to grow.

"YOU DON'T UNDERSTAND," I TELL THERESA. "IT'S A MATTER of potential. I was thinking, right before it happened to me, that it was something I *could* do. I could've, right? I saw my hand on the picnic table there. And I thought maybe if I were to somehow begin, I'd already be finished. Not able to stop, so fast. It scared me to think it." Theresa is listening to me, she always does, but never too hard. We gaze at each other and I discover that I can't tell how old she is, I realize I haven't the first idea; her face is a thick permanent lie. Looking at her I decide it is even possible, maybe, that I am older. I try to fathom it and I find, am surprised, that I would like her to understand me.

"Actually, I was really fucking terrified, Theresa," I tell her. "Truly *terrified,* in a way that changes how you think about the word. I had the maul in my other hand, up over my shoulder." I show her. What she might not understand is how I had the heft of the maul high up along the handle, the way you do for a short clean stroke. I attune myself to the physics of such things, but Theresa might not. She might not care or understand that a few inches' difference in my grip on that handle would have meant it couldn't have happened, that day. And so I just say, "It was already full of that perfect potential, okay? Right here? I judged that if the moment were to arrive—if it were to form—I would barely be able to blink before it was done. I doubted I would blink. And it turned out I was right about that." I smile. I lay my arms down. I show my teeth.

But Theresa looks down at the ruined end of my arm on the table, and somehow hers is the face that is like an animal's. It's hard to say how, but right now she looks very young to me, so much so that there is that kind of danger about her. She leans into me, that look on her face. She says, "I imagine that moment, you know, James? I try to, I do. That moment you always talk about, or the moment right after it. I wonder what you could've been thinking. I wonder," she says, and she squints at me, and she lays her flat-palmed hand down slow and thick on the table near my arm, so near that the stump of my wrist goes into the open arc between her thumb and forefinger, nearly touching, her hand smooth and heavy like clay, and she is whispering, "What were you thinking? What were you *thinking?*" She pats the table with her hand. She says, "And you, you're all calm, James, so calm. You talk like we could share this. As though we were friends," she says, "who could agree on the nature of such an experience." She goes on staring at me, and I wait, her voice so substantial, and then there is this painful thing: I begin to feel a constriction there. There just off the end of my arm where her hand is lying. It slowly becomes a curdling burn. A torrid creep of goose bumps blooms down and around the end of the stump, under the bandages, cold and endlessly crushing across my new skin.

I slide my seething arm from the table, bury it in my lap.

"I don't know," I say. "I don't know what you could even mean, calm." My arm rages between my thighs. "Theresa," I say.

She shrugs again, shakes her head. "But you are calm, James. And that's troubling, I'll tell you. You talk like complicity were available to you. Like if I agreed, it would be absolution. But really, James, you just lost control. You just lost control. You did a cruel thing to yourself. And this sea of calm all around, it doesn't help, it just magnifies that loss of control, which for me—for me, James?—is just an imagined thing anyway. And the size of it is only partly gauged by *this* terrible thing." She throws a gesture over the edge of the table into my lap, where my hands are. "That blemish, all this perfection. It could be considered frightening. Does this make sense?"

I tell her it doesn't. Even her words don't make sense—*cruel?* Her hands are fleshy roots. I say control, *control?* and my face is twisting from the bone; I say, "Theresa, my arm," and I lift it from my lap with the other even though the flesh is burning so bad there I am afraid that whatever it is will run and spread. I cup the stump in my hand and rock in my chair. Theresa stands up.

"Okay," she says, and she cocks her head. She makes a sound I know, a sound like you make when a curiosity has been satisfied. "All right," she says.

THE WOMAN OUTSIDE MY ROOM TWISTS HER HAIR INTO A rope down the middle of her chest. The air inside is still.

I can tell you, the way Theresa says that word, such confidence: *control*. It defeats me. And her ideas, her thick skin; what I can't explain is what makes her word somehow wrong, the measured islands of sense I can clearly recall, like water's press, the feel of the maul's handle in my palm, the wet smooth stringy grip of it, a patient weight across my skin.

Let me admit: fear is heavy, I'm saying it, but then again any substantial burden in my hand runs the danger of becoming so heavy that it turns slick. Maybe this is control, that crushing grip—I can appreciate that. At home I never mow the lawn; this is an example. It makes me uncomfortable, that barely caged blade, the fact that you must walk it. I'm dense with doubt just imagining. And so Celia mows instead, for me. I watch her from the patio when I can. She sways around the mower as it rears through its turns. I watch carefully whenever the mower rises, little clouds of ruin blooming from the underside. The scent of what she does, that scent like thick fruitless juice—the smell of the wet innards bludgeoned from many thousands of blades of grass, it must be—it spills across the lawn.

And Celia mows barefoot, without the catcher. You can imagine. I suspect—and I don't know this firsthand, but I wonder how many do— that a shoe wouldn't do much to stop the blindly chewing blade of the mower. But I guess I don't know about that for sure; I wish she would wear shoes.

Celia's skin, now, it is in my mind a perfection. Maybe this is why I worry. If she mows in the heat her face is flushed brilliant and shining when she is done, the smooth slope below her collarbone wet and long. When she comes up close to me like that, with her hard work still on her, I feel little pieces of a pull like it should be one of those times when I want to lay her down, when I want to water myself with the slick mess her body makes, but instead I drift away. Heat billows off her sickly in fists, like she burns. After, in the cooling bathroom where her leg curls prettily up onto the sink, I see the green ground into and around the cracks in her heel, like a map, a section of a textured globe.

There are strains in the sound made by the woman outside my room that remind me of far-off mower sounds: sounds that circle the house, waxing into windows, fingering their way through curtains. Celia walking barefoot and bare-legged behind the mower, one or two weak whispers of blood on her shins from wading through the debris hashed out by the blade. I can tell you about that blade, that thick blade, toiling savagely in the dark. If you've ever turned over a horseshoe crab on the beach, maybe you will understand me when I say how turning over the mower is always a little like that, and how the mower blade is not the slashing silver devil you'd imagined, but a brute. A surprising heft of metal, a matter of function, more than a little like the dull-edged heavy maul. The head of the maul is blue, did I say that? And no maul is a blade, not really—not like an ax, which is refined. Don't call it an ax; an ax is much too purposeful. The maul works implacably through its weight, blind and crushing, a victim of inertia.

My room goes afternoon quiet. I talk to the woman outside, tell her that I can't believe I am so difficult to understand. I tell her for example that any of us, standing atop a very high place, might imagine a moment of relaxed vigilance where we could step off the edge into gravity, or where just by letting our legs go briefly soft we could crumple quietly over the rim. It isn't rational, after all, to ignore the implications of being so near a lethal, irrevocable action. And if Theresa can't accept this basic human condition, she will never be able to imagine what any such action might be.

"Or rather," I say, "she'll never be able to imagine that inaction could be the cause."

The woman outside my room says nothing.

I say, "Or rather: that inaction is not empty."

The one thing I know for sure is that there is a supple, roaring element inherent in danger, rich with a tigerish allure, thrumming with a deadly dark power, and that power can get in you, by you. What I know is that the weight of all that danger, all those consequences, all the murmuring threat, maybe even the very constraints of the path that does *not* lead to disaster—all of these things enclose and define the shape of the very thing you hope never happens to you, and maybe in a moment of perfect concentration about the matter, the action itself comes forth. I try to explain, but the words are too simple, or too complex. I try to explain how it happens so fast.

"It happens fast," I say.

IT TURNED OUT TO BE MESSY. NOT MESSY LIKE A GLORIOUS movie spill, but messy like things are. The maul missed my wrist where it was aimed and instead went through the back of my hand about a third of the way up to the knuckles. I'm not usually comfortable talking about it except that I will say I miss my thumb. It was the only thing still attached, right after. I remember I knew I could move it, and I did move it before I collapsed; I curled it up against the head of the maul, buried in the top of the picnic table there. The metal was cold. I told the doctors about it, later that day, before the surgery. I told them I could still move my thumb and they said, *I'm afraid that's not possible, Mr. Linden.* Anyway, it's gone now.

They cleaned it all up, my mangled hand, trimmed me down to the wrist where I'd imagined the maul would strike me anyway. So I guess that worked out. I don't know what they did with what they took from me, or with what I left behind in the yard, but probably the paramedics took that. Celia may have cleaned up the rest herself; I never asked her. She never says. I wonder a lot about this stuff, the aftermath I was absent for, I guess just because I'm a practical-minded man. The picnic table and the maul are gone, I'm sure. We had an old hatchet, too, but I never used it, not for anything. Parts of these things must persist in some form, the metal bones, at least. They are somewhere. If you knew enough, you would even be able to discern how far they are from me now.

But anyway for me the aftermath was different, narrow: a lot of pain, pain like icy saltwater, but because it didn't come for a couple of seconds, there was this brief lethal clarity right after it happened, a clarity like when you glance at someone you desperately love and just for a moment, this sad beautiful moment, you have the entire deep delicate structure of her soul in your hand. I saw my fingers on the table. They were living, if not alive. Exquisite. They had been curling over slightly and maybe still were, just barely, the tips trying to dig into the wood, such dear relics. I felt the blood pouring from my arm as it emptied, pressure equalizing. It ran from me, and I thought how perfect an action it was, so integrated, like pouring water from a pitcher that was myself. And it was just as I was beginning to feel the immensity of the moment that had brought my fingers and my open hand to this place, as I was feeling the cold rough head of the maul against my thumb and was recalling the vicious baritone chuff of the maul as it came to rest and how it was not something I'd expected or considered at all—and what had I considered?—it was at just this moment that the pain came like a birth, a hot electric hurt pumping from nerves I hadn't before fathomed, and my right hand peeled away at last from the maul handle rising erect from the table, and I was down on the ground forgetting, where my blood was growing, black in the grass.

CELIA COMES TO SEE ME, BLESS HER. EVEN IF I DIDN'T GET TO talk to her, I would still appreciate her presence, especially here. She is very pretty. Her coming here is a warm transcendent novelty, like a lit candle drifting along a seafloor. She is a broad constant for me, appearing every so often as she does. She endures, persisting through hours, days, when I scarcely think of her, and I admire it. Not that she perseveres, just that she exists. It must be a terror for her simply to be. She goes on through her long absences, when her path becomes a mystery to me, orbiting me like a strolling sun.

She talks when she comes, about work, about the house. I devour her. She tells me she's hung new curtains in the third bedroom, a revelation. I make her tell me about them; I open a space for every detail. The curtains are white, translucent, littered with a handful of haphazardly placed sheer squares that hold simply stitched wildflowers, prettily plain. This is not how she describes them, exactly, but it amounts to that. I think they're lovely. I learn how she hung them, how the curtain rod is black-washed wood, how she kept the red corduroy curtains for scraps. I can picture how the light must be now in that room, the winter sun in those windows turning the room the color of novice ghosts, but I have her tell me anyway. She says it's brighter now. I feel sick, like I should smile.

Celia makes a puzzled face. She tilts her head. "You're so interested," she says.

And then—have I mentioned how I will miss clapping? You should think about it now, while you can. It's a devastating impotence I never imagined. There is a man here whose name I don't know and he claps when he laughs, brutal and slow. His thick hands like cattle, rough mating beasts, a herd of two. Sometimes when Theresa is talking to me I hear this man clapping heavy, out in the hall, at the end of the common area, and because his claps sound like some great hydraulic piece of hammering machinery, or because his claps sound at all, I don't hear anything else. I don't hear what anyone says to me after. I can't help it; talking seems so delicate, so impalpable, so ponderous.

Theresa asks me about Celia. I tell her about the curtains, about what Celia has said to me.

"And so, are you interested?" Theresa says.

"About the curtains," I say, asking. Theresa shrugs her thick shoulders, a massively mute gesture, full of an alien portent. Something an elephant would do.

"You know, your absence," she says. She fingers her wrist. "Something going on that would otherwise be so near to you."

We sit not talking for a while and then Theresa asks me, right out, if I ever worry that I will hurt someone else. I'm not sure I hear her right. It's the first time she's asked me this, and she lays it out so placidly, so heavily, that I'm almost caught up in the sheer inertial implication. I almost say *of course,* which is not exactly what I mean at all.

I wave her off. But I find that I have no answer for her because—and this is true—it hasn't yet occurred to me that I might hurt someone. But we sit and I warm myself to it, and at last I ask her if she means directly.

"Yes," she says.

"Because, I mean, Celia was hurt," I say. "I hurt her. She was there, right after. And still, now, after all this time." I look broadly up and around us, motioning for her around the long green-gray room where we are.

"I don't mean like that," Theresa says. "I mean, you know," and she lifts her hand and makes a swift chopping motion in the air. She says, as she does it: "*Cha.*"

I pick at my bandages.

I say, "So I shout for Celia, and she finds me in the grass, and the grass is all going dark, and her face is rushing in, getting big, but kind of swimming away? And she comes down over me where I am, and I'm like fading on fire but not too far gone to know my place, and I wait for her to ask me what happened. I even think, for one foggy second, that she'll ask me who did this. I'm sure she'll say it: *Who did this to you, James?* But there's only this look in her eyes, this look of like, soft stone."

Or what I say is: "I read somewhere that—the horseshoe crab? You know?"

"Yes, horseshoe crabs," Theresa says, and she carves the quick shape of one on the table with the tips of her index fingers.

"Yeah, they have—their blood is blue."

"Hunh," says Theresa. She says, "I didn't know."

I nod but don't tell her the rest, which is that they tell you the blood of the horseshoe crab turns blue only when exposed to air. To eyes, I guess. I have seen pictures, and I can tell you it's a startling shade of blue, between a cornflower blue and the blue of a robin's egg, a modest dreaming blue like the edges of the sky at noon. But I don't tell Theresa these things. I keep this to myself. You never know; she could surprise me. She could, for example, ask me what it is before it's blue.

Theresa is looking at me still, and we sit there a while longer, and maybe she has nothing to say about the horseshoe crab, or maybe I could talk to her forever before I learned all she might know about color. The gray-green walls of the common area are around us.

THERE IS CELIA PAINTING THE KITCHEN ORANGE. I GUESS I will like it. She would say it's not the fruit orange, it's that harvest orange, a warm orange of welcome and comfort, and I determine for myself that the trim is an edible brown. I'm surprised by it all, and a little rattled by the sounds of her work carrying to me where I am, and I'm a bit bemused by how much tape she's used to protect the edges of everything. She taped everything at once. The room is a sketch. I try to think if I know of a noise as distinct as the harsh sound of new masking tape coming free from the back of itself, if all such sounds become so tiresome. I possess a clear sense of that sound, more suitable for memory than any voice could be. I don't help Celia with the painting. I haven't and I won't start now. She doesn't mind. Or sometimes she does, maybe, and I could stand in the doorway and watch her because she likes when I talk to her, or listen to her, and, speaking of listening I find that the *frisssh* of the brush along the wall isn't so bad when I watch. Sometimes, maybe, I watch her when she doesn't know.

I come in to watch one morning and Celia is already painting on the far wall, wearing just a T-shirt and dark panties, and standing in the doorway watching her I'm instantly, outrageously aroused. Her hair up in a fist. She is stretching up to a high place above the window trim and there are round rectangles of sunlight stretching down her legs, and when she rises to her toes her panties wrinkle dark and deeply into her crotch. Her scar moves in place like a drop of water changing shape as it runs. It has a color I can't quite gather. It threatens translucence, seems to shimmer. Watching, I begin to wonder if I could get Celia to let me do it to her there, there against the wall just now, and because of thinking it, it becomes unbearable. I come up behind her quiet, pull her soft hips into place, her panties down. Higher up, she has her chin on her shoulder now, lobbing sweet fragile objections at me and smiling, and then after a bit she steps half-out of her panties and spreads her feet for me, lays her forearms along the unpainted wall there. I wrap my fingers around the wings of that bone where you can hold a woman from behind. She doesn't let go of the brush while we do it, and I don't know why but I'm glad. It shudders in her hand. Her arms go slowly apart over long moments, walking up the wall, and eventually her empty left hand wanders up to the edge where the fresh orange paint is drying, and in a moment I scarcely see, maybe don't see, her two longfingers and her thumb dip into the paint, out again. She leaves three small rounds there, a dear little cluster, gathered like a swiftly drawn pawprint. Like an animal was running there. I stare at it and stare until I'm through.

Afterward, we sit on the floor in the kitchen, talking. I lean against the counter and she leans against a table leg. She has her panties back up, puddling into them slow. We talk about how that was nice, how the room will look beautiful when it's done, what breakfast could be today. She picks at the paint on her fingertips. She looks up from them, up at the wall. She says goddammit.

"Don't worry about it," I say. She says she'll just paint over it, and I tell her, "Don't bother. We could just have it there." She rolls her eyes at me and looks back up at the wall, and it occurs to me that it would be like her to think I'm not sincere, to assume I'm only inclined to craft some vague and dreamy compliment for her, or us. I doubt she is able to imagine that there's a different way to wish that the mark would stay, that there is an intensely private worth in aspiring to the indelibility of moments.

She gets up. She tries to paint her prints flat, but the wall is already too dry; she brings out a stab of sandpaper instead. I linger. I monkey my bare feet up onto the warm table leg where she was. I tell myself: fingers are the dreams of toes. Celia has the wall rubbed flat again before I make myself aware. You'd never know.

"Okay," she is saying, sidling back to me without looking. I look down at my feet. I picture the long bold tendons there, sliding beneath my skin. I think about what I've learned.

I FIND IT BEST THAT I DON'T TELL THERESA ABOUT THE ACCI-
dent anymore, about the close things I recall. Except about my thumb—
I remember how it moved, and I sometimes dwell on the fact that it wasn't saved. Otherwise I could tell her different things, like: I can feel that my arm is slightly lighter now. The rest is hard enough for me to understand; I can't share my experience more cleanly, especially because every audience is interested in motive. What could I offer that would satisfy? I know that Dr. Lane, at least, doesn't appreciate the context I provide. He distrusts my account in part because it lacks a motivational continuity. He says that. I can't blame him. After all, my greatest dilemmas come from considering the quantum nature of life passing. If time goes by in discrete packets. And maybe you could tell me: Are moments laid like tiles? Or like bricks, or scales? I couldn't say myself. I'm afraid I will venture the kind of guess that will lead Dr. Lane to conclude that I can't be cured. That he could name my affliction, any affliction. That he could describe my mistake in terms that justify the context but don't do justice to the problem, which is that I imagine things could happen. I believe they can, if only for moments. It's a fear I can't live without. How could you?

Theresa asks me if I regret losing my hand. The sun hums in the morningside windows.

"Yes," I tell her. "I miss it. Very much."

"What do you miss about it?" she asks.

"Most?" I say.

"Okay," says Theresa, shrugging. And by the look on her face on this day, maybe I could tell her about the sadness I sometimes feel at having betrayed my own flesh, the way you would betray a lover's confidence. I could tell her how it seems to me now that exposing the hidden strings and meats of my hand was akin to dragging a gelatinous deep-sea creature to the surface of the ocean, into a deadly and blinding alien light, a shape-killing near vacuum. I could tell her elements of truth, of course, but they might not be right. They would only be pieces. I'm not accustomed to thinking in the kind of extremes she asks for.

She lets me think for minutes. At last I tell her, and I've thought about it carefully: "It's quite a novelty, being asymmetrical." I lean to my right to emphasize.

Theresa nods at me slow. "Well isn't that just something?" she says. And then we sit quiet at the table a while.

And maybe someday I will tell her certain other things. I could mention to her, for example, that a sound from that day still haunts me, and it is not the sound of the maul's head exploding into the picnic table or even through the spiderbones of my hand. Instead I recall, as the maul came off my shoulder, the heavy-fisted blast of a roar ripping out of me, barreling up from my chest on a single thick busy breath. The forced exhaust of a vehement exertion, desperate and brief, expelled like the air before a new emerging bullet. My lungs emptied by a crush of furious power, fiery down my trunk.

But this is a part of my experience, which is not the same as my account.

I do not like to talk to Dr. Lane. I see him once a week, briefly, and Theresa is always there too. She is something of a handler on these occasions. From the very beginning, Dr. Lane has gone on asking me things like whether I still want to hurt myself. At first I say no, I *never* did, but that doesn't deter him. In my confusion, I've suspected for a long time that he hopes I'll admit to it, but I realize now that I've misjudged him, his capacity for understanding. What he truly hopes to hear is that I used to fear myself but no longer do. My remorse would make him happy, too, or rather: a display of remorse. Remorse for myself, I mean. I come to this realization lying in my room, and I laugh out loud because of it, because it seems ridiculous that he would choose to care for me in such a manner. How presumptuously shallow, how blind, as if an extra display were needed—what, a narrative? Something oral?

The woman outside my room tells me I am laughing. She is leaning into the bright doorway, making a rich shadow of herself, and she somehow has a lap even though she stands. She is that kind of creature. I can't see into her lap, into her dark, but I can hear her fingernails grating and popping soft together there. Her shoulders, I think, shiver from it.

"I am, I know," I say. She folds out of sight, talking.

"It's a fact," she is saying, again and again.

I roll onto my stomach, bury my hand in my gut. I wish I could say: *remorse would be a relief.*

THE NEXT TIME I TALK TO THERESA, I CRY. AS I BEGIN, ALL THE lines disappear from her face, a symptom of her surprise, I think. I've never seen it. But I don't blame her; the strange cooling paths of the water moving from me, down my cheeks, across my lips and salty into my mouth, dripping. I might laugh again. Theresa stares smooth-faced and as she does I raise my missing hand and stare toward my palm and I say into it, meaningfully, that I hate myself for this. I don't bother to draw on the weakening muscles that are meant to curl my fingers, but I try to look as though I were. Out to my other side, out of sight, I hold my other hand splayed and calmly straining against the tabletop. My fingertips, I know without looking, are like the bony roots of trees. Theresa looks where I look, at my missing hand, says my name. She would never think to notice my other hand, I am certain that she wouldn't, but I try not to let her anyway. I say what I've said again. I say it again. This happening gets back to Celia. Whenever she comes, often before she sees me, she talks to Dr. Lane. A gathered delicacy garnishes her talk then when we meet—her gestures, her voice, her working face.

We sit on my bed. I see her expression as she is turning to sit beside me there on my right—that is, there beside me on the bed instead of across from me in the chair—and her look is blankly intense as she moves to sit, a look I recognize, though not on her: the look of distant surprise you feel when you find that an otherwise tiny decision has become an issue of consequence. She has that on her face as she thinks about sitting beside me; you can imagine. But anyway she goes ahead, and she sits beside me there on the bed, and in the space between us, the width of a leg, the thin sheet wrinkles roundly. She opens her mouth into quiet, leaves it open as though she only needed it to breathe. She has all her fingers shimmed between her knees, her laced feet tucked up into the bedframe.

After a little while I say, "You've never asked me how the food is here."

"What?" she says, dipping her head and twisting it toward me. She curls her lips: she is making a smile. Her short hair swings. Her neck.

"I'm just saying," I say. "Celia. It's strange. All this time."

"And so how is the food?" she asks me.

"It's good, actually," I tell her.

"What do you like to eat?" she says. "I mean, what is good?" And then there is a little shift beneath the skin of her face, a swift and subtle movement of plates, and her eyes go to soft spilling glass. She slides to her feet, swallowing sounds, laughing over them like you do.

"Whoo, James," she says, turning toward me and stepping away. She wipes her face and shakes out her hands, and now she is smiling red-faced, and I wish I could say that we talk more before she leaves.

Later I tell Theresa I might like to begin keeping a journal. She frowns. But she speaks to Dr. Lane about it anyway and he offers me, the next time he sees me, a bright sympathetic encouragement. Picture me there, writing in my blank book late at the desk in my room, or over empty afternoons in the common area, holding the left-hand pages down with the paperweight potency of my clubbed arm. I write things in it about myself, things that are not strictly true; or rather, things I don't truly know. I write along a narrow, purposeful path, a space that touches both what I suspect about myself and what I believe Dr. Lane would like to hear. I write, for example, this clever sentence: *Now I'm beginning to realize that it's fear that's given shape to so much of what I've done.* Or this one, which I choose because I'm certain it's already been said, by others: *I've made a certain peace with myself, realizing that only after I forgive myself will others be able to forgive me too.*

I ground my talk in a hopeful present. I imply change.

I WILL MAKE A LAST CONFESSION: I WORRY INCESSANTLY about all the water pipes that lace my house at home. How they are forever full of all the waiting water that was arrested abruptly at each faucet, in the shower, at a rusted nozzle sleeping on the lawn, at machine-controlled outlets I only imagine—all those dark feet of water just barely too late to be necessary. Think of the deadly electric streams, dormant in the wiring, dammed at open switches. Or the brooding clouds of gas gathering in the bellies of the furnace, the stove, escaping scarcely and silently under pressure, thin burning threads drawn by tiny patient flames. I worry, I do, how the whole house must be holding its breath, overfull and ready, built to burst: trembling with availability.

There was this apartment we lived in once. The one with black-and-white checkerboard tiles in the kitchen. It was in an old house with four other apartments, but we knew—you could tell—that our kitchen was the real one. We liked that; it meant no one else's was. Our front door there led into that kitchen, and it fed out into a black-floored stairway up the heart of the house, and the outside surface of the door was bare wood, with a stain that had bled away in patches like a too-heavy tan. I don't remember what apartment number it was, but whatever it was, it hung there. It was silver.

I am thinking of that door now because of the woman outside my room, and because of the sound of Celia's knife grazing the counter at home, and because someone had scratched into the soft wood on the front of that old door. The scratches were shallow, wide and round, pale. The kind fingernails would make; I can't be sure. They had the broad randomness that is the product of a too-tightly focused purpose, an order like worm trails in old sticks.

We lived there for a long time, and it wasn't until we had nearly moved on that I realized the scratches made letters, that they were letters scratched into the stain by hand, long irregular lopsided ones, madly malformed, and because I knew they had been laid there I stood breathing on the door trying to realize them, slowly naming them. Some were nearly as long as my torso, some smaller than my palm. I stepped back, back up onto the stairs leading to the second floor, and the letters came together for me at last, in one of those slick moments of recognition that you can't take back, and I saw on that day as we were leaving that they spelled out *I was there,* and then below that, in a space of its own: a lean tumbling question mark. All in a long angular scrawl I had seen a hundred times but never known for words until that moment, and I am thinking now, as I consider how Celia's knife is able to carefully push the tomato apart into pieces: I never told her about that. I never did. And I think, maybe, that it's because that sliding instant of discovery was so peculiarly mine, such a singularity of experience, that to tell her about it would have been a disservice to the moment, to myself.

ON THE DAY DR. LANE TELLS CELIA THAT I MIGHT BE READY to go home, very soon, Celia is wearing a yellow dress I don't know. The lapels are large. We sit in the common area.

"Dr. Lane has been encouraging," Celia says. She has her head lowered quietly at me, her fingertips together in their pairs atop the table.

She brings her palms together and apart slowly, so that her fingers fan slightly and deepen their kisses, roll back to their tips. She does it at the pace of flat dying waves sliding in succession over sand. I imagine that she does not know that she does it.

"Yes," I say, and I keep my eyes low. She sits with me in that small quiet space for a while, uncertainty bubbling up blue under her pink face, until gradually, eventually, maybe she recognizes me a little there in that place. I imagine she does. At least, I sense that the air goes loose between us, and she says, "You should see the garden."

I do not know what she means.

"Oh yes?" I say.

"Yes, I've done sweet peas. They've flowered, it's unbelievable. I have beans and peppers, zucchini; pumpkins, but they might not make it. I'm even trying potatoes. Sunflowers all up at the north end, it's crazy." She speaks a laugh.

"Well," I say. "That sounds purely amazing, Celia," I say, and I mean it. I try to picture what she describes, a riot I'm not prepared for, and I find a refracted memory in which I build her a raised garden bed from railroad ties, lay it down in a day beyond the last big hackberry in the yard. What she describes to me now could never be held there, I'm sure of it. I try sludgily to imagine where the garden could have grown to and how, where she was able to find more sun between the hackberry and the glut of buckthorns along the property line, what the flower of the sweet pea could be. And those railroad ties, they lay like long bricks along the hard ground when I first put them down, but you could barely discern them when I saw them last, and I wonder: do things sink into the earth or does the earth rise around them, swelling? My stomach broods like an animal.

And Theresa is talking to me, her voice spinning, and I try to anchor my gaze on her across the table there, but it is Celia after all, and she is saying, "James? James?"

"Celia. Yes," I say. She is draping a crooked smile across her chin.

"I'm wondering if this is something you can do." She nods. "I need this to be something you can do, okay? Can you talk to me, James?"

And she waits for me to speak, she always does, she has always known to, but I watch her hands and I'm having a hard time pretending that thoughts could ever slow into words. I'm not given to lie to her. I'm not even sure what motive I would have to lie, what I want, what the meaning of *possible* is, what colors bleed from her garden, how the notion of promise was promoted from a quality to a deed. But I know that I slide my hand between her talking palms, and that I make a sound like a sigh. And there is this: her skin.

Her fingers crumble down over my hand. She squeezes till it hurts.

"James," she says, and she looks up across my face like you look up at the underside of a belonging that must be carefully cleaned. She says, "James, can you do this? I need to know."

She is terribly beautiful, looking at me like that. Radiantly beautiful, in a way I can't recall her being. I open my mouth. I open my mouth and I tell her: I imagine I can.

She goes on crushing, crushing my hand.

I AM GOING HOME. IT'S A PROBLEM OF PERSPECTIVE. WHEN Dr. Lane says good-bye, he shakes my hand hard. He is the kind of person who would prefer to surround your hand with both of his own, I can tell, but he doesn't do that. He nods at me, tells me I'll do well. He embraces Celia. Their eyes are bright and warm and sharp. Theresa is there, frowning, looking hard at me as though I cannot see her. She scratches one wrist with the other. We hug awkwardly, one arm apiece, and when I say good-bye to her I tell her that I will miss her, that I would like to thank her.

"Okay then, James," she says, and after that we leave.

We take a cab to the station. I have asked Celia if we can take the train; I thought I knew why. The late winter sun is going down. The air is cool and dark, massive. The streets are loud, the sounds of cars. In the cab, sheets of streetlight glide over us now, and now, and again.

I tell Celia that I'm a little scared. She tells me not to be. She looks out the window. Celia rears the fingers of her raised hand back, knocks her knuckles against the glass, lets out breath. Cords and grooves in her wrist rise and fall. I have seen her naked.

I say I would like to see those curtains, and she says yes, but she says it in a way that makes me think she doesn't understand me.

"The white ones," I say.

"Oh yes," she says, and then a few minutes later she tells me something else startling, she tells me that she has finally gotten around to painting the kitchen. She says it's the color she always wanted now. She says this, and I catch a little cup of my own breath in the foot of my throat, let it out like a bird. I can't recall if this is something we always talked about or not, painting the kitchen, if it is something we always wanted to do. It sounds as if I am to assume so. And what color was the kitchen, if it was, or what color did she want it to be? White, or orange.

Moving slips of light pass backward over Celia, crossing her. Some of it must be falling into the holes of her eyes, making some shifting shape inside there and some color, some evolving color. Maybe it's true that just such a color could be preserved in there, held in some unknowable state, the hue of absorption itself, some pooling and immeasurable potential, like the kept blood of the horseshoe crab. Or maybe nothing could ever be untrue in there. What a thought. I close my eyes against it, and against a greater danger, slowly dawning: my suspicion that sight itself could become visible.

So I don't ask Celia what color, what color the kitchen is now, but she describes it anyway, and as she talks I begin to understand that no interesting color has a simple name. I don't listen well, but I hear her talking keenly and I work hard at imagining the kitchen, at imagining her acting in such a way at all, at what it means, whether our mutual interest is a matter of communion or confinement; it's something I'm going home to, I guess. She talks, her voice through the cab like movement in water. I sit and think richly my threaded living thoughts that go on even after we arrive at the station.

And now we are waiting, here on the bare edge of the platform along the tracks under yellow lights, and I am looking down at my feet, afraid just standing here thinking, the world big and multipotent around us. Celia stands close on my right, just ahead of me, just slightly turned away, and she squints up into the dark, into the clouded sky. While I am staring at her she spots me out of the corner of her eye, a flicker darting my way, but she doesn't turn to me. It could mean anything.

Down the platform to my left, a tall wide woman stands facing us, the only other person here, standing like the long exposed tip of a great stone. I have dismissed her—after a momentary disorienting swell of recognition—as not Theresa. This woman wears a long black rain poncho, the thin cheap kind. It's dry and dull. You can still see the fold marks making sketchy square planes, no two lit alike, a dozen nearly identical shades of gray. She carries a small green laundry basket filled with neat vertical files—thickly filled, round-bottomed manila folders. Her legs are spread so wide. She holds the basket out in front, between her hands, and it's weighing her down, her center of gravity. And now she is staring back at me blandly.

I turn to Celia beside me. She is leaning out, looking down the tracks, away from me. Her toes are into the yellow line at the platform's edge. Her left arm trails out to her side and back, toward me, and there— did I say this?—she has a weightless hanging grip on the hem of my jacket, just between her thumb and fingers. It pulls me, grounds me; I'm already heavy in her direction. She looks strangely slim-hipped. It's un-settling, but she must always have been that way. It gives her—barely— the top-heavy carriage of a man.

I clear my throat. I glance over at the tall woman, back to Celia. I close my eyes, open them. I hear close sounds across my shoulders, tap-ping: rain.

"The train comes through here," I say. Celia turns her head to look at me over her shoulder.

"Yes, of course it does."

"The usual train," I say, and I mean the one into the city, the one I know.

"Yes, James, of course. The train." She means there is just the one, but it seems strange.

"It looks different."

Celia laughs and turns away again. She looks up into the rain, goes on staring down the tracks.

"Well, I don't think you've ever been to this station before, James." But she gestures out broadly into the air off the platform's edge, says, "I guess we would've been by here, though." And she is right. I haven't been here, of course, though now that I think of it I know I have been just there where Celia gestures, plenty of times, just there out above the tracks, in the empty narrow corridor where the trains run by. I try to gauge it, some unanchored space in midair, and I guess I would have been just there, a few feet up and out in some imagined passenger car. Through a green window. Just there, or there. These things may not mean much, might mean everything. It may not even be true that the sameness of any place ever endures. That thought fills me a little, makes me a little heavy and small, and sad I think, like your reflection makes you sad sometimes. Or *sad* is not really the word I mean; it might be more like happy.

The rain piddles around us. I hold out my left arm, twist it so that my wrist is upturned. I try to capture with my eyes the phenomenon of a raindrop passing just through the open air at the empty end of my sleeve. It's funny, a marvel, a wondrous thing; I feel a giddy choked contraction behind my eyes, down my throat, up from my chest. "Celia," I say, I think.

Off to my side the tall woman has the laundry basket down on the ground, is bent over into it, straight-legged, rifling through it intently. She is turning the folders on their sides. They hiss softly and slap. Her head comes up briefly and she looks down the tracks, startlingly alert, like a mantis. She glances at me, goes back to her work. I drop my

arm. I hear the train. Celia is talking to me now, and her talk comes
up the tracks with that other blooming sound; I couldn't say what she
says. Her brows are together. I step up into her, into the fading yellow
stripe, and now my good hand—my hand—is between us, and I flex it
by thinking. I work it fine. The sturdy warming tracks lie below and
I marvel that their audacious disguise is so intact, that you could dig
them up, that they would come up in pieces. They are wet, or shiny.
Celia is still talking, saying my name. And there is this: I try but cannot
see the opening of my own eye as I look out from myself. Is the outline
of that opening blindness? Or maybe it is too constant a sight for me
to even perceive it now.

Celia is here and her shoes are black, there beneath my raised hand.
Just beyond her, just down the tracks, the train is nearly here, taking
shape behind the glare of growing lights. I feel flattened in its shine; a
revelatory compression comes over me, a great breadth given to me. I
believe it may be that I can't move, or that everything is given power
to move around me. Celia turns and now her broad narrowing back is
before me, the curve of her shoulders beneath her coat. She still has her
hand on my jacket, just so. I am not at all afraid. We are waiting for the
train.

The fingers of Celia's hand begin to curl. I press my own hand against
my belly slow as the train closes in, knead my feet inside my shoes atop
the platform. I am aware of my weight, coiled in the muscles of my legs.
The platform seems very high, a foreign height above the tracks below.
I begin to wonder how quickly the moment could go by, how purposeful I will be.

The Heart as a Fist

MARTIN CANNOT LISTEN. HE HAS TRAINED HIS HEART TO OBEY.

Martin sleeps with a woman who tells him that if you speak to your heart, it will begin to hear you. She tells him to breathe, breathe, and she describes what he already knows, which is that as you fill your lungs, the heart races to harvest. Breathe in, she says, and feel your heart hurry.

She sits astride him, her feet curled beneath the strung undersides of his thighs, her folded knees cupping his hips. Her hair swings, her breasts.

Martin opens his hand inside the warm sink water. He feels the water roll across his palm, billowing. He cups his hand slow, and when it becomes an open-topped channel, a space that could almost own the water it holds, he stops to contemplate that body of water, trying to believe in it, how it could be held, and how it resembles a rope, the hot intestine of an animal, the tiny arc of a fluid circuit. He waits until he has learned all he can know now about that water, his fingers like fibers, the weight in his palm finite, and then he briefly draws a fist, lets it fall instantly open again into the same cupped shape beneath the surface. His hand empties, squelching mutely, and then silently refills as it opens. He thinks: *water is substance.* He makes a fist, releases it, makes a fist. He listens for the sound of his heart in his ear, takes from it its rhythm. He closes, releases, closes, releases. He thinks: *fist. fist. fist.* He takes and gives, takes and gives.

And in the park when the woman speaks, her talk pools around him, a presence he cannot grasp. He is already busy grasping, palming forward his own mysterious machine. How funny to imagine that she might work the same. He hears her voice but not the words, he is too busy listening, talking, he clings handlessly to the grip of her fingers on his shoulder, the ground is flat and near, the world is broad and he is tired, so tired but just beginning he says silently *fist.*

fist.

fist.

fist.

fist.

fist.

fist.

fist.

fist.

fist.

fist.

fist.

fist.

fist.

fist.

fist.

fist.

fist.

fist.

fist.

fist.

fist.

fist.

fist.

fist.

fist

fist

fist

fist

fist

fist

A bird blusters down from its flight at his feet.

Deer in the Road

SO HERE IS ME, AND THE MANNER IN WHICH MY CURRENT PRE-
dicament unfolds suggests I've got time, though my predicament itself
is otherwise. As I launch from the guardrail like a stunt guy who meant
to, as I'm into this slow spiral up off of everything and over the edge
of the embankment, the whole car and me turning upside down, I see
how it's going to go and I'm calm, I'm potent, filled with a panic so
pure it picks apart each instant like you might (if you had the patience,
or the time) pull the finer and finer veins from a leaf that's nothing but.
This steering wheel in my hands now, for instance. It's everything I
hold dear. By which I mean I cling to it; why wouldn't I? It's sick in my
grip, wobbly and loose with the slump of tires not used to being pointless. But this is the burden my arms now bear—devoting themselves to
the pursuit of straightness while the horizon eats me up.

My blinker is on. I mean it is on right now, lit. It troubles me because it's the wrong blinker, though if I keep spinning (if I make it all
the way around) that situation will rectify itself. Elements of this entire
endeavor resemble situations rectifying themselves. It helps to invent
that thought. And the blinker's got it into my head that I might actually
make it all the way around, but frankly I'm skeptical. I drive straight
ahead, my arms like posts. My hands at ten and two. And here now: my
blinker is off. I wonder if I breathe.

The one thing I can't stop thinking is how sorry I am, although that is not at all what I really am thinking. Although I've noted the *presence* of what I am really thinking—the notation its own act of discovery— the thought itself resists unearthing. This unexcavated thought, the one I can't stop thinking, it resembles a stomach sickness and relates to the absence of everything but this act, everyplace but here. Or it resembles some clean rush of anguish and relates cruelly but prudently to nothing but itself. I can't say more, or learn more about what I mean. This one thought remains ineligible for dissection.

Other thoughts do not. For example, I have a palm beneath the thread of every separate sound made around me now. I'm certain that I do. Items of mine, or others that are not mine per se (or maybe forgotten items that belong to no individual so much as to the car itself), these things tumble around me. Each lays down a discrete rosary of sound, and some of these I can name: the prance of a box of tissues; the thump and slither of an umbrella; the jangle of my hanging keys; an explosive bluster that escaped me at first but that I now recognize as the photo albums rumbling from the backseat. Such strange artifacts, these. As strange, but more recent, a new sound has risen into the rest, a faint skittery sound pattering all around me—the floor emptying itself of the loose sand that we never vacuumed out. From the lake last summer, I'm certain of it, I remember as much (although this is not so much a memory as it is a thing I believe in). Memory struggles here against such a lavish experience as this. For example, underneath all these distinct sounds, and others, a handful of more resolute noises persist: the descending roar of the engine, several toneless layers of wind rushing, a stupid and agonal drone I make myself. None of these sounds will stop, all of them so piercingly true, like names or colors I hadn't known.

Of course, I'd tumble myself if I weren't strapped in—and then what a sound I'd make. I'm a little out of my seat as it is, and isn't it funny how the seatbelt had the sense to lock itself? It digs into my shoulder, my lap, heavy and keen as a tourniquet. But I'm not the only suspended thing, not at all, no, not here. For example: the stuff hung from the mirror—that tiny cloth bag, some beads, a strung stone the color of ice cream—would fall if they knew how to, or even whether to, tethered like they are.

Here is another disappointment I've already discovered. I don't blame myself, considering, no I don't. My rearview mirror, spinning with me now, is supposed to be a backward place, I know that it is, but as I look into it (I don't know why—maybe to spot that deer) I see that the view behind me, faded but still faintly sunlit, spins in the same direction as the one I'm headed into. This spin seems wrong—the mirror disguising its own misdirection—but of course it isn't. And though I've come to terms with it, the normalcy has stolen a little wonder from me. I otherwise feel like the water in a twisted rag, wrung out slowly by the conspiracy of the ends. The side mirrors both give up the same poor view. Also, they are not the kind of mirrors in which objects are closer than they appear. It's hard to say what I think about that.

But ahead of me now, there—a damn compelling show. For a little while I'm rapt, I'm glued to the view, I'm *part of the action*. I'm headed down diving into a concrete creekbed, a sloping shallow V, coarse like a cat tongue and dry with a stain that says I came at the wrong time to find water. Like water would do. The flattened shapes and shadows of all the crap at the bottom sway and leer in the wash of the headlights. I spy thick black weeds groping out of cracks, battered hides of paper and a puzzling sheet of huge plastic, a fine selection of all the things people drink from. I'd wonder how each of them got here but I'm already going over them, mostly I am. I'm going to make it to the far side, which lies like a wall from where I sit dropping out of space. I'll allow myself this conceit: it's going to be a hell of a crash.

I'm close now, and another sound I've known but not named becomes clear to me. A heavy something just over my head begins to graze my hair—I suspect I might flinch, of all things. But I know now with clarity that it's the shoe, the shoe left behind in this old car when we bought it, a single shoe belonging to the car's previous owner, or the previous. Again, these are facts and not recollections, precisely. Fact: Kathy said let's leave it there, and we did. Fact: I do not recall her reasons, or mine.

Fact: an old man's shoe, a right shoe, black and broad and round at the
toes, and wrinkled at the ball like a neck, the tread worn smooth, the
sole walked as thin as skin—the sole having been left behind everywhere it'd been, making black skid marks of itself (or engaging in a
more subtle dispersal, unwitnessed). Fact: nonetheless, the shoe as a
whole remained substantial. Grown top-heavy over time, full of weight.
It hardly matters if I recall this now, or invent it. If I choose, the shoe's
movement can remain the loudest thing around me now.

But here now, no, none of that will matter for long—no, it won't. I
have my direction and the shoe has its, both of us involved in the natural
process of settling. Every moving substance means to settle; momentum
is a myth, it's true. For example, though I'm a bit past straight upside
down now (and I wait for a new, giddy sense of rising) I'm either coming
down too fast or I've got too much faith in my trajectory—I feel like I'm
only going round. I won't make it even close to all the way upright. Fact:
I'm sorry about Kathy's car.

And now I'm there, I'm there, nearly there. I can't see or picture what
hits exactly first but when it does the offended patch barks resentfully.
The headlights swallow themselves and I'm plunged into a startling
dark. I imagine the dashboard still glows, but I'm all ears as the rest of
the car begins to barrel on into itself where its nose has come to rest,
that first chirp becoming another ten, becoming a hundred, becoming a
hue. Crueler noises begin to erupt from more vital metal organs. Now
little bursts of orange light litter my view, streaking, all I can see (if I'm
seeing them at all). The steering wheel lurches and jams, seizing in my
still-straining hands. I imagine how the hood crumples toward me, a
jagged wave in ruined shallows, looming in my view if only I could see
it, but I can't see it and anyway, maybe, it is not precisely what will kill
me. I have a great deal left to discover—facts, I believe.

Pain replaces my legs. There's no room for them anymore. I've ar-
rived, come to a strange place I'd scarcely considered—a place where
I'm still moving forward but nothing in front of me is. Something strikes
me in the head, and fuck, fuck, I'd like to know what, and I swear I feel

the red strokes, the first little tendrils of anger beginning to bloom—but they are so far, so slow. And here now: the steering wheel begins to collapse beneath me, certainly it does. Elephants on my chest. I listen for sounds but a great tuneless hum has risen around me, making me thin. I cannot recall what I bring with me, what I've found or been given. How silly my name is. I cannot read the dashboard clock, a streaking block of blue. All my held air leaves me, surprising and silent (or maybe it's married to the din I'm drowning in) and as I'm crushed by what's carried me I think: I was in the other seat; I was in the other seat when Kathy hit a deer one time. A time like this one, or not at all. That time, a doe came surging fleetly out from Kathy's side of the woods and ran up alongside us, frantic, blindly headed the way we were headed, and Kathy cried out and turned the wheel, just as the deer met the front bumper. The deer, she peeled away at the same moment, but not before she touched us, not before we saw the shadows of her ribs in the headlight, not before the corner of the car pushed a brief dimple into her hide that I saw, I saw, and as the deer ran back to the trees we pulled over, cussing and shining—breathing, breathing. We got out in wonder. We met at the front of the car and there, in time, we bent to find hairs, fine and brown, glinting in the trim of the headlight.

Airbag

Three

ONCE TRITI'S GONE UP AFTER DORLENE, TAKING MY KEYS WITH her, I walk over to Jim. He's lying down now, up against the door of the corncrib, runners of his thick fur bulging out through the slits. I stick the toe of my shoe through one, into his side. I do it again, harder. He doesn't even move. I do it a third time, straining my toes, and now he licks his chops and looks back at me.

"What's wrong with you?" I ask him, and then I leave.

At the car, Dorlene's bag is gone. I discover my cigarettes have already been opened. I decide I'll add one more to the missing, and as I smoke my way up to the house, I see the brushpile is finally alight. I head that way. The whole operation's been shifted over on top of the burning gas can. Tom's orchestrating as the kids roll bigger logs over to the blooming fire. I don't see Triti or Dorlene. I try to envision what either of them might be doing in this instant. On the way down toward Tom, I pass dark figures filing in the other direction, and one graceful swinging shape holds out a wine bottle to me as she passes. She places it practically inside my hand, and the audacity almost makes me let it fall.

"Hey," I protest, turning, holding the bottle back out to her.

She lifts her hands and goes on by. It's just some pretty girl I've never seen. She lays her hands on her chest. "It's known no other lover," she croons low, backstepping into the dark.

It's some cheap red, a screw-top bottle, nearly full. I'm not much for drinking, but I hang on to it—mostly because I'm not sure how to do anything else. I'm standing there still looking at it when Tom comes up.

"So the fire is happening," he says.

"Yeah. And you're alive."

"Well, I'm something. Where were you?"

"Walking."

"You and Dorlene," he declares.

"Just walking. And talking." I finger my cheek with my tongue. I hold the wine like a football. "I told her about Lisa."

Tom shakes his head. "Oh, fuck me."

"What?"

He crosses his arms over his belly. He laughs to himself for me. "Let me just say this." He rocks back, looking up into the sky for his thoughts. "I think it may be that these are the kinds of conversations, okay, that in certain situations could get you into trouble." He peers at me, questioning.

"I know," I say, but I don't.

He searches the sky again. "Well, I think that maybe in this case it doesn't matter, okay, but I'm gonna suggest that it's worth thinking about."

I keep myself from asking him why it doesn't matter, not sure he even knows what he's talking about. I hold up the bottle of wine. "Someone gave me this."

"Who?"

"I don't know; some girl."

He looks down at his feet now, that head still shaking, still that constant grin. He points at the wine with his pinky. "In no way should you take this as an indication of your worth as a human being."

"When do I ever?" I say, and for some reason that cracks him up.

We pass the bottle, drinking from the neck. The wine is sweet and thick, and as we drink Tom recounts to me the several clever comments that have been directed his way since the near-miss with the gas can.

I remind him about the lighter fluid and he tells me lighter fluid is for pussies.

I eyeball the house once in a while, but somewhere along the line—long after Tom and I have taken a seat in the grass, and long after the wine bottle has ceased being heavy, and a good long while after Tom has waded genially into a story I've already heard about the time he pulled a woman from a river—I stop looking. And it's not until Triti is standing right there in front of us that I think about either her or Dorlene at all. She comes up and I realize—or imagine—that I've smelled her before I've seen her.

"Here," she says, reaching. My car keys dangle from her hand.

Tom blurts, "What the fuck is this?" He turns from side to side, pantomiming befuddlement.

"How did it go?" I ask Triti.

"Strangely."

"Where is she?"

Tom says between us, "This is Dorlene you're talking about."

"She's in my room." Triti looks very tall. Her tits seem huge from down here. "She told me my bathtub was transcendent."

I summon up the sight. The tub's an old claw-foot tub, freestanding. Jarringly, there's a cheap plastic skylight directly overhead, a crude blot of renovation. Because the skylight's so unexpected, and because the tub has a white shower curtain that goes all the way around, being in there always feels a little like being in a vessel, like a pod in space, or a chrysalis maybe, or a broken bone. Plus for Dorlene, being so short and all, the sight up that white oval chute and out into the night high overhead—trying to visualize it makes me a little woozy, displaces me.

I say, "I think . . . I think maybe it is."

Tom toddles ponderously to his feet. "Okay then," he says. He lumbers off toward the fire, throwing a wave back at us.

"You found some wine," Triti says when he's gone.

"*Found* would be giving me too much credit."

"Ah."

"Or not enough."

"That sounds likely."

"What did you do with Dorlene's clothes?" I have no idea why I'm asking that, I don't.

"I put them in the laundry."

"She handed them out to you?"

"Oh Jesus, Dave."

"No, no, it's not that. It's not like that."

"You want to know what she looks like naked? You want me to go check?"

I get a flash of Dorlene's little legs, bare in the dark—just her legs and nothing else. "No, no, no."

"She came out after she showered and gave me her clothes. In a plastic bag I gave her. And then I put them in the laundry for her."

"She let you do that?"

"She didn't want to go in the basement."

"Oh."

"She doesn't like stairs."

"Oh."

"She was sweet, she apologized like a million times. Thanked me." Triti turns and looks back over her shoulder at the house. "She kissed me on the cheek."

"Really?"

"She smells funny."

"I know."

"I know," Triti tells me, and I'm just starting to feel the thrill of that when she says, "I wish you were standing."

I peer up at her. "I wish you were sitting."

"Well then," she says.

"Anyway, I have to pee." And it's true. I stand up. I swirl the bottle of wine and upend it; a dark dribble trickles out and disappears. "And I need more wine."

"And I . . . ," Triti begins, and she looks around us in the dark, everywhere but at me. "I guess I'm going down to the fire."

"If you think it's safe."

"I'll risk it."

"Bold of you."

"Don't mess with anything in my room."

I rock a little. "Why would I?"

"Don't dig through my panties or anything."

"Jesus. I wouldn't do that," I say, but I know I'm going to. We just stand there a minute, and somehow she makes it so that I have to walk away first.

It's very dark, and the air bites. The wine's hitting me hard; I guess I haven't eaten much. I head toward the back steps and next thing I know I'm up them and into the back porch, and somewhere along the way I've lost the wine bottle, and I wonder if maybe Triti took it from me somehow, or cleaned it up after me. All I know is, I'm in the porch alone and the bottle is gone. It's very bright and I can't see outside at all. It's too warm in here, and cramped.

People talk in the kitchen. I can tell it's no crowd, but that makes it harder to go in. As I stand there—working up the fortitude and wondering how much I'm swaying—I hear Dorlene. Her voice pierces like a pin, but I can't make out a word. And then I hear Ernest, lower but clearer: "That's not what you are." Dorlene drones nasally again.

I step closer. It occurs to me that I can be seen from the invisible outside, standing in here doing nothing but waiting. I try to look indifferent, patient. For just a moment my mind ports outside to the side yard here, sees me as I must look from that dark, and I'm two places at once. Two people, maybe. And then the voices bring me back, sharper now.

"There are kinds," Ernest is saying.

"Oh yes, many varieties," says Dorlene, the last word coming out as a quaint, watery quiver.

"And your kind—your variety—looks like this," Ernest says.

"Sometimes. I got lucky. I'm very proportionate."

"Yes, you are," says Ernest. "And it's all genetic?"

I walk into the kitchen then, just as Dorlene sighs. She is standing in front of the kitchen sink, looking down at herself. "Yes," she says. She's wearing a long purple skirt that skims the ground, and a black cardigan. Under the cardigan she has on a camisole top that—unbelievably—is too small for her. A thin slice of her belly is bared, and her breasts are pert and tight beneath her top. She clearly isn't wearing a bra. She holds a giant red cup by the edge in one hand, letting it swing like a bucket, not seeing me. Ernest nods at me. Fat Susan is here too, back in her usual seat. She offers a two-finger wave. "But it really starts in the womb," Dorlene says, tilting her head, her high voice going almost musical. She draws out the word *womb* into a sad coo. She lays her free hand on herself as she says it, down on her abdomen, but not even where her womb would be, if she even has a womb. She lays it down lower, denting her skirt.

She looks up then, midgesture, and sees me. "David!" she cries, throwing up her hands. A slop of clear liquid swings from her cup and slaps to the floor. "Come here, come here." I do, but almost flinch as she reaches out and hugs my leg, presses her face against my thigh. She releases me, and in a screeching stage whisper says up to me, "Let's not tell them what happened earlier. It'll be our little secret." She throws a mischievous glance at the others.

"What happened?" Susan says.

"I said it was secret," says Dorlene.

I pull away. "I have to pee." I blunder on through to the dining room. The long table of food is looking carcassy, and out in the parlor the video game kids are gone. Someone's in there, but I don't see who. My thigh burns from where Dorlene wrapped me up.

I don't let myself slow through the fastidious clutter of Triti's room. It's just like I remember, crowded and pristine—partly the nature of her nesting and partly a gesture of compactness, living in a house she doesn't own. The smell shocks me back, rising maybe from the old things she gathers: a blue velvet love seat, a wicker birdcage full of origami cranes, an almost life-sized plastic deer that lights up from the inside. It's got the sterile musk of a museum. And maybe it is a museum. Over her white steamer trunk, just for instance, she's got the quilt she made and tried to give me two Christmases ago. I don't know what she thought I would do with it, where I would keep it. But here it is now. And there's other stuff, too, stuff I don't want to try to place.

I sail through. I use the bathroom, the smell of the place hitting me like a hospital. I peek into the shower when I'm done; it's still damp. I look at myself in the mirror. I look wild and alert.

On my way out I peek into Triti's dresser. I think maybe I will find condoms in there, or something along those lines, but I don't. Instead it's just panties, a soft sea of nothing but cotton. I slip my hand into a pair, graze the inner crotch with my finger. I think to myself: *Right there*. I almost don't close the drawer before I leave—on purpose, I mean—but I do. I fumble back to the kitchen. When I enter, everyone is looking at me quiet.

"I want some wine," I say. "Is there wine?"

"Oh, honey," says Fat Susan, "you see me, don't you?" She tinkles her fingers against a gallon jug of wine in the center of the table, so big and squat that I didn't even recognize it for what it was. I get a cup. Susan pours and pours until it's dangerously full. She titters and she sets the jug back down. We do a little mock toast to the air.

I slump back against the counter between Ernest and Dorlene. "So what are we talking about?"

"Dorlene," says Ernest.

Dorlene says, "It's true."

I swing toward Ernest. "What do you want to know?" I say, and the kitchen gets quiet again. Fat Susan looks at her hands. I sip my wine like all of this is nothing.

"Dave and I used to be neighbors," Ernest says to the room.

"Is that right?" Dorlene squeaks. I've no idea if this is news to her.

"Yes, he and I—and our former wives—used to play Scrabble together."

The memory of this comes back to me like a yearbook photo, comic and only half-real. "We did," I say.

"Dirty Scrabble, do you remember that?"

"Dirty Scrabble," Susan says.

I dig back for it. "Right. Extra points for being obscene."

"Yes, double word score for every vulgar word. But it always devolved into arguments over ambiguous words." He stabs at the air with a flat hand. "*Hump. Bone. Swap.* You were the envelope pusher, as I recall."

"*Finger,*" Dorlene says, and a laugh squirts out of me, I don't know why.

Ernest nods. "Yes, exactly, though you'd get no resistance from me on that one."

"Or me," I say. Fat Susan drinks her wine.

"I'm hungry," Dorlene says. "I've been hungry all this day." She bends at the waist, folding in two like one of those drinking-bird toys, and sets her cup on the floor. She goes over to the fridge and tugs at the door, kicking back hard. I expect the door to fly open—or to stay firmly shut, maybe—but it comes open real gentle and she just stands there, peering inside.

We all stare. It's a spectacle, no doubt about it: around and above Dorlene, the fridge is huge and unreasonable, like a thing a person shouldn't own. The crisper drawer is chest high, and the higher shelves look out of reach, and all that stuff in there, all the containers and the greenstuffs and the few packed-away extras of party things, it's all just . . . *more.* Bigger, yeah, but also just more—too plentiful, an absurd extravagance, like food for an army, or for a terrible duration. Milk in massive gallons, two of them. Up on the top shelf, Triti's little herd of sports bottles stands like a forest, thick and multicolored. They don't seem like bottles at all just now—more like a place you could go. All the colors seem thicker, or deeper or something, and the light coming down from way over Dorlene's little head glows out around her.

Ernest says, "That is a sight."

Dorlene dips her chin over her shoulder, spreads a coy smile. "Ernest, are you looking at my bottom?"

A little dark arrow dents my gut. Ernest purses his lips. "Not just then, no."

"*Bottom,*" I say.

Dorlene shakes her head, looks into the fridge again. "My, my. I'm serious to god—you boys."

"*Boys,*" I say. I drink.

Dorlene reaches up and sets her fingertips against a smooth blue bowl filled with brown eggs. She cocks her head. "These belong to Tweedy. From her chickens. Are they boiled?"

I hesitate. Ernest's eyes are already on me, his chin tucked in. "Dave would know," he says, and Dorlene looks back at me.

"I'm sure they are," I say, like it's an educated guess, but of course the blue bowl has always been for nothing else.

Dorlene's face is a question. "Tweedy is very lovely. So truly kind, and helpful. And David, do you think she would mind if I had one?"

"No, I guess. I guess not."

Dorlene lifts an egg from the bowl. It's the size of a pear. She shakes it beside her ear with both hands, like a present. "And is there a spoon handy?" I'm right in front of the silverware drawer, but I walk all the way down the counter and pluck a spoon from the drain board.

We all watch as Dorlene cracks the egg open with the handle of the spoon, which—in her grip—is as thick as a tool. She taps deftly all the way around the longest circumference of the egg. She removes the top oval in a single piece and slides it beneath the bottom. Holding the egg like a bowl—it fills her palm—she sets to it with her spoon. Like it was ice cream. She wanders to my side and leans against the cabinets. She carves out bean-sized bites. Outside voices surge and ebb through the window. Dorlene's teeth graze the spoon now and again.

"I feel terrible. I feel like it must bother you," Susan says to her suddenly, as if she's been keeping a secret.

"What must, Susan dear?"

"It doesn't bother her," says Ernest.

"How do you know?" Susan says.

"It doesn't," he tells the room again, offering up a broad, flat-handed shrug.

"What's this now?" Dorlene says.

Ernest says, "Us watching. People staring. The way it was when you walked in here earlier tonight."

"Oh, that." Dorlene unearths the yolk. The yolk is bright and clean, the shocking fluorescent yellow of farm eggs. "Ooh," she says, delighted.

Ernest says, "It doesn't. It couldn't. It's inevitable."

"I wonder what the fuck would you know about it," I say to him. He just looks back at me quizzically, like I'm a shape he can't make out.

Dorlene goes on eating. "Well, it is true that I can't let it bother me. And I am used to it."

"Your whole life," Ernest says.

"Naturally. And I'm not just anyone." She shaves off another crescent of egg. "I'm very short, even among the small."

I remember something she told me, way back in the car as she chipped away at the clumsy silence. "The seventh-shortest woman in the country," I say.

"Person," says Dorlene. "On record," she says, and now Fat Susan *oohs.*

"No shit," says Ernest. "How do they know a thing like that?"

"I said *on record.*"

We slip into another lull. Somewhere outside, someone releases a giddy cascade of laughter. Dorlene eats. Ernest taps out an intricate little rhythm on the countertop. I look down Dorlene's shirt.

"How short is the shortest person?" Ernest says.

"Two foot two. She's barely alive, though."

"How old is she?"

"Forty-three."

I pull my eyes out of Dorlene's top. "Forty-three? What's wrong with her?"

Dorlene looks over at Ernest. She lifts her arms into the air. She crosses her wrists. She starts to do a slow slinky spin there on the tile. She keeps her eyes on Ernest until he's behind her, and then she looks up at me. "Why, David," she says. "This, of course."

A struggling, awful sound burbles out of Susan, pulling all our heads toward her. She's crying. She holds up a chubby hand, apologizing. "I've been drinking," she explains. She sits there and chokes back the noise, but tears keep coming. "I'm just a mess."

Dorlene drops what's left of the egg into the garbage can bristling with plates. She hands the spoon to me. She hops in place. Her tits bounce. "This is fun. What else, what else?"

Ernest steps right in, like he's been making a list. "What was high school like?"

"Lovely. I was very popular."

"Did you date?"

"I did."

"What do you do now?"

"For dates?"

Ernest smiles. "No, for work. What do you do for a living?"

"Oh, I don't."

"You don't."

"That's right."

"Do you drive?"

"Oh goodness, no."

Ernest drops his chin and looks at her, almost sternly. "But have you ever?"

She hesitates, giving him a flinty kind of look back. "I've steered. Somebody else had to do the gas, of course. The brakes."

I'm still working through the mechanics of that when Ernest says: "Do you menstruate?"

Fat Susan titters. My stomach lurches.

"My goodness," Dorlene breathes. She practically bats her eyes.

"Not right now, no."

I push away from the counter then. I say I'm going to check the fire. I steer myself outside, where it smells like cold and burning. I make it down to the fire without running into anyone I know, without passing anybody at all, I think. There are people, but I don't see them. I'm not looking. But when I get down to the fire, there are maybe a half dozen people around it, sitting mostly quiet on the grass or upright chunks of log, and Triti is one of them. I arc toward her.

The fire's massive now, a proper bonfire. A handful of torso-sized trunk lengths are propped up in there and torching, along with some scrap lumber and what looks like planks of siding. Someone's even dragged out a huge and splintering sheet of plywood and propped it upright across the middle of the fire. Green shoots of flame are fluttering out the edge of the plywood here and there, deep in the orange blaze, and not long after I sit Triti begins wondering aloud what we might be inhaling, whether it will cause us or our offspring any disfigurements, and how hilarious such disfigurements might be.

"Frog hands," I suggest.

"Elbow face," she says.

"Uncool. Beaver hands."

"You already said hands. And anyway, I'm not sure I'm getting that. Would your hands have buckteeth?"

"Beaver-tail hands," I clarify.

"Thumb gigantism," she says.

I look at my thumbs. I think I'll say *Dorlenery* next, but something stops me. I can see Ernest's head through the kitchen window, small and black and sleek. "That's hands, too," I tell Triti.

We watch the fire. I'm feeling sludgy and wide, something in the neighborhood of—but not—happy. I put what's left of my cup of wine down between my feet. Triti doesn't drink, of course, and while she doesn't exactly disapprove—not exactly—there's a point you can get to where she starts to think of you as like a toddler, or a tottering pile of breakables. I don't need that at all.

"Sorry about earlier," she says. "The Dorlene."

"The Dorlene," I say.

"I get confused sometimes. Like things aren't real. Dorlene isn't helping much."

I nod. I feel a puckering sadness for Dorlene that I'm not sure anyone's earned. Maybe this was what Fat Susan was crying about.

Triti waves a hand. "Plus I'm not sure this place helps."

One of the kids, a burly guy who wants to be seen, staggers up to the fire with a massive log between his hands. He's bent sideways, holding the log upright like it's a stack of dishes. He bends with his knees and lays the log against the fire. The pile shifts but holds, and a massive argument of sparks flies up and away. Somebody claps.

"Yeah, this place," I say to Triti. "How is this place?"

"Oh, you know. Peachy."

"Are you—?" *Sick of it,* I'm about to say, but the question starts to feel cruel. "Do you miss town?"

"Mmm—I miss the bus. The bus was fun." She tilts stiffly toward me. "I liked how the whole bus leans over for crippled people."

She holds her imitation, stressing it. And this is the comfort I'm talking about. It's easy to let it rise. I reach for another swallow of wine. "You don't even have to be crippled. You could just be old and fat. I worry that one day the bus will kneel prematurely for me."

She straightens. "I don't think you need to worry about that for a while. You should worry about how many people with TB are on the bus at any given time."

I swirl a finger at her. "I get it. You don't miss the bus. You miss hating the bus."

She looks into the fire a while. Her face is alive, her eyes as dark as a dog's. "Well, there's a lot of coughing on the bus. Maybe you think I miss caution?"

"Sure. Anyway—on the bus—it's not TB you have to worry about, it's schizophrenia."

"I always wore my headphones."

"That's just prophylactic."

"You're trying to out-clever me."

"I thought that's what you wanted from me."

She chops out a laugh. Not a funny laugh. She chews her lip. "Yeah, I'll put you on my list of people to out-wile."

"Ah, yeah, the list of people to out-wile. That's also the short list of people you respect."

"That's the list you think you're on?"

A shadow comes over us, and the heat of the fire gets shut down. Tom is there, twinkling.

"You're blocking the heat," Triti tells him.

"I doubt that," says Tom.

"It's factual."

"I just came to say I'm leaving." We both just nod. "I'll see you to-morrow?" he asks Triti.

"I'll be here." She says it like it's a job.

"You good?" Tom says to me.

"Good." He stands there. I know he's thinking what else he ought to tell Triti before he leaves, something to resolidify the illusion that he owns the place and she just lives here. It's the way he always colors his departure. We wait through it. "If you have trouble getting people out of here tonight," he says finally, "just call me. Some of these kids, I mean." He grins and drops a dismissive wave at me, like I'm the future. "You know what I mean."

"I do, and I don't foresee any problems," says Triti.

He stands there a minute longer anyway, looking off and nodding, and then starts in on some other tedious stuff—people he needs to call, a furnace check for winter, something about the dog. Triti says okay, got it, fine.

He gives us a last low look, spinning his keys around his finger. "Okay," he says, and he starts his slow turn away. He says, "Take it easy," spreading his words through the turn, fanning them like he's a sprinkler, leaving us to say nothing or say it to his back. "That's a nice fire somebody made," he comments as he passes the blaze, and he disappears around the far side. We hear him talking up the slope, saying fuck you to someone up there and laughing.

"How much has he had to drink?" Triti asks.

"Jesus Christ," I say.

Triti reaches between her legs and picks a finger of bark from her stump, tosses it into the fire. It skitters down into the bed of coals, catching at once. For some reason—as we both watch it go—my mind jumps back to smoking that first cigarette with Dorlene down at the car, the way we each lasted as long as the other. If that was a gesture we were both making, I'm lost trying to figure who had to work harder at it. But the more the time goes quiet now, here by the fire, the more I decide maybe that's the story of everything.

The bark's become an orange husk by the time either of us decides to talk. I say, "So you're staying for another winter?"

Triti shrugs. "I don't know what I'm doing, Dave."

"Well you seem like you do."

"I don't know to whom."

"To everyone."

"Well, everyone is stupid."

"Winter was awesome out here," I say. "I remember that. All that snow, everywhere. It was like a fortress out here."

"*Out* here," she says. "Why is it always *out*? Maybe you're out."

"I probably am," I say. I try to drink the last of my wine, but I've gauged it badly in the cup—I take a two-swallow swig and I'm still not done. I feel her eyes.

She says, "I wonder sometimes if you'll ever come visit."

I swirl the last wine, watch it stain the white sides and fall. "I'm visiting now." Another slug of bark goes into the fire, cartwheeling. "I don't know, Triti," I say. "It's hard out here even now." I wave my hands through the air, gesturing at the house, the lawn, the sky. "All this *you*."

"There's going to be me wherever I go."

More quiet. After a few minutes Triti straightens herself and puts her hair up. For a moment she is all mindless, perfect grace: balletic arms, sure strong hands, bent neck newly bare and long, her face as simple and clean and old as girlhood itself. All of this lit by firelight. The pink in her hair glints red. And god I just about die. Because let me tell you, if there's a sight that'll kill you more sweetly than a beautiful young woman putting up her hair, I don't want to know what it is. I swear to myself that if I could go the rest of my life witnessing only this womanly act and no other, I would be all right.

Triti props her hands into the stump beside her hips. Her eyes are sad and long. She gives me a squat smile, all lips. "I miss you," she says. "I don't know if you know that, but you ought to. I'm not saying I even want you here, but I want you to know that I liked how things were, and I'm sad they're not anymore."

I chew on it. My heart pounds. "How things were," I say.

"Yes." Her jaw goes strong. "Certain things. Not all of it. I know you understand me."

I nod and stare into the burning pile, watching a highway of flame feather over a gridwork of cracks on a gray, deepfire log. "I don't even know," I say, "what to miss or how to miss it. Relative to what, you know? It seems like . . . seems to me like everything is always absent."

"Yeah, well, it's either everything or you." This sinks into me slow, like a welcome knife, deep and true, and right then I swear I'm so in love with her I feel like I could get to my feet and take us both unflinching into the fire.

But I don't even rise, and neither does she. The fire exhales its great long breath and throws glitter at the stars, and we let the burn of it draw our fronts while the cold erases our backs, and we look at each other now and then in nothing but that light. We don't even start to speak. People talk around us instead, quiet and dear. We let them make words that don't reach us.

Eventually, I don't know how much later—the fire a whole new pet—Triti does rise. She gets to her feet and makes her excuses to the group at large, just a few hangers-on now. She includes me. She talks about getting to bed. A sprinkling of friendly good-nights sprout from the quiet circle around the fire. I straighten, and I think we touch eyes a last time, and maybe I mumble a parting something. She walks away, becomes a rumor, footsteps and murmurings. A few moments later she appears as a silhouette on the back step, distant and flat, and I watch her up the stairs and in, and once she's gone I do get up, I do, because this is how I'm choosing to hear myself talk now: *stand, balance, step, step*—the long grass thick as hands in the dark. I walk straight down the lawn, headed away from the house. I have no idea where Dorlene is or even could be, or what I owe her. No one's told me enough.

I leave the heat and then the light of the fire. I pass beneath the softly buzzing sodium light beside the dwindling cars, into the shadow of the corncrib. I remember Lord Jim, wonder if he has been released yet. I peer through the slits, picturing a shapeless heaving patch of clouded moon, dirty and ragged and quiet. "Jim," I call out, circling. "Lord Jim." I stumble and drop my empty cup into the weeds, where it alights like a leaf on water.

The heavy crib door is wedged shut. I yank it open with a sound like an ax being sunk into wood. The sodium light's haze slices and drapes through here like bones, a violence of black and yellow, shadows and lines, steps and dividers. In the daytime, up in the loft, the slotted walls let the sun in soft, and haydust lays stripes in the air, but in this dark, this light, all the depth has been rubbed clean and the shadows are long and mad, and I can't tell what's floor what's wall what's pit. I sway in the door, my voice going out and not coming back. I listen for movement, look for sliding shadows. "Hello," I say. "Anyone."

A station wagon crunches by, going out the back way. Beyond, voices and car doors float and bark. I head deeper into the property. I go straight through the tall grass, up over my waist.

Almost right away—that's how it feels—I come to the drinking trough, its low shape surprising me there against the earth, oval and still. Stars float in the black water, a great and vivid swath of them, dim and clear. I've wandered out into Tom's mown pathway, into the exact steps, maybe, I took before. Dorlene and I were right here, me on my knees, her up into me like a lover.

I go down again. I shift until I'm precisely where I feel I was earlier and I hold out my hands, embracing the space before me and bending over, trying to gather to myself again the sensation of Dorlene's smallness in my arms. I feel I could almost do it, she was so close to nothing. And as I try to get it back, my body decides to teach me again the only right answer to this moment, or to that one. The same swollen push announces itself, rude and heavy, the crease of my jeans cutting into me painfully. I unbutton my pants, releasing myself. A sigh escapes me, too, but there's nothing around, no one, and so I bring my knees together and let my pants fall, the cool air prickling the skin of my ass. I lift up my shirtfront and pin it under my chin. I draw myself taut with my off hand. I go after it, right there up against the side of the trough. It won't be long. I could set the air on fire. I try to be quiet. I breathe through my teeth. It takes no time at all, of course it doesn't, I'm so heavy there, and when the relief of the certainty arrives, it draws me down into the smallest nugget of thought I know how to have. I lose my balance and I catch myself on the edge of the trough, my hand slipping between two of the rotten boards, into a mess of cobwebs. I heave and heave, not caring, emptying myself. I lean there still while I catch my breath real quiet, while I squeeze and finger myself clean. I wipe both hands on the ground. Talk drifts down from the house, from the pool of cars, but I am in the dark. Even right in front of me, right down on this ground, I can't see my stuff at all, the strings that must be laid out here in this growing grass.

I stand and tuck myself back into my pants, still too thick to be comfortable, but somehow I like the confinement, the way I'm leaking, the way none of this feels like me. I breathe and breathe. I let the coolness calm me back to life. I ought to find Dorlene now, figure out where she's going, see what she needs. A couch, a hotel.

I go deeper along the mown path. The slumped shape of the collapsing barn—elegant and sad in the daytime—rises across the sky, an accident in the dark. I stoop and dig through the grass until I find a stone. I heave it. It clicks and natters through the wreckage. I imagine the size of the stone—or the number of pebbles—that would be needed to bring the crumpled barn all the way to its belly. I think of the dust and ruckus it would raise.

I'm cold. My thighs ache. I leave the path and wander along the property line behind the pigshack, at the edge of the cornfield, heading back toward the house and the road. The corn whispers, shedding its own dim woven light. My line takes me back by the fire. People are still around it. There's a guitar. I don't see or hear Dorlene. I leave it again, passing beyond the glow. I imagine that some animal could come and drag me off into the corn, something angular and entomological, something I couldn't or wouldn't fight. I feel cold and wet and loose in my pants.

Up at the house, the kitchen lights still burn, the porch. Triti must still be up after all. Maybe I will see her through a kitchen window, any second now as I move, as my view of the room opens up. I walk and watch and wonder how much longer I can continue to believe it, when I'm jolted: far up ahead in the road, the screech of a car jamming to a halt, the blurt of horn. A muted thump.

I swing into a sloppy trot. Behind me, the guitar cuts off and gentle interrogations rise. I hear Dorlene's voice ahead, piercing. I cross the driveway, into the yard proper, stumbling loose up the slope beside the house. I can't see the ground, but I'm heady with momentum and not worried—almost curious—about falling.

As I pass the porch, the front door bangs open and Triti barrels out. She is wearing a thin-strapped top and pajama bottoms. Her breasts swing. She takes the stairs in one heavy step, landing right in my path.

I cry out and veer aside. She glances over at me, half-lit by porchlight, dark-eyed, her lips parted. There is no hint of recognition in her at all. For me, I mean. Her gaze swings over me the way it might swing over a stranger, or a wall. I witness this. I've no idea what look I give her in return, but I do know it isn't that.

She pulls easily ahead, her thick legs pumping. The textured whisk of her pantlegs brushing together, the feathered thump of her bare feet in the grass, so purposeful and sure.

I round the house. In the unlaned road out front, a collage of light hangs. A stopped car, brake and headlights blaring, dome light on. The engine idles sleepily and exhaust billows red out the back. Through the windows and the open passenger door, the interior glows warm and yellow, empty as a coffin. In the dirty white light washing over the road ahead, a ragged unmoving shape hunches. The dog is lying in the road. As I draw nearer, an element of that shape shifts and becomes new: Dorlene's face, grotesque and gaping and maudlin, made of dots. Her lower half is lost in the dog's white mass.

I slow. Triti pulls away. She churns up the embankment and out into the pouring light like she has stepped into a photograph, or onto a stage. I see now that Ernest is there, too, that the car is his, that he has been standing there all along perfectly still, so close to the bumper of his car that he's lit only to his knees. His flat hands cross over his mouth like a bandage. Triti speaks to him and drops to the road.

I climb the berm and stop beside the car, my toes just into the gravel shoulder. I can't tell if I am seen. In the car, an undigestible sight: a crinkly white mass pouring from the dash onto the passenger seat. A bundled sheet, or a trash bag. A fungus. It's not until I see another one sprouting from the steering wheel that I understand—the airbags have blown.

Triti sits cross-legged in front of the car, draped in the stark light, her hands hanging into her open lap. She has her head cocked slightly to her right. Dorlene holds the dog; his limp, wrecking ball head over-spills her. Her tiny arms wrap around his neck and jaw, as though she's wrestled him here. Her cardigan is gone. Her shoulders gleam. She looks from him to Triti, her face stricken, her mouth working, her eyes nothing but color. Threads of Jim's fur rise through the light. I step out into the road then. I think I want to see. I come up beside Triti, right over the scene. Dorlene tips her head back. The dog is dead. His torn and bloodied face shines—torn away, really, along his muzzle. The wound bares his teeth, his strange wide molars the whitest thing in my eyes, far whiter than his coat. The gaping flesh gives him a hideous snarl, makes him seem savagely angry, and Dorlene appears to be restraining him, an exquisite sight—one of her forearms is cinched tightly around the dog's snout. On Jim's shoulder and the buckle of his jaw, rude patches of his fur have been ripped from him, his pink flesh exposed, seeping blood like sweat. He is bleeding on Dorlene. She has blood on her arms, her face.

Closer to me, Triti sits at the dog's feet. Jim's front leg is shattered—it looks counterfeit, bent at a repugnant angle and broken open like candy. And I see now that Triti strokes the paw of this wrecked leg with a single finger, as light as breath, a gesture that looks mindless but that I know is torrid.

Dorlene's little mouth opens and closes. She is keening almost inaudibly, a noise like the squeal of wet wood on fire, threaded through the rumble of the engine.

"Who was driving?" I say out into this, and my voice is a sacrilege but I don't stop. I look over at Ernest. "Was it you?"

Ernest slides his hands through his hair and into his pockets. "I didn't see him. He ran right out." Dorlene looks up at him.

"It was both of you," I tell the two of them. "You were doing the thing—the steering and the brakes." I can't say it right, but I know they understand. Dorlene shakes her head. I say to her, "You were driving but he was under you, doing the brakes, the gas. The dog ran out—or maybe he was here already—"

"That's not how it happened," says Ernest.

"—and the airbags went off," I say, not to anyone in particular, to the dog maybe, lying there. I can't make any picture besides the one I've already conjured: Dorlene standing at the wheel and calling out shrill directions. Ernest, bent eagerly with the pedals in his hands, the two of them laughing clever until the moment Dorlene spots the dog. Ernest has stepped back out of the light, all but vanishing. I realize the blood on Dorlene's face is coming from her own nose, from the corner of one of her own eyes.

I want to not be standing. I go around the dog, to where his great back curves across the road, putting him between me and Triti. I sit on the pavement. I tell Ernest to turn off the car, the lights, and I think someone will tell me no but no one does. The car goes dead and dark. We plunge into black. We sit there quiet. Cricketsong rises like a pulse.

As my eyes adjust, the scene before us—the scene we are in—slides and becomes new, over and over, the slow arrival of a print in a darkroom. I can't tell if Jim's ghostly body is fading or growing brighter. I'm spending almost all my sight on Triti anyhow; I have to. She's made no sound, the only one of all of us. She hasn't moved except for the single finger stroking slow. I begin to gather the expression poured like stone into her face: she doesn't even look at the dog, not directly, her eyes set on a point further away along the ground, just beside where I now sit, so that the dog seems to be lying under her gaze, contained—and so that her attention to him is an almost unwitnessable act. And I can't call her face sad, not really, but rather perfectly sculpted by this consequence, flawlessly full of whatever this moment means to Triti and to no one else, and her face hasn't troubled itself with knowing even this fact about itself. And because she is taking in or reaching out to no one right now she is as calmly and thoroughly alive as a forest. I could sit here all night and watch her, getting lost in my absence from her stare—my absence just for instance—and envy her. Because, I'll be honest, I can't seem to measure any of this stuff against myself, not any of it—not this night at all, not my arrival in this place, the sight of Triti being river-still, the fact of Dorlene even existing, the dog getting out and into the road, Lisa in our house alone or not alone, the smells of burnt wood and wet dog, the sound of this deed being done, the spent airbags hanging loose like just more corpses—none of it, none of it.

We sit in silence a while longer, all of us. I feel like I ought to do something that none of us has thought of yet. Triti's hand just hangs there between her knees, beside the dog's paw. She gives nothing away. She goes on moving that one finger so slightly that I know—I honestly do—that I am the only one who sees it.

And then Dorlene pipes up, setting that voice loose in the air. She tilts her head from one to another of us. "I don't know what to say, I'm serious to god. What is there to even say? David—David?"

The blood trickling from the corner of her eye has carved an arc across her delicate cheek, a black curve rendered in a trembling hand. She kneads her fingers like worms through the dog's rough fur. Her mouth is a pleading ring. I lean toward her, take her tiny arm. "Tell me it's true you could've died," I say.

Assembly

PETER LUMLEY ASSEMBLES THE MACHINE.

The parts of the machine gleam silver and smooth. Their edges run sharp and clean. When Peter Lumley holds any one of them in his hand, its weight surprises him. They assume the size of chestnuts, fingers, pushpins, peas.

Peter Lumley builds a machine that utters his name. It speaks like a metronome, in a voice like a woman's or a child's, talking his name over and over. An element of the machine rocks back and forth calmly, like the needle of a metronome, but through a horizontal plane. The machine does not produce the tock of a metronome, only the sound of Peter Lumley's name, and beneath the sound of his name, the soft complex slide of perfect gears. The machine does not slow or stop. Peter Lumley sleeps to the sound of the machine for several nights.

Peter Lumley disassembles the parts of the machine. He reassembles them, building a lilting machine with an animal's shape: a long-footed, top-heavy, thin-ankled animal—like a baby kangaroo, he realizes, long after he has finished, though he has never seen a baby kangaroo. The machine rocks lightly on the toes of the machine, cylindrical bearings in its ankles working noiselessly, the hunched crescent of its body floating, like the crown of a tree, and the spindled legs are so thin—so close, Peter Lumley realizes, to the lowest limit necessary to bear the weight of the machine—that the machine does not seem to be borne. He sets a dish of water out for the machine. He draws a kitchen chair to the table where the machine rocks over the water. He sleeps in the chair near the table. He dreams of fantastic thirst.

Peter Lumley slices carrots on the counter near the sink. Peter Lumley makes stew. He washes the stewpot, the water dish, the knife.

Peter Lumley, in a practical state of mind, builds a machine that produces, detects, and obscures unpleasant smells. The machine is shaped like a dense, loafish bed of earnest and ornate flowers, neatly arranged. Peter Lumley appreciates this machine but becomes quickly bored with it, because the machine lacks visible moving parts. He notes the importance of this to himself, takes the machine apart hours after assembling it.

Peter Lumley builds a breathing machine. A finely whirring machine, splendidly humming, producing an invisible cloud the same humidity and temperature as the air in the room. Peter Lumley bends over the machine each morning and breathes, breathes.

Peter Lumley gets nosebleeds. He undertakes the studious application of ice. He watches television obliquely, his head thrown over the back of his chair.

Peter Lumley builds a silent machine that is adept at staying out of Peter Lumley's sight. He becomes very fond of this machine. He imagines its exact appearance. He thinks of the machine often. Often, he talks to the machine—or for no audience in particular, but in such a way that the machine would be able to hear him. He feels that the machine trusts him. He lives with it without incident for over a month, until one evening, stepping backward away from the sink, he treads on the machine, hears it fall intricately to pieces on the tile.

Peter Lumley arranges the parts of the machine on his bed. He arranges them according to extravagance of form, beginning with the smallest pins and spheres and ending with the shape that reminds him of the alphabet bent turbulently into a bow. He acknowledges arbitrary choices he makes at certain small levels of the array but pleases himself with the gradient of the whole. He then selects every sixth piece, beginning in the upper right-hand corner of the bed. He builds a small thoughtful machine using these parts— every sixth piece from the arrangement of the whole—and then the thoughtful machine trolls over the bed, selecting additional parts from the parts that remain. The thoughtful machine devises a complex system of selection. Peter Lumley understands that the complexity of the system escapes him; he recognizes only that a system exists. Belatedly, he suspects that a series of images could have been detected in the arrangements of the parts left behind by the thoughtful machine. After the thoughtful machine completes its work, Peter Lumley finds himself unable to build anything from the parts it has selected. He considers this a failure on his part. He sits on the floor for some time, within the crescent of the chosen parts strewn about him on the floor. Eventually, he becomes witness instead to the increasingly arcane act of the thoughtful machine disassembling itself.

Peter Lumley eschews every light in his room except for a bent-neck, drooping lamp with a deeply pink glass shade. He considers the light cast by the shade, wonders if it is womblike, frees the lamp with an extension cord, carries the lamp with him from corner to corner at night for a week.

Peter Lumley spends over a month attempting to build a perfectly spherical machine. He does not know for certain whether the parts in his possession will allow him to accomplish this.

Peter Lumley builds an undulating machine that prevents shadows from being cast. He stands in front of this machine and does not see his shadow, even when he makes shapes with his hands. He begins to blame his hands for this, to develop a distaste for his hands. He washes his hands, repeatedly, in very hot water. He lets them redden. He stands in front of the machine for over a day, turning the pink lamp on and off, on and off.

Peter Lumley builds a flying machine that does not fly. Instead, it lumbers across the floor like a crumple-winged moth. Peter Lumley, watching, momentarily considers crushing the machine, but before he can begin to accurately imagine such a thing, the machine whirs and unfolds, erupts absurdly into the briefest fluorescence, a tumescent shape like a toadstool, then collapses swiftly into a wide and smooth shallow bowl, shimmering, and then back into the lumbering winged thing again. Peter Lumley stays up deep into the night, watching the machine.

Peter Lumley mails a piece of the machine. He selects a piece at random, a piece that looks like a triangle from one direction, the shell of a nautilus from another. Peter Lumley mails the piece to himself. He includes his return address. He uses insufficient postage. The piece of the machine settles naturally into a lower corner of the envelope, buckles the paper, weighs the envelope down uneasily.

Peter Lumley builds an almost perfectly spherical machine. He had not known this could be done. The surface teems with the inner workings of the machine, not an unbroken plane at all but the exposed points and protrusions of rods, gears, pistons, flywheels,

mesh—only the smallest of parts, but all so tightly packed together, so
keenly aligned, that the nearly spherical machine feels textureless
in the hand. He drops the machine into his pocket. He understands
that he had known he would be able to. It works against his thigh.

Peter Lumley begins to notice discolorations beneath certain of his
nails: finger and toe. He cannot recall what this might mean, though
he believes it means something misfortunate. The discolorations are
purple-black, white, cadaveric.

Peter Lumley begins to wonder if he has been parting his hair on the
wrong side. He aspires to build a mirrored machine that will reflect
an unreversed image of himself, but instead he dreams he builds—
purely by accident—a dull, throbbing disc that is only visible if
Peter Lumley is in motion.

Peter Lumley takes to keeping single, small pieces of the machine in
his mouth. He does this for hours at a time. They taste exquisitely
bitter, almost sweet. He cups them with his tongue, keeps them—
mostly—from his teeth. He salivates profusely over them. He rinses
them in the sink. They each possess, in his mouth, the faint tingle
of batteries.

Peter Lumley begins to build a machine in which each part connects
to exactly three others. The machine quickly becomes large and
improbably cornered, but it only slowly grows large enough. At
regular intervals, he takes apart sections of the machine, puts them
back together. He carefully never takes apart the entire machine, but
he intends that when the machine is finished, there will be no section
still intact that has remained intact throughout. He works on
the machine for days in a row, fusses through many layers of
assembly, disassembly, reassembly. As the machine nears completion,
Peter Lumley becomes suspicious. He begins to suspect that the work

progresses with an intent he had not foreseen, although he can name neither the intent nor its symptoms. He blames the machine, works deep into the night.

Peter Lumley sleeps.

Peter Lumley wakes and works on the machine.

When it is complete, the machine assumes the precise size and shape and color and texture of Peter Lumley's room. This confirms the suspicion that has been growing in Peter Lumley, and he knows what has happened the moment he finishes, because he loses sight of the machine. He searches for the machine. He uses his hands. He lifts pillows from his bed, but he knows that certain elements of the machine are meant to be pillow-like. He opens the window onto the street, but the machine has been built with such features in mind. He runs water in the sink. The machine provides this amenity. Peter Lumley fingers and palms his hair. He considers his surroundings. He examines the surface of a mirror.

Peter Lumley sits on a kitchen chair until long after it becomes too dark to see.

Peter Lumley packs his belongings. Peter Lumley leaves certain things behind, does not know for certain what this means. He packs toothpaste, underwear, soaps, mail, his toolkit, the pendulous pink lamp. Peter Lumley leaves certain things behind.

Peter Lumley lives elsewhere. He subscribes to magazines full of deeply shining pictures. He reads up on the unfamiliar. He pays to have food delivered to him. He walks in the early mornings.

He invents a game in which trivia questions are asked about himself. He enjoys this game. He finds it surprisingly difficult, not at all sad.

He cares for his teeth. He possesses a healthy respect for the
mechanics of flossing. He wraps the floss sturdily around
his fingertips. His fingers turn purple and white.

He takes up paper-folding. He has purchased colored paper for the
purpose. He has followed difficult paper-folding instructions,
has made an angelback frog, a seven-cornered star, a snowcapped
mountain, a dromedary. He memorizes the steps involved in
the creation of basic forms. He refines his technique. He makes
a castle keep, a hawk approaching, a collapsible looking-glass,
an unfortunate dog. He has come to the conclusion that the best folds
are those he draws through the bite of his incisors. He presses the
fine cuts in his fingers closed, applies droplets of clear, potent glue.

Peter Lumley receives a piece of the machine in the mail, returned
and forwarded to himself. He appraises the handwriting
on the envelope.

He maintains a display of the shapes he has folded from paper.
He fusses with the arrangement.

He implements a regimen of stretching in the morning. He is
surprised to discover how far he cannot bend. He commits himself
to deriving satisfaction from the regimen.

He devotes himself to exploring the countless permutations of
various cheeses, various crackers. He learns the difference between
fontina and fontinella. He fails to encounter a perfectly satisfying
cracker. This occupies him for several weeks.

Peter Lumley fingers the machine part through the worn, crinkled
thickness of the envelope. He contemplates the intricacy of what
he discerns.

Peter Lumley remarks to himself how every day, he dresses himself in the ordinary fashion.

Peter Lumley gathers certain of his belongings. Peter Lumley combs his hair.

Peter Lumley returns to his room. He finds Peter Lumley there, bent over parts of the machine. Peter Lumley rises and begins to talk rapidly about the machine. He tells Peter Lumley that he has spent over a month counting wrinkles in his skin. From certain parts of the machine, he has constructed an aperture through which objects, such as himself, can be seen greatly magnified. He asserts that he has developed a new appreciation for the nature of a wrinkle, for its tendency to propagate endlessly at finer and finer scales, for the ever-more canyonesque quality of his skin. He explains that he has since disassembled this machine.

Peter Lumley participates in the unpacking of Peter Lumley's things. Peter Lumley asks about the pink lamp.

Peter Lumley and Peter Lumley come to work quietly over parts of the machine. They sit through the night. By morning, they complete a noise-dampening device—possibly by accident—and cannot speak to one another for most of the afternoon, except with gestures. They are surprised not to understand each other better.

That evening, Peter Lumley and Peter Lumley construct a device that briefly causes forgetfulness. Later, hesitantly, they blame each other for this.

Both Peter Lumley and Peter Lumley insist that the other take the bed but Peter Lumley refuses.

They build a machine like a long, twisted tank tread, a sagging belt like a strip of ammunition. They watch as it trundles around the room, dedicated to a specific sinuous circuit. Peter Lumley observes that it is a Möbius strip, that its interior becomes its exterior as it rolls, and so forth. Peter Lumley observes that every unique point of the machine touches the floor in the same unique spot each time the machine circles the room. Peter Lumley draws attention to the pleasantness of the sound made by the machine. Peter Lumley concurs. The sound remains pleasant for several days.

Peter Lumley and Peter Lumley build a bulbous machine that seems to do nothing. It reminds them of something they cannot recall.

Peter Lumley and Peter Lumley construct an angular, spinning device whose purpose is a source of contention.

Peter Lumley and Peter Lumley build a box with no outside.

Every other night, Peter Lumley sleeps in the bed. An unspoken understanding allows this to occur naturally. Peter Lumley sleeps in the chair on these occasions. Peter Lumley is an excellent cook, a quietly tidy man, a decent enough companion, sensible on the whole.

In time, Peter Lumley and Peter Lumley build a tiny machine that trembles and causes maternal yearnings in those who cup it in their palm. They admit to themselves, huddled quietly around the machine, a different intent.

The Peter Lumleys contend that the trembling machine is pleasant to sleep with.

Peter Lumley trims Peter Lumley's hair. He attempts to style it like his own.

Peter Lumley wonders aloud if the trembling machine seems to express certain needs. Peter Lumley explains that the machine cannot express need, only function. He describes, in detail, the theoretical mediums for a fabricated expression of need. Peter Lumley hands Peter Lumley the trembling machine.

Peter Lumley considers his surroundings. Peter Lumley recalls basic forms used in the folding of paper. The trembling machine is always with Peter Lumley.

Occasionally, Peter Lumley speaks sentimentally about the Möbius-strip machine. Peter Lumley perfects an imitation of the sound it made. Peter Lumley asks if Peter Lumley remembers the forgetful machine. Peter Lumley wonders aloud what would have resulted if the box with no outside had been built inside out.

The Peter Lumleys slowly begin to verbalize certain complicated needs to each other.

The trembling machine is disassembled.

Peter Lumley and Peter Lumley begin to build a machine that slowly takes the shape of Peter Lumley. Peter Lumley feels a strange warmth begin to spread across his face as he becomes aware of the fact. He comes to believe he recognizes this same sensation manifesting itself on the face of Peter Lumley. The work progresses quickly. Parts of the machine settle deftly into place. Peter Lumley is surprised to find a process something like memory at play in his fingers. They work through the night and through the morning and they finish in the afternoon.

Peter Lumley and Peter Lumley congratulate themselves.

They dress Peter Lumley in Peter Lumley's clothes. At one point early in this process, Peter Lumley, Peter Lumley, and Peter Lumley spend several murmuring minutes in a circle, examining the skin on one another's backs.

Peter Lumley tidies up. Peter Lumley bathes. Peter Lumley preheats the oven, begins peeling potatoes, makes a glass pitcher of iced tea.

The Peter Lumleys sit down over dinner. They eat beef tenderloin and potatoes, pale green beans, cranberry sauce from a can. Peter Lumley slices the tenderloin. Peter Lumley explains that the tenderness of this meat has to do with the location of the muscle along the spine of the animal, its infrequent use. Peter Lumley describes the way the tenderloin, in deer, can be pulled out easily by hand. The Peter Lumleys pass the salt. Peter Lumley praises the mashed potatoes, agrees they are creamy, adds pat after pat after pat of butter. Peter Lumley mentions a pain in his side. The Peter Lumleys share a look. Peter Lumley bends in his chair, reaches for his side. He grimaces. He continues eating. The Peter Lumleys all do the same. Peter Lumley tugs at the corner of the tablecloth, straightens a wrinkle with a brisk brush of fingers. They drink tea from thick, green glasses. Peter Lumley uses plenty of ice. Dessert is the remainder of a fat chocolate cake. They discuss how best to divide the cake. Peter Lumley recalls the egalitarian solution whereby one person slices, one person chooses. Peter Lumley objects, invents a variation whereby Peter Lumley cuts the first slice, Peter Lumley cuts the second slice, Peter Lumley chooses, Peter Lumley chooses. Peter Lumley declares he no longer feels like cake.

After dinner, the Peter Lumleys play the game Peter Lumley has invented. They enjoy the game immensely and play it deep into the evening, until Peter Lumley fails to answer a question asked by Peter Lumley. The question has to do with recent developments.

The Peter Lumleys watch television. They do not speak. Peter Lumley
drinks tea, coffee, milk.

The Peter Lumleys, deep into the night around the table, sort
aimlessly through the leftover parts of the machine. Peter Lumley
talks softly with himself.

Peter Lumley nods off. Peter Lumley snores monstrously. Peter
Lumley nudges Peter Lumley awake.

Peter Lumley and Peter Lumley begin to disassemble Peter Lumley.
They begin with his hands, prudently. His skin looks rosy beneath
the light of the pink lamp. Peter Lumley remarks what a sad affair it is.
Peter Lumley marvels at the complexity of the machine in question.
Peter Lumley watches their work unfold, flexes his tongue inside his
mouth. As he watches he hums to himself—as ably as he might—a
circumscript, invented tune.

Acknowledgments

The stories in this book have appeared in the following publications:

"Jane," *The Southern Review*
"Assembly," *Confrontation*
"Obit," *The Indiana Review* and *PEN/O'Henry Prize Stories 2010*
"Flounder," *The Gettysburg Review*
"Momentary," *The Massachusetts Review*
"The Lion," *Black Warrior Review*
"Deer in the Road," *Berkeley Fiction Review*
"Putting the Lizard to Sleep," *The Georgia Review*

Thanks to Neil Archer, who is incapable of not stating the obvious, and who helped get this all going. Thanks to Richard Powers, for bringing the massive fist of his intellect to bear on these stories. Much gratitude also to Alex Shakar, Michael Madonick, Philip Graham, and Audrey Petty, for all their time and insight and support. Thanks to my classmates at UIUC. Thanks to Katie Dublinski and everyone else at Graywolf, and to the dedicated folks at Bread Loaf.

Thanks to my parents, and my son Rowan. Thanks to Jodee, for everything she does and is; so much would never have happened without her. Much gratitude and affection for all the friends and readers and shapers, named and unnamed here, for letting a part of your lives be a part of mine. Life will always be the thing, the story that can't really be told.

Bread Loaf and the Bakeless Prizes

The Katharine Bakeless Nason Literary Publication Prizes were established in 1995 to expand the Bread Loaf Writers' Conference's commitment to the support of emerging writers. Endowed by the LZ Francis Foundation, the prizes commemorate Middlebury College patron Katharine Bakeless Nason and launch the publication career of a poet, a fiction writer, and a creative nonfiction writer annually. Winning manuscripts are chosen in an open national competition by a distinguished judge in each genre. Winners are published by Graywolf Press.

2011 Judges

Carl Phillips
Poetry

Stacey D'Erasmo
Fiction

Lynn Freed
Creative Nonfiction

Ted Sanders's stories and essays have appeared in journals such as the *Georgia Review, Black Warrior Review, Cincinnati Review,* the *Gettysburg Review,* and the *Massachusetts Review.* His work has been featured in the *O. Henry Prize Stories,* and he was the recipient of a 2012 NEA Literature Fellowship Grant. He has lived in Illinois for most of his life and now resides in Urbana with his family. He holds an MFA in fiction from the University of Illinois at Urbana-Champaign, where he currently teaches writing.

The text of *No Animals We Could Name* is set in Sabon MT Pro, an old-style serif typeface based on the types of Claude Garamond and designed by the German-born typographer and designer Jan Tschichold (1902–1974) in 1964. Book design by Ann Sudmeier. Composition by BookMobile Design and Publishing Services, Minneapolis, Minnesota. Manufactured by Versa Press on acid-free, 30 percent postconsumer wastepaper.